TOUCH OF DEATH

ORDER OF THE ELEMENTS: BOOK TWO

EMMA L. ADAMS

PREFACE

The magically gifted have always lived among us.

After centuries of living in hiding, a group of mages banded together and created their own parallel world to the everyday one, a paradise designed as a home for the magically inclined. Mages, vampires, elves, shapeshifters and many others flocked there, and for centuries, they flourished, ruled over by the council of the Elements.

Then, several decades ago, the spirit mages turned on their fellow Elements and slaughtered them. The resulting war brought an end to the elemental council and left the magical world in ruins.

Since then, it has remained fractured. Clans of shapeshifters, vampires, and others rule the cities, while the Court of the Dead dominates the areas even magical beings fear to tread. It may be a paradise no longer, but to many of the magically inclined, it's still home.

Welcome to the Parallel.

I woke up to a blast of air hitting me in the face. Not a breeze from an open window, but a hurricane-like torrent that lifted me from my bed and slammed me into the wall so hard that starbursts of light winked before my eyes.

My gaze snapped open to the sight of the Death King's Air Element standing over my bed, eyes narrowed in anger.

"Who did you tell?" they demanded.

I blinked, the back of my head throbbing. "Who—what? What are you talking about?"

Ryan raised a hand and slammed me into the wall again. Pretty lights twinkled in front of my vision, blurring the figure standing over the bed. Their hair was shaved to stubble, their nose pierced, and their armoured clothing a toned-down version of the clothes they wore when they rode a skeletal horse alongside their king. They stood a good five inches taller than me at just under six feet, which made their looming presence even more alarming when I was half awake and not wearing my glasses.

"Ow!" I yelped. "What the hell are you doing?"

"You betrayed us," said the Air Element.

I'd done nothing of the sort. "I thought we weren't enemies any longer."

Okay, the King of the Dead *had* locked me in jail and ripped out my boyfriend's soul, but that was the result of a misunderstanding after I'd accidentally stolen the amulet containing his own life essence. The Air Element and I had worked together to take down the rogue wannabe-spirit mage and returned the amulet to their king, and while I'd refused the Death King's offer of a job, we hadn't parted vowing to kill one another. So whatever the Air Element's problem might be, I had nothing to do with it.

Another gust of air ripped through the room, and my bookshelf fell over, spilling volumes of manga all over the floor. "You told someone of my master's secrets. Don't deny it."

"Who?" I said. "What secrets? I really don't have the faintest idea what you're talking about."

Ryan frowned. "You don't know."

"Of course I don't." I shivered, my bare legs and arms exposed to the chill air stirred up by the Air Element's arrival. I wore only a thin pair of pyjamas, with no weapons or even my lucky dice, but I still felt more exasperated and confused than frightened. Which probably said something about how screwed up my priorities were lately. "What does His Deathly Highness want, then? What's got his tail in a twist?"

"You ought to show him more respect," they said.

"After the trouble you put him through, he was generous enough to offer you a job. Which you turned down."

"Yeah, and I haven't forgotten how he locked me in jail." I sat up on the bed, my neck and back protesting at the movement after my surprise collision with the wall. "I might add that I also saved his life, so he has some nerve sending you here to threaten me. I didn't tell anyone his secrets."

Mostly because his secrets were mine, too. I'd used forbidden spirit magic to return his soul to its original vessel after Mr Cobb had tried to claim it as his own, and since I was the one who'd moved his soul into a new vessel to begin with—under duress, I might add—not blabbing worked in my favour as much as his.

Mr Cobb had nursed a bitter grudge towards the Order of the Elements for taking away his magic and had seen stealing the Death King's soul as his only way to regain his lost glory. His grudge had also extended to me, since he and I had shared the same mentor, Dirk Alban. While Cobb had paid the price with his magic, the Order had spared me the same fate on account of my being underage. Instead, they'd removed all my memories of my training in spirit magic, which amounted to over two years of my life. Yet I still suspected the Death King could come up with a worse punishment than the Order if I told anyone that the notorious immortal death lord had a weakness after all.

Ryan gave me a long look. "You'd better be telling the truth."

"It would help if you told me which secrets I'm supposed to have shared, and with whom." The Death

King had a whole castle's worth of them, and I'd hardly scratched the surface.

Ryan didn't answer my query. "If it wasn't you, then someone else is sharing our private business with outsiders."

"Did you ever catch that lich?" I asked. "The one who betrayed your king?"

From the Air Element's disgruntled expression, I'd guess not. No surprises there, because all the liches in the court had turned on their master when Mr Cobb had briefly claimed the Death King's soul. Since I was the only person who'd actually seen the traitorous lich scheming behind his back and all the liches looked the same to my human eyes, I hadn't been able to pin down the traitor's identity.

I'd always thought of the Death King as an all-powerful entity, so the idea that he could be thwarted had shaken me. Even more that I'd held his soul in my own hands… an experience I had zero desire to repeat. After all, the guy was infuriating, ruthless, and had a +5 in Annoying the Shit Out of Liv. All of which were good reasons for me to turn down his offer of a job even before he'd sent his Elemental Soldier to break into my house.

"You are invited to come and talk to my master to discuss this further," they said. "I won't discuss private matters in public."

"If you didn't want anyone listening in, you shouldn't have broken into my house," I pointed out.

"I didn't know the node came out directly into your home."

If that was an attempt at an apology, I wasn't having any of it. My head was throbbing, my bookshelves were a mess, and I was irked as hell at the Death King for not just calling me like a normal person. It wasn't like he couldn't have astral projected over here.

Okay… maybe I didn't want that. I hadn't forgotten the time he'd paid a visit to my mum and her wife, Elise—a horrifying event which I hoped would never be repeated. *Bloody lich lords.*

"Fine," I said. "I'll consider taking His Deathly Highness up on his offer."

As the Air Element turned on the spot and vanished into the node, my *Death Note* poster fell off the wall with a crackle of finality. Wonderful.

Sitting up, I grabbed my glasses and put them on to survey the damage to my room. Luckily, Brant wasn't here, or his fire magic might have caused a more permanent backlash. He had a tendency to overreact to any forms of hostility, especially against me. My books, manga and DVD shelves lay in a pile on the floor, while most of my posters had seen better days, but I'd got off easy, considering the Elemental Soldiers' magic was the very best the Parallel had to offer.

The buzz of the node which went through the house had thoroughly banished any remnants of tiredness from my body, so I set about returning my room to its former state. As I set the bookshelves upright, Devon came into the room, her hair messy from sleep. The tips were dyed blue today, while she wore her Totoro onesie.

"What in the Elements' name is going on?" she said. "I thought you and Brant were having really rough sex until I heard the crashing."

"Nope. I got attacked by an Air Element."

"You mean *the* Air Element?" She looked around at the carnage. "The Death King's soldier?"

"You've got it." I grabbed a stack of manga and set about arranging the volumes into the right order. "Rather than knocking on the door, they jumped through the node and woke me up by slamming my head into the wall a few times. Supposedly, someone's sharing His Royal Deadliness's secrets with outsiders."

I'd known my brief history with the Death King was bound to get me into trouble again sooner or later, but I'd expected the trouble to come from the man himself. Maybe he was the one who'd told the Air Element to use force. It wouldn't surprise me.

"Which secrets?" asked Devon.

"I tried asking and got zero response." I shoved a stack of Fullmetal Alchemist manga onto the shelf. "I'm guessing it's to do with His Highness's detachable soul. Everyone knows about Cobb's attempted coup by now, even if they don't know how he came so close to besting the Death King."

Devon clucked her tongue. "Who is it you're supposed to have told, then? The Order?"

"I think the Order must already know." I finished filling one shelf and moved to the next. "They've been allies with the Death King forever. That hasn't changed after what Cobb did, as far as I know."

Mr Cobb had tried to get me arrested along with him by bringing up my history of spirit magic at his trial, and only the Death King's timely arrival had prevented me from winding up with another black mark on my record. I'd been doing my best to keep my head down and stay out of trouble in the weeks following my close call, but it seemed not everyone was following that advice.

"So they just… hopped through the node?" she said. "In the middle of our house?"

"Supposedly, they didn't know it was here." Which might well be the truth. I'd done my level best to keep the Death King from finding out our address. We had a difficult enough time keeping customers without the King of the Dead showing up here, thanks. "They want me to speak to the Death King, which absolutely isn't happening now. I have a coffee date with Brant, besides."

Aka, the one Element I could actually stand to be around at the moment. My boyfriend had a long-term permit from the Order so he could be here, which was a major sacrifice on his part considering his magic was dampened on this side of the nodes. But if it meant we could spend time together without running for our lives, he insisted it was worth it.

"Fun," she said. "No missions from the Order, then?

"Nope." Yet another reason to avoid tempting fate. The official rule was that crossings into the Parallel outside of official Order business were prohibited, and while most people broke that rule whenever they could get away with it, that didn't mean I wanted to risk drawing the Order's attention by following the Air Element back to their master's castle.

Things had been different, once. The original Spirit Elements, who'd created the Parallel to begin with, had been held in high regard by the entire magical world, but during the elemental war a few decades back, the carnage they'd wreaked had wiped out the entire Council of the Elements and resulted in the Order outright banning spirit magic from use. No exceptions. Now Mr Cobb sat rotting in a jail cell, while I remained none the wiser as to how much he'd learned from Dirk Alban before I'd come to find myself standing beside our mutual mentor's dead body when the Order had shown up to pass judgement on the pair of us.

"Better hope we get a shit-ton of business, then," Devon said. "The landlord upped our rent again."

"Shit, really? You never said." She'd probably forgotten to. "I'm not holding out much hope that the Order will send me on any high-ranked missions soon."

Our only other source of income came from the cantrips Devon sold, but since she could only sell to magical practitioners, that meant the bulk of our customers worked for or were associated with the Order. Yet another way they held us both under their control.

"Yeah, I know," she said. "If you ask me, Judith told half the Order we're to blame for those deaths."

I pulled a face. "I wish I didn't think you were right."

A number of Order personnel had been killed in the battle with Cobb and his allies, and since I was the one who'd led them into the conflict, many of them had been vocal about their disappointment that I'd got away without any serious punishment from the Order. That had been the Death King's doing, which was yet another reason it made no sense for him to send one of his people to threaten me.

Devon backed out of my room. "I'm heading downstairs. There'd better not be any more Elements down there, because the next one's getting a taster of my anti-gravity cantrip."

"That's what you're calling it?" Devon's lack of any

custom jobs lately had prompted her to start inventing new cantrips using her spares, including one that sent anyone who touched it floating into the air like a balloon. It was a really good job I'd only set that one off inside the shop, or I'd probably have ended up drifting over the Atlantic Ocean. A bored Devon was a very dangerous thing.

Devon closed the door behind her, while I finished fixing up the bookshelves and then dressed in jeans and a T-shirt. I tugged a brush through my chin-length brown hair and popped in my contacts, then I grabbed my Parallel bag, telling myself it was just a precaution. In case Brant decided to hop over the nearest node to give the Death King a piece of his mind, for instance. He'd almost lost his soul protecting me, and he was a lot less forgiving of the Death King's actions than I was.

My Parallel bag contained all the necessities for a mission on the other side. Clothes, snacks, water, torch, sleeping bag. It also contained my lucky dice, which the Death King had returned to me after his people had taken my possessions off me while I'd been in jail. It was a weird decision on his part, one I still didn't know how to interpret. An apology for locking me up, a gesture of kindness, or another piece of leverage to use against me. Or maybe he didn't want my crap littering his castle. Anyone's guess.

It wasn't worth trying to figure out the motives of an undead immortal who'd been around the Parallel for longer than I'd been alive, so I put the thought out of mind and went out to meet Brant.

2

———————

Brant and I met outside Starbucks. He wore a long coat with the collar turned up against the cold, his hair shaved on the sides and longer on top. My heart gave a skip, half happiness, half nerves at the inevitable shit storm that would ensue when I told him about the morning's incident. I did my best to put it out of my mind when he wrapped both arms around me and kissed me, his warm embrace welcome in the freezing air.

We walked into the café, where I ordered a cappuccino and he ordered a black coffee. I also got a blueberry muffin, and absently nibbled on it while I tried to figure out how best to broach the subject of the King of the Dead.

Coffee dates weren't my usual thing, especially with a fire mage who'd spent more years in the Parallel than on earth. Brant had spurned the Order from the start, and while we'd met in the course of one of my missions for them a couple of years back, he'd once tried to convince me to go and live with him in the Parallel, which had led to our first breakup. He hadn't brought up the subject since, and given recent events, he'd probably figured that I needed time to adjust to the knowledge that I was still a spirit mage in everything but name. The Death King's request that I move into the Parallel and work for him had been weird enough, thanks.

I stirred my coffee with a spoon. "Do you remember the Death King's Air Element?"

"Armoured soldier with an attitude problem? Yes." Brant sipped his own coffee. How he could drink it without sugar or milk was a mystery to me. "Why?"

"They paid me a visit this morning," I said. "An explosive one."

Brant's eyebrows crept higher with every word I spoke, and finally, he rose to his feet. "That's trespassing, that is. Does the Death King know?"

"Ryan claimed to have forgotten the node came out directly into my house," I said. "Not that that's an excuse for the violence. Sit down, Brant. Don't go declaring war on anyone."

He sat down, his mouth pulling in a scowl. "This is bullshit. I thought your agreement with the Death King was over."

"It's not about our agreement. Someone's supposedly sharing the Death Court's deepest secrets. It's more likely to be one of his liches than me. It's insulting, really. I saved his soul and he repaid me by sending one of his soldiers after me."

"Why not return the favour?" he said.

"What, barge into his castle in the middle of the night?" I arched a brow. "I doubt I'd be able to take him by surprise, even if I got past his security. Besides, I don't have a permit from the Order, and it's not worth risking a reprimand just because the Death King's having a paranoid blip after his near-death experience. I mean nearer-death. Whichever."

Brant was silent for a moment. "How about going to visit him using your powers, then? That's not breaking the law."

"Using my…" Right. "Astral projecting? Not sure he'd like that any better, to be honest."

Astral projecting—aka, travelling into the Parallel as a spirit without my body—neatly skipped over the Order's rules against crossing without a permit, but that didn't make it any less risky.

He drummed his fingers on the table. "You have the skills, it's a shame to waste them."

"Speaking like a typical mage."

Forcing an elemental mage to live without magic was like asking someone who lived both on land and in the water to pick one over the other, so most mages left Earth as soon as they were aware there was an alternative. The Order enforced so many rules on those of us who opted to remain behind that most elemental mages went behind their backs on the most mundane issues.

The difference was, regular mages weren't breaking the law every single time they used magic.

"You're a mage," he pointed out. "I know you have Devon and your other friends to think of, but the Parallel is safer than the Order in a lot of ways."

"Aside from the vampires, phantoms, liches… and let's not forget the countless unscrupulous elemental mages out to get me." I ticked them off on my fingers. "Also, the lack of adequate plumbing. And public transport."

"I thought you hated the bus anyway."

"Yes, but at least I can get around without having to shortcut through underground tunnels crawling with monsters." I lifted my coffee cup. "Also, where could I get a decent cappuccino on the other side?"

"Just listing the pros and cons," he said. "I know the Order makes it so that you feel you have to choose one world or the other, but that might change one day."

"Huh?" I frowned. "What do you mean by that?"

He shrugged. "Nothing really. Just rumours. You know, the Order's rules have only been as stringent as they are since after the war. They used to be much more lenient before then."

"Which is longer than both of us have been alive," I reminded him. "What's going on that makes you think they're going to change anytime soon?"

"Nothing," he said. "But I'm sure not everyone at the Order is thrilled that they lose pretty much every mage to the Parallel as soon as we're old enough to make up our minds about learning magic."

"True, but look what happened when the Elements were allowed to do whatever they liked," I said. "War, destruction, chaos…"

"Cobb almost started a war anyway."

A chill raced down my back at the mention of the jailed spirit mage's name. "Yes. I know. I'm not saying I agree with anything the Order does, but imagine the Spirit Elements had done to this world what they did to the Parallel. I might not agree with what the Order did to me, but I understand it."

After all, I'd known what I was getting into when I'd signed up to study spirit magic with Dirk Alban back at the academy. Just because I couldn't remember why I'd said yes didn't erase the fact that I'd walked in with my eyes wide open.

His hand reached for mine across the table. "That's ancient history. I don't want the Order to guide your decisions."

Sometimes, the guy just missed the mark entirely. "They ripped two years of my memories out of my head. Forgive me if I don't want to lose anything else."

His hand faltered. "That was tactless. Sorry."

"I'm just in a twitchy mood today," I admitted. "On account of the rude awakening I had this morning. Maybe I *will* hop over to the swamp to figure out what's got the Death King sending his Elements out to threaten me."

I'd sworn that I'd stay out of any dangerous Parallel-related business, and the Death King definitely fell into that category. But then again, so did Brant himself, despite his assertions to the contrary. The Parallel was teeming with unscrupulous individuals out for themselves alone, and while I didn't count Brant among them, sometimes he said things that made me wonder if people ever really changed.

"You don't have to do anything you're not comfortable with." He reached and squeezed my hand across the table again. This time, I squeezed back.

"What're you up to, anyway?" I asked. "Any jobs?"

Most mages in the Parallel made a living through barter and trade—in rare objects or information—and while the Order left them to it, if they grabbed the wrong item at the wrong time, they'd find themselves the target of one of the Order's retrievers. Which would explain why I didn't get on with Brant's friends. I mean, if you ignored the fact that one of them had locked me in a cage a few weeks ago. I'd assumed the incident would prompt Brant to take a long hard look at who he did business with, but from what he'd just said, I doubted that was the case. Then again, what had I really expected?

Brant was silent for a long moment before saying, "The usual. Working, listening out for trouble. Haven't heard anything odd from the Death King's direction, but I can't say I've been anywhere near the swampland."

"It's better for your survival that way." Now I'd bought up the subject, though, I wouldn't put it past him to march up and knock on the Death King's door and wind up locked in a cell. Again.

He had a point… I *could* astral project into the Parallel without leaving my own home. Or without my body leaving it, anyway. As long as the Order's people didn't catch me in the act, nobody would have to know. I'd get in and out without trouble.

Granted, the Death King was the very definition of trouble, but he had no reason to harm me. Right?

———

Back home, Devon had opened the shop for the day, and sat behind the counter, spinning a blank cantrip underneath her thumb. Cantrips were made out of a rare metal found only in the Parallel, inscribed with symbols depending on their function. In their blank form, they resembled pale gold coins, slightly larger than regular money. A number of thin instruments covered the desk, the tools Devon used to carve the coins with the necessary symbols for each spell.

"What's that one for?" I indicated the coin she was spinning.

She caught the coin in her fingertips. "It's a spare. I never have spares. What the hell are the Order doing, going totally magic-free?"

"Are you expecting anyone from the Order to show up today?" I asked.

"Not anytime soon. Why?"

"I'm planning a little astral projection," I told her. "I'll stay in the back room, but I'd like to be forewarned if I'm going to be interrupted.

"Wait, you're going to the other side?" She put the coin down on the desk. "To the Death King?"

"I figured it'd be less risky than visiting him in person," I said. "If he throws a tantrum, I'll come straight back with no harm done."

"You're still leaving your body behind, though," she said doubtfully. "Did Brant tell you to do it?"

"He gave me the idea," I said, "but it's less risky than walking there on foot."

"Everything's risky where the liches are concerned," she said. "But go on, if you must. I'll watch the desk."

"Cheers." I headed for the narrow wooden door behind the counter. "I'd rather not, but if I don't, Brant might find himself minus a soul again."

I went through the door into the back room, which was around half the size of the shop. While it was originally designed to be a storeroom, Devon's cantrips didn't take up much space, so we'd turned it into a gaming cave complete with a table set up for our weekly D&D game. Along the wall stood our TV and games consoles—all second-hand courtesy of a friend of Devon's who worked at a game shop—while the kitchen lay in an alcove on the right-hand side.

I cleared an Xbox controller out of the way and sat down on the sofa, so I wouldn't end up coming back into my body to find my legs cramping from standing too long.

Then I stepped out of my body, into the path of the node humming beneath the house. At once, the vibrant current of magic came to life around and inside me. Hovering on the spot, I pictured the hidden world on the other side, and the node's light carried me through.

I came out of the node in the stretch of desolate swampland in front of the Death King's castle. I'd assumed that if he could build a castle in a place where castles had never existed, he could make the surroundings look a bit more appealing, but perhaps he liked living in a place filled with murky swampland and twisting trees and not much in the way of wildlife unless you counted the phantoms drifting around. The ghostly shapes didn't bother me as a spirit myself, so we ignored one another as I floated up to the gates surrounding the huge dark-bricked castle dominating the swampland.

Most people in this part of the Parallel—if you could call them *people*—belonged to the Death King. First were the wights, skeletal beasts who rode around on horseback and fought tirelessly for their king. Then there were the liches—tall, shadowy and ghostlike. If killed, they'd simply come back in a new, identical body, courtesy of the amulets in which they kept their life essence. Not a fate I'd have chosen for myself, that was for sure. Two of them stood on either side of the gates, but none said a word to challenge my presence. A sweeping gesture indicated that

I could go in, so I did, floating straight through the gate and into the castle grounds.

No liches hovered on this side of the gates, though I should have known better than to expect the Death King himself to come out and greet me. Or one of his chosen Elemental Soldiers, each hand-picked as a representative of the four elements of air, earth, water, and fire. The last time we'd seen one another, he'd unexpectedly offered me a job as his own personal Spirit Element, which I'd turned down mostly out of shock. After he'd locked me in jail and ripped out Brant's soul—temporarily turning him into a lich—I'd assumed any chances we'd had of ever being allies had crumbled to ashes. As it was, I'd helped him regain his throne from the dickhead who'd stolen his soul, while he'd helped me survive the aftermath of the fight and ensured the Order hadn't punished me for the laws I'd broken.

We hadn't spoken a word to one another since. Truth be told, I hadn't the faintest idea what to say to him after all that, but if he thought I'd turned on him, I'd be more than happy to put him right on the matter.

I floated up to the castle doors, which were made of dark wood that matched the bricks, surprised to find no liches on guard duty like there normally were. I hovered awkwardly on the spot, not wanting to float through the doors in case I got ambushed for trespassing. It wouldn't be the first time, but back then, it'd been a total accident.

I looked around for any signs of life... or death... but even my friend Dex was nowhere to be seen. Granted, the fire sprite wasn't the Death King's biggest fan, either.

I reached out to knock on the door, and my hand passed through the wood. So much for that idea. Huge pillars embedded with grinning skulls stood on either side of the gates. The Death King had once hinted that the skulls belonged to people who'd annoyed him, and he wasn't the type to joke around.

"Alas, poor Yorrick," I said to one of the grinning skulls. "I knew him, Horatio. I wonder what you did to deserve this fate. Trod on the Death King's foot, probably."

I stiffened, sensing someone watching me. A tall, shadowy figure had passed through the doors without opening them, silent and still. The Death King wore a long dark cloak and an equally dark suit of armour which moulded to his body. His dark mask concealed his features, though I was fairly certain nothing at all lay beneath. Yet somehow, I still knew he was staring at me.

"How long have you been standing there?" I asked.

"Long enough. You're quoting Shakespeare."

"Yes. I am." Why was he looking at me like that? I didn't think I'd done *that* bad a job at my Hamlet impersonation. "Where are your guards?"

"Dealing with important business," he said. "I'm somewhat surprised to see you here like this." He gave a sweeping gesture at my transparent form.

"I didn't think it was worth the hassle of coming here in the flesh," I told him. "What do you want?"

"I don't recall asking you for help."

"Excuse me?" I folded my arms across my chest. "What was the point in sending your Air Element to give me a rude wakeup call, then? They woke me up and accused me of spreading your secrets."

"Not on my orders, they didn't."

"It's a good job I didn't bother breaking the law to

come here in the flesh, then." Nobody managed to infuriate me quite like the Death King. "What was the accusation for? Did you get bored and decide you needed to start a feud with someone?"

"I meant they weren't supposed to threaten you," he corrected. "I did ask them to bring you to speak to me."

"What do you want with me, then?" I frowned. "What's so important that you couldn't come to see me in person?"

He beckoned me to follow him into the castle. "Someone is killing my liches."

3

I stared at the Death King for a moment. "What? Someone's killing your people? How is that possible?"

"I imagine you know how."

"No, I really don't." Liches were immortal. Kill one and they just got up again, courtesy of their souls' separation from their bodies and stored in a— "Oh. The soul amulets?"

"Yes." His voice tightened with anger, and I pictured the expression on the face that lay beneath his mask turning to rage. Or rather, the face that had once been his, back when he'd been human. He put on an illusion of his human guise whenever he crossed over to Earth—a handy way to avoid freaking people out—but most of the time he played the Grim Reaper. Effectively, I might add.

"What happened?" I asked. "Someone stole one of your souls again?"

"So it seems." The fury in his words hit me like a whip, and I barely suppressed a flinch. "I don't yet know how they did it, but it's only possible for one of us to be killed if the vessel holding their soul is compromised."

Well, shit. "You think the lich who betrayed you is still around? Or Cobb told someone else how to break into your hall of souls?"

"That, or he and his allies took more than one soul during the original theft," he said. "There is no other way for one of us to die."

"I'll take your word for it on that," I said. "But if you don't know who's responsible, then I'm not sure if I can be much help."

"You have more experience in the area than the average person, and you remain the only living person who has seen what the inside of my hall of souls looks like," he said. "Except for my Elemental Soldiers, of course."

What was he implying? "I didn't *tell* anyone. And I wouldn't have known if any of the other souls were missing. Didn't you put extra security outside after the incident a few weeks ago?"

"I did," he said. "Nobody has ever stolen anything of mine aside from the recent transgression, so I can only assume it's connected to the individual who took my own soul amulet out of my hands."

No kidding. The place was a fortress, and of all our enemies, only the traitorous lich had survived—by virtue of blending in among the other liches. While the Death King distinguished himself by the armoured clothing he wore, the others were near-identical. Picking one out of a line-up would be all but impossible.

"If someone stole more soul amulets, were there any

signs of a break-in recently?" I asked. "Are you certain they disappeared at the same time as yours?"

"No, but the victims' soul amulets are all unaccounted for," he said. "I want you to find them."

"How am I supposed to do that?" I said. "I can hardly walk around the market asking about stolen soul amulets, can I? People will recognise me from the battle. I'm as big a target as you are."

"Do you really believe that?" he said. "How many times have you been recognised here in the Parallel since the battle?"

Well... none. Not that I paid social calls to the residents of Arcadia most of the time, unless I was sent to confiscate illegal artefacts on the Order's behalf. While the Death King's soldiers recognised me as the person who'd saved their master's soul, to ordinary people, I remained a nobody.

"Okay, I see your point," I allowed. "But you're making a lot of assumptions about what the Order will let me do. They only let me off without punishment last time because they didn't find out I used spirit magic, but it'll only take one slip-up for me to end up getting slapped with a memory spell again. What's to stop you from walking around the city and questioning people yourself? I'm pretty sure anyone will talk to you if you ask."

"You'd be surprised," he said. "Most people don't react well to force."

I raised an eyebrow. "You might want to try telling that to those Elemental Soldiers of yours."

He ignored the jab. "If it was possible for me to investigate on the ground myself, I would, but I have too many other matters to attend to, and I will not leave my castle unattended."

"So you want *me* to?" My voice rose in surprise. "What about your four Elements? The Air Element seems to be taking matters into their own hands, anyway."

He shook his head. "My Elemental Soldiers are needed to defend the castle. Besides, they're not trained in espionage."

"Uh, neither am I," I told him. "I'm a retriever for the Order. I find dangerous shit that's been stolen and return it to a secure location. I don't spy on people."

"Precisely," he said. "If any of my liches' soul amulets have been removed from the hall of souls, I'm sure I can rely on you to track them down, given your contacts."

Meaning, Brant. "Why me? You're not my employer. The Order is. Not only are you asking me to go out of my way as a favour, you're potentially asking me to go against the people who actually pay me."

"I wouldn't expect you to go uncompensated for your efforts," he said. "I should have made that plainer at the start. I can pay you generously."

Of course he would offer me money at a time that I desperately needed it. And if he'd been anyone else, I might have considered taking him up on the offer... if not for his apparent obliviousness to the fact that my own soul was more fragile than his. "I already turned down the offer of working with you, on account of the fact that spirit magic is *illegal*. We can't all have endless second chances at life."

"I have no intention of asking you to use spirit magic," he said. "I'm simply requesting that you keep an eye out for any missing amulets. I'm sure it won't be impossible for you and the fire mage to talk to traders at the markets you frequent."

"Now you're making assumptions about my boyfriend *and* the Order."

"I was under the impression questioning rogue mages isn't new territory for you." His tone was slightly peeved, as though he was disappointed by my refusal. "I'm not asking you to break the laws."

Yeah, that's because you make *the laws here.* Though the vampires ruled the city, and they and the Death King had a long-standing rivalry. Maybe that was why he refused to leave his castle to question people in the city. The vampires were forever wanting to expand their territory... which was just one more reason for me to stay the hell out of their business.

He kept looking at me, not to be contented with silence. Fine, then. "I'll see what the Order says about me taking on a side job in the Parallel for another employer."

Which meant, *no way in hell.* He couldn't be that desperate, surely. I was the *last* person he should be asking for help, and whatever he thought, involving me was more trouble than it was worth. For all of us.

"Very well," the Death King said. "I'll be waiting for you next time, Olivia."

I opened my mouth to tell him to call me Liv—only the Order called me Olivia—then caught myself just in time. That would be too friendly. Not to mention I was pretty sure his real name wasn't *Death King,* but he'd never told me what it was, and I didn't want to spend any more time with him than I had to.

I turned and floated back through the castle doors and down the stone steps, towards the rippling point of the node in front of the castle. As soon as I moved into its path, energy rushed through me, and I crossed back into the house on the other side.

Devon's muffled laughter greeted me, along with someone else's. Trix sat beside my body on the sofa and burst into hysterical giggles at the sight of me. Tall and slender with pointed ears and silky hair, the elf must have shown up while I was on the other side.

"What's so funny?" I said.

Devon grinned. "You might want to look in a mirror."

"Oh, for the Elements' sakes." I floated downward and peered at the body I'd left behind. My face had been carefully painted to resemble one of the ogres from our D&D campaign. "Hilarious. How old are you two, really?"

Trix snickered. "What were you doing that you didn't need your body for?"

"Astral projecting into the Parallel to talk to the Death King." I slipped back into my body and sat up, stretching out the kinks in my neck. Then I rose to my feet and walked into the kitchen to clean my face. "This is a waste of your decent makeup, Devon."

"Hey, I have to get some practise in before comic con."

I scrubbed my face over the sink while Trix got the laughter out of his system. By the time I'd returned to join them, he was still snickering at my misfortune.

"Are you done?" I rolled my eyes and sat down next to Devon. "I take it your customers didn't show up, then?"

"You haven't been gone that long," she responded. "Nobody's shopping for cantrips."

"Why, did a rival business open up down the road and nobody told us about it?" I was joking, but Trix sat up straighter, no longer laughing.

"In the Parallel, yes," he said.

"What?" Devon frowned at him. "What d'you mean?"

"I thought you knew," said the elf. "The Collective of Spells, also known as the COS. They're new at the market, and they sell state-of-the-art cantrips. Everyone buys from there."

"Seriously?" I blinked. "First I've heard. Who is this COS?"

"I don't know."

Brant might know. There was little he missed when it came to the workings of the markets in the city. He probably wouldn't have thought to mention a new source of cantrips, but if this new collective was taking away our business, we needed to know about it. The reason so many practitioners came to Devon in the first place was because she didn't come with the usual risks of buying a cantrip in the Parallel—namely, the risk of it backfiring in the user's face. Despite years of complaints, the vampires who ruled the city of Arcadia refused to allow any kind of legislation which would lower the risk levels, and if a legitimate business had stepped in, they might have filled a gap in the market for people who didn't want to risk being caught by the Order when they came to Devon's shop to buy their cantrips.

I turned to Trix again. "When did they set up their business?"

"A few weeks ago," he said. "They pretty much appeared overnight."

"Can't have happened overnight," said Devon. "You need the right materials to make spells. Not to mention skills most practitioners don't have the patience to learn."

It was a point of contention for Devon, because the

Order had refused to listen to her appeal after she'd failed her exams at the academy and had assumed that she spent all her time making cantrips instead of studying was a choice rather than a symptom of undiagnosed ADHD. By the time she'd got the diagnosis, it was already too late. That was how we'd met, as two dropouts below the Order's lowest rung, yet we'd clawed our way up from rock bottom once before. Like hell would I let anyone take away everything we'd managed to gain in the last few years.

Trix fidgeted. "I don't know, you'll have to ask them."

"I might just do that." Whoever these newcomers were, they surely couldn't be new to the Parallel itself, so maybe they'd heard if someone was still trading in soul amulets. I'd see what Brant said when I brought up the subject.

And here I was, actually thinking about taking the Death King up on his offer. *You should know better than that, Liv.*

"You haven't said what the Death King wanted," Devon said. "Go on, spill. Is he really pissed at you?"

"He's trying to hire me as a private investigator and spy, despite the fact that it isn't my job and he isn't my employer." I gave her the rundown. As predicted, Devon gained a calculating expression when I mentioned his offer of 'generous' compensation.

"He's probably loaded, given that he lives in a castle," she said. "He can't have much to spend his fortune on, either, being dead."

"He might have done a better job decorating the place, considering," I said. "I know he's an ancient immortal, but still. I can't take money from him. He probably stole it all from the people he's murdered."

I didn't know how long he'd been Death King, but his Court had ruled that part of the Parallel since before the war. They'd outlived the Elements and anyone else who'd ever held power … ironic, considering their undead state. Which was probably *why* nobody had killed them off.

No wonder he was worried that someone might have found out his liches' weakness lay in the soul amulets— but I didn't know nearly enough about how it all worked to figure out how this particular killer was operating. He hadn't even told me how the liches had died.

"Money is money, and we're almost out," said Devon. "Take the job. You can always back out and say the Order doesn't want you working with him if it turns bad."

"You're supposed to tell me not to take risks," I said. "Also, he works *with* the Order, so it wouldn't surprise me if I walked into the office to find him sitting there again trying to blackmail me."

"He's not trying to kill you anymore, though," said Devon. "I know, I'm the last person who should be encouraging you to cooperate with him, but this job is just what we need to get us out of this hole."

Yeah, right. Still, if I took my request to the Order and gained a permit to get into the Parallel, I might at least be able to see how much of a threat this Collective of Spells was. I could also ask around about soul amulets, and if it turned out they didn't know anything, then I'd leave it there. I wouldn't take any permanent jobs from the Death King, not in a million years. He was manipulative, cruel, and inhuman, and he could crush me in the palm of his hand if so inclined.

Yet considering all that, he must feel he had no choice

if he'd opted to ask *me* for help. His supposed enemy. A living spirit mage with too much to lose.

Despite everything, it was reassuring to think that no matter what the universe threw my way, I could always count on my enmity with the Death King.

4

I wouldn't have put it past His Deathly Highness to find out if I didn't keep my word, so off to the Order's office I went. I was actually starting to entertain the idea of using him as a cover story. If the Order thought I was working hand in hand with the notorious King of the Dead, they might start treating me a little less like pond scum. Already, some people had taken to avoiding eye contact with me in the corridors, based on the Death King's intervention with Mr Cobb's trial. Better than their disdainful mutters about the black mark on my record and my abysmal grades at the academy.

On the other hand, basing the Death King's potential actions on one favour he'd done for me was a dangerous idea. He might not step in to save my neck the next time I wound up on the chopping block, and without his own life on the line, there was nothing to stop him from leaving the Order to hang me out to dry.

I rode the bus into town to walk to the Order's HQ and shot Brant a text on the way asking him to meet me by the nearby node to the Parallel—assuming the Order gave me permission to go, that is. I decided against telling him my plan until we met in person. I didn't *think* he'd flip out and flat-out refuse to let me take on the Death King's mission, but his request was too bizarre to accurately convey via text message.

I showed my Order ID to the guards outside the narrow brick building which served as the Order's local branch—both of whom made a big show of goggling at the black mark on my ID, as usual—and walked through the reception area to the stairs leading down to the retrieval unit. The head of the department, Mrs Carlisle, occupied the desk with the computer, while boxes filled the rest of the space inside the basement. Judging by their hand-written labels, they must have come from the Parallel.

"What's in here?" I peered through the gap in the nearest box's seal, which revealed a number of gleaming coins. Cantrips, already pre-made. Where'd they materialised from?

"New tools for our staff," said Mrs Carlisle. "After the incident a few weeks ago, the upper room gave us permission to update our repertoire of defensive spells for use in battle."

"You commissioned cantrips for the retrieval unit?" I said. "Wait, if they're from the Parallel, how do you know they're safe to use? I thought most cantrips made over on that side were either duds or dangerous."

The Order's regulations only covered this side of the nodes. Everyone knew that.

"Our new supplier is different," said Mrs Carlisle. "We have reassurance that they're in compliance with Order standards, and these cantrips have been thoroughly tested before being distributed among our staff."

"Damn," I said. "I guess that's why we haven't had much business lately."

"That's right, your friend makes cantrips, doesn't she?" Mrs Carlisle looked up from the computer screen, wearing a calculating expression I didn't like. "Pity."

"What does that mean?" I said. "Isn't it more convenient for you that you have someone on this side you can buy from? I mean, the Parallel isn't known for sticking with standardised safety regulations. The vampires don't have any need for them."

"I wouldn't expect you to understand, Olivia." She tapped on the keyboard, her attention on the computer screen again. "It's beyond your level."

Now that was just patronising. "If you're wondering why I'm here, the Death King came to me with a job offer and requested that I visit him in the Parallel. I'm going to need a permit."

She halted, her hand on the computer mouse. "The Death King came to you?"

More or less. I didn't need to mention the fact that I'd used astral projection. It'd be easier if they assumed that he'd come to visit me instead of the other way around. "Yes, he did. He has a job that only I can do."

"Which is...?"

"Confidential."

"No." She shook her head. "I can't give you a permit without any more details."

"Ask the Death King himself," I said. "Or you can send someone to tag along after me into the swamplands of the dead if you really want to."

Her mouth thinned. It was a low blow given how many Order people had died in the battle in the swamplands, but even if that hadn't been the site of our final stand against Mr Cobb, nobody wanted to go to the Death King's home anyway. Even the Order knew better than to draw the ire of the most powerful individual in the Parallel.

"Fine." Mrs Carlisle held out a hand, and I pushed my ID book across the desk to her. She stamped it one-handedly without looking at me. "Don't be surprised if you're subject to interrogation upon your return."

"As I said, you're welcome to ask the Death King for further details." I rose to my feet and climbed up the stairs to the reception area, where practitioners milled around in groups, either returning from trips to the Parallel or chatting between missions. While the notion of the retrieval unit gaining better equipment wasn't an unappealing one, we were a long way off from the funding the upper levels got. Like proper clothing designed for the unpredictable conditions of the Parallel. My once-squeaky-clean new boots were already dyed mud-brown from traipsing through the swampland, as were the frayed hems of my jeans, while the unpredictable climate and hostile inhabitants had pretty much destroyed most of my wardrobe.

I left the Order's HQ and made my way to meet Brant. He greeted me with a kiss, his worried gaze raking me up and down. "You're going to the Parallel? I thought you were going to take my advice and see the Death King the other way. Not in person."

"I did." I dropped my voice. "Astral project, I mean. He's just a cover story so I could get a permit to go to

Arcadia and have a look around. There's something fishy going on at the market."

I told him about the new cantrip business Trix had mentioned as we headed towards the node leading into the Parallel.

"Damn," he said. "First I've heard of it. I haven't been in the market much lately, but they must have set up shop fast."

"Apparently, and not only are they stealing our independent clients, they've snagged the Order, too, by sticking to their regulations," I said. "Which is kind of weird for a Parallel-owned business."

The Order's notoriously finicky nature meant anyone who wanted to sell to them had to fill out reams of paperwork. Most people in the Parallel were just trying to stay alive, so even the legitimate practitioners discounted the Order's members as a potential market because they didn't have time for that shit.

"No kidding," he said. "That's not what the Death King wanted to speak to you about, is it?"

"No…" If the Death King found out I'd told Brant about his request, he'd be displeased to say the least, and the very last thing I wanted was for Brant to part company with his soul again. "He's concerned because the lich insider wasn't caught and he's growing paranoid about someone sharing his secrets with outsiders. Which is why the Air Element decided to take matters into their own hands."

He frowned. "What does he expect you to do about that?"

"Question people at the market who might know about illegal trade in soul amulets." I halted beside the node. "Needless to say, I'm not his lapdog, but it gave me a handy excuse to grab a permit so I can snoop around the market. If the Order's people decide to ask him if he really gave me permission to be there, I'll be forced to comply with his orders, but I'll leave it up to them to decide whether to take the risk of angering His Deathly Highness."

Brant grinned. "Hey, if it gives you an excuse to go into the Parallel without the Order kicking up a fuss, maybe you should play that card more often."

"I'll pretend the Death King and I are BFFs." I might be skirting his orders, but he must know I wasn't a spy or a professional investigator. If I happened to find any clues at the market, I'd pass them to him if I had to, but I wasn't holding my breath. As for not telling Brant? It wasn't a light decision, but anything that could kill a lich could do much worse to a living person.

Brant and I stepped through the node in a rush of energy which woke me up more thoroughly than a triple espresso shot. Revelling in the sudden burst of power in my veins, I didn't see the revenants until we landed on top of them.

Three figures appeared from the light, and Brant got between me and them, his hands alight with fire. I grabbed for my pouch of cantrips and flung a paralysis spell in their direction. The revenants all froze mid-motion, teeth bared and hands outstretched. They were shaped like skinny hairless humanoid beings with sharp nails and teeth. Vampires without the sex appeal, who fed on the energy from the nodes. *Note to self: look before you leap next time.*

Brant blasted them with fire, and their papery skin

ignited. Within seconds, all three turned into piles of ashes which scattered onto the rain-damp earth.

"I'm guessing they were snacking on the node when we landed on top of them." I ran my foot over the ashy ground, glad one of us had enough firepower to take them out without causing too much of a scene.

"They don't normally come to the surface, though," Brant said.

Fair point. While revenants and their vampire counterparts weren't allergic to sunlight, they preferred the night hours. The day was overcast, admittedly, but the tunnels weren't far from here. Strange for them to come aboveground, but maybe another group had driven them out of their usual hangout.

Brant and I made our way through the winding dirt road to the tangle of warehouses on the outskirts of the city of Arcadia. For whatever reason, the vampires had ordered the central warehouse to be the designated area for all official magic-based trade, so most practitioners congregated around that area. This side of the city was also popular with mages, while elves, vampires, shapeshifters and other magical folk generally stuck to living among their own kind. Despite that, the markets were full of an eclectic bunch of people who came there on a daily basis for their magic fix.

I looked up at the dull cloudy sky. "I should find Dex. I haven't seen him for a while."

"Are you sure you want to take him into the market with you?" he said. "Fires spread in close quarters."

"Hey, I'm taking *you* with me." I shot him a playful grin. "Didn't you once set your own house on fire?"

His cheeks turned adorably pink. "That was when I was a kid and I couldn't control it."

Brant, like many mages, had been disowned by his regular human family after one fire too many and had ended up running away into the Parallel. He hadn't had an easy life, and it'd be hypocritical of me to judge him for doing whatever was necessary to survive. The guy had an ethical code, which was more than I could say for most mages I'd met.

The warehouse doors stood wide open to allow us to enter the market, which consisted of a collection of stalls selling everything from enchanted clothing to magical delicacies. Cantrips were widespread, ranging from expensive transformation spells to more everyday charms like insect repellents and water-breathing spells. The flow of foot traffic was aggressive enough that stopping to take a look ran the risk of being trampled by overeager practitioners searching for the latest bargains. Even the vampires, who didn't usually venture outside during the day, were walking around with their hoods pulled up, their pale eyes scanning the wares on offer.

The third time someone trod on my foot, I gave Brant an exasperated look. "Why not just ask someone for directions?"

Brant, who'd rather cut off his own tongue than ask for assistance, shook his head, so I accosted a middle-aged man with a scarred face. "Hey, there. Any new practitioners in here?"

He grunted. "There always are."

"Is there a group who are selling legit cantrips to the Order, then?" I elaborated.

His head snapped up. "You're with them? Get out of here."

Well, now. I hadn't expected a direct answer, much less an overt display of aggression. "Why?"

"I don't trade with Order lackeys," he said flatly.

"We're not with the Order," Brant interjected. "We're curious as to who these new practitioners are. It seems they're snapping up a lot of the local business."

"Of course they are," he said. "What do you expect? This place is littered with so-called magicians who'll as soon as hex your testicles off as give you a protective charm."

"He's not wrong there," I whispered to Brant. "Whereabouts might we find these new practitioners?"

"That way." He pointed towards the back of the warehouse, the more run-down area where the ceiling leaked when it rained, and draughts snuck in through gaps in the walls.

So the practitioners were overtly selling to the Order in front of witnesses? Interesting, and not typical of the Parallel. Despite the Order's authority back on Earth, a lot of people in the Parallel didn't trust them, and with good reason. The original Order of the Elements had been the ruling authority before the Council had been obliterated in the war, and the new authorities had kept the same name afterwards despite the unpleasant connotations. Which seemed a weird move to me, knowing what I now knew about spirit magic.

The Parallel had been fractured long before the war, but when the Council of the Elements had been in charge, they'd at least tried to keep the population alive and thriving. Now, with the vampires ruling the city, they only needed to ensure enough humans survived to maintain their food supply. The rest of us could die for all they cared. The lack of safety regulations in here was testament enough to that, and I had to stop a kid of barely sixteen from buying a dud cantrip which was nothing more than a regular ten-pence piece covered in sharpie.

"Hey, fuck off," the seller said. "Mind your own business."

"Stop selling your shit to desperate kids, then." I flicked the cantrip back into his face, and his shouts pursued me through the market stalls.

Brant caught my arm. "Don't go wandering off like that."

"I wasn't about to get that kid get taken in," I said, more irritable than usual due to the heat and the crowds and the general atmosphere of aggressive bartering.

Then my gaze fell on the back row of stalls, an area which seemed positively pristine compared to the rest of the market. The back wall looked to have been completely rebuilt, while the ceiling no longer dripped the remnants of recent rainfall onto anyone unlucky enough to have their stalls set up below. A pair of long wooden tables dominated the rear of the warehouse, lined with endless coin-shaped cantrips arranged in rows of a dozen. Far too many to have been hand-crafted by a single person. A banner adorned the wall behind the tables. *Collective of Spells.* This was it.

"Can I help you?" said a dark-skinned young woman with braided hair, stepping up behind the rows of cantrips.

"Yes," I said. "Did you make all these yourself?"

"Oh, we're not the manufacturers," she said. "We just

sell them."

Brant and I exchanged baffled looks. Partnerships like Devon's and mine were common enough, but not on this scale. Each of the more complex spells would take hours to make, regardless of the practitioner's skill level, and the materials alone would cost a lower-ranked Order employee several months of wages.

"When you say you're not the manufacturers, who made them?" asked Brant.

"You'll have to talk to a supervisor," she said.

"Meaning…?" I began.

A short man elbowed past me and started negotiating for a price on sleeping spells as though I wasn't there. Trying to quash my irritation, I stepped aside to speak to Brant.

"That's not one person's work," he said, echoing my thoughts.

"So there's some kind of factory mass-producing cantrips?" That didn't sound right, either. No machine could mimic a practitioner, and I'd always assumed there weren't nearly enough people with a gift for spellwork within the city to form a collective.

"No way," he said. "That wouldn't be possible even if this place wasn't stuck in the Dark Ages."

"I wonder if the vampire council approved this," I said in an undertone. "It seems set to shake up things in a major way."

The Death King wouldn't care, most likely, but then again, his people had everything they wanted and needed. Being dead had its perks, that was for sure. The vampires, on the other hand, were control freaks, if not to the same degree as the Order was. They wouldn't stand for anybody upending their status at the top of the food chain.

A faint breeze drifted overhead, but not from a gap in the warehouse wall. Then, as though conjured up by my thoughts, the Air Element walked past the table, dressed in full armour with the Death King's symbol on full display.

"Great," I murmured. "You know, I can see why the Death King wanted me to do the espionage part. His soldiers are as subtle as a house fire."

Mutters and whispers followed the Air Element's path through the market. Everyone knew that uniform, if the expression of disdain and superiority wasn't enough on its own. The breeze stirred up in the soldier's wake sent several practitioners scrambling to stop their tables from falling over.

And the prize for the most dramatic entrance of the week goes to...

Resigned, I walked up to Ryan and halted before them. "Let me guess, you want to know why I'm slacking off on duty."

"I'm not here for you," Ryan informed me.

"That's nice," I said. "You forgot to add, *I'm sorry for crashing into your bedroom and attacking you for a crime you never committed.*"

Too late, I remembered Brant... whose hands were sparking with fire. Oh, crap.

"Apologise to her," he said in a warning tone.

Dammit. I had to get him out of here before the two of them kicked off a full-on brawl which might well end with half the market on fire.

I grabbed Brant's elbow. "We'll talk later. C'mon, we don't need to make a scene."

Ignoring the stares, I all but hauled Brant after me through the crowd towards the warehouse doors. After a moment, he stopped resisting, though his face remained twisted in a scowl. I released him when we reached the street, leaving the warehouse's crowd behind.

"What was that about?" I said. "Brant, put out the fire. People are staring."

He let the flames die down. "I don't trust those Elements."

"Nor me. I wonder who they were looking for in there." I took a few steps away from the warehouse door, keeping one eye on Brant. "I expected to get my ear chewed off for wandering around the market instead of going to see the Death King like I told the Order, but I guess the Elemental Soldiers didn't hear about that. They weren't around when I saw the Death King at his castle, either."

"Maybe he sent them to spy for him."

"I thought that was supposed to be my job," I said. "Maybe the Death King asked them to check out the market, then. He must know about our new competitors."

"I don't doubt it," he said. "I'll talk to my contacts, see who might know the brains behind the operation. There's got to be a whole network involved with this Collective of Spells."

"Has to be, if they're complying with Order standards." Unease trickled down my spine. "I don't like this."

Brant had mentioned changes in the Parallel, but he seemed as stumped by the new development as I was.

"Nor do I," he said. "Do you want to head home? Or… were you serious about checking in with the Death King?"

"I would if I had anything to report to him," I said. "I didn't even think to ask at the market."

"What, about potential lich traitors passing on his secrets?" he said. "I doubt anyone out here would know. Besides, it's probably too soon after the battle to bring up the subject."

"Yeah," I murmured. "I don't know what the Death King was thinking, offering me a job."

He glanced at me. "Did he offer to pay you well?"

"Yes. That's part of the problem." I dug my hands in my pockets. "Since thanks to our friends back there, Devon and I are heading full-speed towards big trouble."

"Speaking of trouble…" He trailed off, pointed at three skeletal figures staggering in our direction.

Ah, shit. The revenants from earlier had brought friends.

5

Brant leapt in with flaming hands, while I dug into the pouch at my waist. One of the revenants lunged at me, but I flicked a D20 at him and it hit it in the forehead, knocking it straight into the path of Brant's flames. I scooped up the die before it fell victim to his fiery attack. The second revenant tried to take a bite out of my face, but I slammed my foot into its knee. Bone crunched, and it fell sideways into the path of Brant's fire.

Flames ate away at the revenants' bones, turning all three of them into ashes.

"What the hell is with these revenants?" I said. "They don't normally come aboveground during the day, if at all."

"I know." Brant shook a dusting of ashes from his hands, looking perturbed. "I reckon something drove them out of their nest."

My gaze fell on a nearby set of stairs leading into the tunnels that lay beneath the city. "They came from in there."

"Don't tell me you want to go and look."

I answered by walking over to the stairs and peering down into the gloom. "Might as well do something constructive."

Brant groaned. "You know what, I'd have preferred it if you'd opted to visit the Death King. This sort of thing never ends well."

"I *have* played over two hundred hours of Skyrim, you know." I pulled a cantrip infused with a light spell from my pocket. "I'm also wondering if Dex might be hiding underground. It's strange for him not to at least show up and say hi."

I understood why Dex would avoid enclosed spaces after his bad experience in the Death King's jail, but my curiosity about those revenants refused to be sated. What had happened to drive them away from the underground node?

I flicked on my light spell and climbed downstairs, halting halfway to shine the light over the murky walls. *The intrepid sorceress rolls a perception check.* Nothing stirred in the darkness below. So far, so good.

Brant descended behind me, grumbling under his breath. I continued until my feet touched down on solid ground, using the spell to light the gloom and wishing Dex was with me. It was odd for him to avoid me, but he wasn't Brant's biggest fan, and the two of us had been spending a lot more time together over the last few weeks.

Brant reached the foot of the stairs behind me. He cupped a flame in his hands, his own handy torch. "I hope you know where you're going."

"The node is that way." I pointed through the murky

tunnel. "I had to find my way out of here pretty fast a few weeks ago."

That, and I could feel the node's current of magical energy thrumming below the earth like the pounding of a subterranean waterfall crashing onto the rocks below. Brant gave me a sideways look. "You sure that's why, and not your sixth sense?"

"My spider-senses are dead-on." I shot him a grin, turning right down a tunnel. Brant fell into step with me, sliding his hand into mine. He didn't need to hold my hand, but I didn't push him away. I was still working on rebuilding trust between us. Since losing my memories, good friends were hard to come by. Opening my heart to a romantic relationship, even harder. Brant had been nothing but patient with me so far, thankfully.

As the node's buzzing grew stronger, a horrible smell rose from the tunnel ahead, like a drain clogged with decomposing rats.

I gagged. "What the hell is that?"

"Something dead," said Brant grimly. "It's been rotting down here for a while, I'm guessing."

"Ugh." I slipped my hand out of his and pulled my coat over my nose and mouth. "I'd blame it for scaring off the revenants, but they don't have any sense of smell. They're foul enough on their own."

The node's buzzing intensified, and the tips of my fingers tingled with static. I was too close to turn back now, so I finished rounding the corner. Brant halted mid-step, cursing under his breath. I squinted ahead, trying to see what his more effective eyesight had picked out, and my gorge rose.

A pile of bodies lay in front of the surging energy of

the node, roughly heaped on top of one another. Revenants, by the look of things, and not killed by anything human. Claw marks ripped through their papery skin, revealing splintered bones and torn flesh. No wonder those other revenants had run to the surface to feed. But what could have killed them in such a manner? Being undead, they were stronger and faster than regular humans, though I doubted a person had ripped them up. No, some kind of monster had ambushed them here in the darkness.

"Creepy," I murmured. "What do the vamps think of all this?"

Revenants were cousins of sorts to the vampires, created when a vamp drained a human entirely of blood without feeding them vampire blood in order to complete the reanimation ritual. As a result, revenants fed on the energy of the nodes rather than drinking blood from living beings, so the vampires who ruled the city tended to leave them be. That didn't make the fact that they'd been left to rot down here in the darkness any less strange.

"Let's get out of here." Brant's face appeared greenish in the half-light. "Better leave those to whatever killed them."

"I don't think it expected to get a meal out of them." My gaze snagged on the node, a torrent of unbroken energy, and alarm sparked within me. "What if whatever killed them got out through the node? It might have ended up on Earth."

He shot me a look tinged with concern. "I just had the same thought, but the Order would know if something dangerous was at risk of crossing over."

"If not, I can always report it." I gave a grim smile. "I'm *sure* they won't pin the blame on me this time."

Meaning, no way in hell would I be the one to enlighten the Order on the possibility of there being some unknown monster at large with enough power to rip through revenants. Knowing them, they wouldn't believe me unless I brought proof. But there was someone who *might* believe me… and who I was supposed to be meeting with anyway.

Brant and I returned to the surface on swift feet, the horrible smell pursuing us like a persistent ghost. By the time I clambered up the ladder to the surface, my hands were shaking, and the taste of bile coated the back of my throat.

"I think you should go home," Brant insisted. "The last thing you need is a meeting with His Deathly Highness after seeing that."

"I like how that's his official title now," I said. "Good job I haven't accidentally let it slip in front of him. Or about how he inspired a villain in our D&D campaign…" I trailed off. A familiar pair of armour-wearing figures stood at the edge of the alleyway as though they'd been waiting for us to climb to the surface. One was the Air Element, while the other was a tall lanky guy with dark hair and a scowl on his pale face. He wore a cloak identical to the Air Element's, except lined with dark red instead of green.

"You," said Ryan. "What were you saying about my master?"

Uh-oh. "Nothing important. What are you doing here?"

"I saw you going into the tunnel, so I decided to wait

until you came to the surface," said Ryan. "This is Davies, the Death King's Fire Element."

"Hey," I said to him. "I'm Liv."

The Fire Element grunted in acknowledgement. Then his gaze fell on Brant, and his eyes narrowed. "Didn't my master turn you into a lich?"

Brant's expression turned equally hostile. Oh, boy. Fire mages in general didn't get along with one another at the best of times, and Brant had a short fuse. It looked like this dude did, too.

"Nobody is getting turned into a lich!" I took a step forward, placing myself between Davies and Brant. "I'm guessing you waited for me because your master wants to ask me a favour again?"

"He wants your report, of course," said Ryan, apparently not noticing the fiery tension next to us.

"He's not her employer," said Brant.

The Fire Element scoffed. "Can't she speak for herself?"

"Yes, she can." I shot Brant a warning look. "I find it interesting that none of the authorities here are talking about the state of the tunnels. Does your master know there's a pile of dead revenants down there?"

Ryan frowned. "The tunnels aren't part of my master's jurisdiction, so it's none of our business what happens down there."

That figured. The underground was the lowest level of the city of Arcadia, but that didn't mean whatever had attacked those revenants wouldn't find its way to the surface. If it hadn't already.

Davies scoffed. "C'mon, Ryan. If those two want to slum it with the revenants, they're welcome to."

He swept around and walked away, his cloak billowing behind him. After a moment, Ryan followed. Brant made to ambush the Fire Element from behind, but I caught his arm, dodging the flames that sparked on his hands.

"Brant," I said out of the corner of my mouth. "You can either stay here and ask more questions at the market or come with me and promise not to set the Death King's castle on fire. I went through hell to get your soul back into your body once and I'd rather not do it again."

"Fine," he said. "I'll stay here, but if those arseholes try anything, I'd be more than happy to teach them a lesson."

"I'd rather your soul stays put." I leant in to brush my lips against his. "Don't let the Elements get you down."

His mouth twitched. "Isn't that usually my line?"

"Not in so many words." I turned after the retreating Elemental Soldiers. "See you later."

I caught up to the two armoured soldiers at the edge of the expanse of swampland leading up to the Death King's castle. Ryan whistled, and a skeletal horse trotted over to them. A second horse kicked moodily at the marshy ground, the bone of its skull gleaming in the weak sunlight. The Fire Element swung up onto its back with ease, cantering away across the marshy ground.

Ryan whistled again, and a third skeletal horse materialised. "Do you want to ride?"

"Me?" My voice rose in surprise. I didn't particularly fancy wading through the swamp while those two ran miles ahead of me, but the horse was... well, *dead*. "I've never ridden a horse in my life. Living or otherwise." I was a city girl, after all.

"It's easy." Ryan handed me the reins of the first beast. "This is Neddie. He's friendly to new riders."

A zombie horse called Neddie. Why not.

I gave the skeletal horse a sceptical look. "Okay, mate. Let's give this a go."

The horse bent its head, which gleamed smooth and white. Trying not to think about how fragile it looked, I climbed into the stirrup and positioned myself on the saddle.

The Fire Element had already taken off, but Ryan held back to keep pace with me, which was oddly kind. An attempt to make up for breaking into my house, maybe. The ride was almost relaxing if I didn't look down and remind myself that I was riding a skeleton, reanimated by magic and held together by little more than a fragment of spirit energy.

"Why dead horses?" I asked. "Why not bring in live ones?"

"It's easier to use a reanimation spell than tame a living horse," said Ryan. "Living horses wouldn't come near this place, anyway."

"Sensible animals." My hips protested at the jolting movement as we shuddered to a stop beside the gates leading to the castle.

The two liches on guard were identical on the outside, tall and dressed in black. They parted without speaking, and the gates creaked inward to let us into the castle grounds.

Getting off the horse was harder than getting on its back. My foot got stuck in the stirrup, and I'd have fallen on my arse in the mud if the Air Element hadn't used their magic to steady me. A current of air pushed me back upright and I climbed down more carefully this time.

"Thanks." I landed on my feet, facing the castle steps. "I think I'll astral project here in future."

"It does take some getting used to." Ryan led the way through the doors to the castle, which opened to reveal a large, opulent hall.

The Death King stood in his usual spot on the dais at the back of the hall. Tall and forbidding with his hood pulled up to conceal his face, he nevertheless projected an expectant look in my direction. "I take it you have news to report?"

"Kind of." Crap, I should have rehearsed what I'd say, but my thoughts had been knocked off balance by what I'd found in the tunnels and the surreal experience of riding on the back of an undead steed.

"So you don't have anything to report," he said.

His disdainful tone bothered me more than I'd have expected. "You gave me almost no information. You didn't even tell me how your people died. I need way more to go by than 'someone's killing my liches' before I can turn into a super-spy."

"What do you want me to tell you?" he said. "I was under the impression you were going to ask about the illegal trade in souls."

So I was. I'd forgotten to bring up the subject to anyone at the market after our discovery of the Collective of Spells and their mysterious acquisition of hundreds of cantrips. "There's a new trader who's taken over half the market with mass-produced cantrips. I didn't see any souls for sale, but if the liches are already dead, wouldn't their soul amulets be… well, worthless?"

If he'd had a visible face, he'd probably have shot me a glare for that comment. "Not to the right trader."

"Is that what you think happened?" I pressed. "Someone stole some of your souls and then… sold the empty amulets? Are they definitely missing?"

"Yes, but there is no telling when they were taken," he said. "I have now barred access to the hall of souls for everyone except for my closest allies, but others might have been taken during the time I was unaware of a traitor within my army."

It seemed a major risk to let anyone into the room that contained the souls of his entire army as it was, but I supposed he'd always thought he and his fellow liches were invincible.

My thoughts must have shown in my face, because he added, "The price for treachery is steep. Few would be foolish enough to risk their own soul."

"Uh-huh," I said. "How did the victims die, exactly? You said they were definitely dead, with or without their soul amulets, but not how it happened."

"You wish to see the bodies?" He stepped down off the dais. "Come with me."

Oh, boy. I suspected he was about to make me pay for failing to turn up any useful information. In fairness, I should have asked about the trade in souls while I'd been at the market, but I'd been too distracted by the new cantrips and stopping Brant from starting a fight with the Air Element. Not much of an excuse, but no thief would have been foolish enough to bring a *soul amulet* to a public market. If anyone bought it, their throat would be cut and their prize taken away before they reached the doors.

The Death King glided through a door on the right-hand side of the hall, and I hurried to catch it before it swung shut in my face. A short corridor carpeted in blue contained several more featureless doors. Apprehension warred with curiosity about seeing more of the Death King's domain, and my nervousness quadrupled as he led the way through another wooden door into a small stone-walled room.

I reached the doorway and recoiled. Two bodies lay decomposing on a table in the centre, their decaying flesh buzzing with flies. Vicious slash marks ripped each body open from shoulder to hip, revealing putrefying organs inside.

I pressed a hand to my mouth. So that's what a dead lich looked like. I could have lived a long and happy life without seeing that, thanks. "What killed them?"

"They were found in that state," he said. "As though their souls were returned to their bodies for long enough for them to die a normal death, but not long enough for their bodies to fully regenerate before decomposing. If a soul amulet is destroyed, we normally fade away."

"So it wasn't a spirit mage?" I backed up a step to get away from the smell, swallowing hard. Something with very sharp claws had killed them… but judging by the state of the bodies, something else had returned them to life first. And just where had their amulets disappeared to?

"I never said that," he said. "It should be impossible to reverse the spell turning a person into a lich—that is, for anyone who isn't like us."

"Yeah, I'm lost." I ducked into the corridor, trying hard not to vomit in front of him. "If the soul amulets are miss-ing, maybe they contain the answers. Where were the bodies found?"

"On my territory," he said. "The soul amulets have yet to be accounted for, but neither is inside the hall of souls."

I squeezed my eyes shut, feeling an oncoming headache. "I think I might be the last person you should be asking about unknown magic."

I mean, I barely knew my *own* magic.

"So you refuse to help me." He stepped into the corridor and closed the door behind him, mercifully cutting off the smell of decaying flesh. The image of the liches' half-decomposed bodies was more difficult to shake loose.

"I don't *refuse.*" I breathed through my nose and out through my mouth, walking back to the entrance hall in order to put as much distance between myself and the slaughtered liches as possible. "As a matter of fact, I found something weird in the tunnels earlier."

"Oh?" He halted beside the dais. "In what way?"

"Some kind of unknown creature with sharp claws has been slaughtering revenants," I said. "The other revenants were freaked out enough that they've started running to the surface to feed on the nodes instead of underground, which is a major pain for anyone crossing over."

"I imagine it would be." He gave me a long look I couldn't read, what with his face being hidden. "You think there's a connection."

"I have no idea," I said. "You couldn't pay me to go into those tunnels again and face whatever killed them."

"Couldn't I?"

Right. He'd already offered me cash. With our business in peril, Devon and I needed to figure out a way forward, one way or another—but my knowledge on faceless monsters that killed the dead was about as substantial as my knowledge of high fashion or water sports. That is, non-existent.

"I don't know that there's definitely a link," I said. "I'm only pointing out that both deaths involved creatures that should have already been dead ending up slaughtered. If you don't know what's responsible, I sure as hell don't. It's out of my area."

"Out of your area," he echoed. "Is nothing in your life connected to the Parallel?"

"Don't be absurd." I dug my hands in my pockets. "I'm not dead. You are. That makes it more your problem than mine."

The room seemed to grow colder with each word I spoke, as though the Death King's temper frosted the very air itself. "If that's your decision, I will honour it. Is there anything else you wish to tell me?"

"Uh." Crap. I had the distinct impression I'd made a huge mistake, but had he really expected me to throw myself headlong into the investigation after seeing the state of those bodies? "Weird question, but have you seen Dex lately? My fire sprite companion."

"No, I haven't. Any reason?"

"He usually shows up to annoy me whenever I visit the Parallel," I said. "Then again, he's not your biggest fan, seeing as how you locked him in jail that one time."

"I expect not," he said. "He's the one whose life you saved during the battle."

There was an undercurrent of meaning to his voice, meaning he knew I hadn't just saved his life… I'd brought him *back* to life, using spirit magic. Dex had died, scattered into fragments under the impact of Cobb's power.

Power he'd borrowed from the Death King.

Even spirits didn't last forever, but what I'd done—reversing Dex's death—shouldn't even be possible according to the regular laws of magic. Yet I'd done it, and the man in front of me might be the one person who could actually give me some answers. If I stepped further over the line that'd cost me two years of memories and cost my mentor his life, that is.

"Never mind," I said. "He's probably lying low, if he has any sense."

"I expect he is." His tone was neutral, with no underlying hints except those in the gaps of my imagination. Like a hidden invitation to take him up on his offer.

I shook off the thought and turned my back. "Until next time, then."

I felt the Death King watching me as I left the castle, pursued by a sense of disquiet which wasn't entirely connected to the bodies of the dead liches. I'd been right in assuming there was nothing I could do about them, nor their killer, and even the Death King was bound to accept that soon enough.

As for the fire sprite, Dex must have his reasons for being absent. I'd saved his life in as literal sense as possible. It was bound to have shaken him up a little, and if I were him, I'd want to lie low for a while. That didn't mean he was in trouble. *I hope.*

6

To no surprise, Devon was less than thrilled to learn of my latest discoveries at the market in the Parallel. Once I'd left the Death King's castle, I'd hopped straight through the node to home without bothering to check into the Order on the way back. If they wanted to know what I'd been up to, they were more than welcome to take it up with His Deathly Highness himself.

"Who the bloody hell *are* the COS?" She tugged at a loose stitch on the coat she was sewing as part of her costume for the local comic con later this month. "Who are they to think they can get away with stealing my business?"

"I'm not sure they know they're stealing it," I said. "Frankly, I'm surprised it didn't happen sooner. Even in the Parallel, people have to realise that teaming up is more efficient than going it alone."

"Yeah, *that's* not a surprise," she said. "I'm more pissed at the Order for going directly to them for all their supplies. The Order doesn't just jump headfirst into buying from an unknown supplier in the Parallel without assessing the risks first. They must have made this decision a while back"

"I suppose the Parallel is easier for them in some ways," I said. "Given how close the node near the market is to their headquarters."

She grunted, grabbing a handful of fresh thread. "Yeah, but they've bought custom cantrips from me for years. Now all this business with Cobb happens and suddenly they want nothing to do with us. Sure, maybe the COS was already in the works, but the Order stepped in to buy from them pretty damn quickly."

"Maybe it's someone from the Order who's making the cantrips," I suggested. "Must be a practitioner. A fairly substantial group of them, given how many cantrips they were selling. Nobody else can create them."

They must have asked permission from the vampires who ruled the city in order to operate, too. Small businesses or individuals could do whatever they liked until they drew the wrong attention, but a huge operation like that would get shut down hard if they stepped on the wrong toes. The vampires didn't like ceding power. I'd assumed they were indifferent at best to the Order, but that might well change if the Order's people stepped onto their turf.

"Why would the Order sell cantrips to their own members all the way over there?" she said. "They wouldn't need to bother setting up in the Parallel if that's what they wanted to do."

"Good point," I said. "Maybe it's an ex-Order

employee, then. Or they're sending some of their people over to set up a permanent base in Arcadia."

I'd thought the last thing the Order wanted was to actively work within the Parallel, the place they sent anyone too dangerous to live in the ordinary world: a definition that covered anyone who didn't want to obey the Order's stringent rules. To anyone born in the decades since the war, the idea of being able to freely walk between the two worlds seemed as distant a dream as the notion of being able to use spirit magic without consequence.

Devon stabbed the fabric with a needle. "If they're asking for volunteers, I'm not moving into the fucking Parallel."

"Ditto." As out of place as I felt among the ordinary humans here in the middle of England, the Parallel's lack of any regulations had nearly cost me my life countless times. I was as likely to die there from a paper cut as anything else. If the Order had moved in with the intention of improving life for the people living over there, it could only be a good thing... but I somehow doubted that was the case. The vampires wouldn't give up their city that easily.

Devon began stitching the seams of the coat together. "At this rate, I'll end up living off commissions for the next month."

Guilt twisted inside me for turning down the Death King's offer. But really, how did he expect me to solve his liches' murders? I was no detective, and besides, whatever could turn a lich into a decomposing corpse was as far from my knowledge as humanly possible. "I'm sure it'll turn around. I guarantee whoever runs this COS business can't possibly have every single variety of cantrip. They look mass-made, not custom. I bet their creators took so many shortcuts that half of them will fall to bits before they can be used."

"I'll just wait for the custom orders to roll in when people figure it out." She stood up and walked into the kitchen to check on the pizzas she'd shoved in the oven.

"It's just a slow season." I turned on the Xbox to distract myself with a game of Skyrim. "Maybe it'll turn out the COS is making cantrips out of dead rats or something. Things like that always turn out to be too good to be true."

Devon snorted. "Yeah, maybe. Did you see anything else in the market?"

"I met the Fire Element," I said. "He's a colossal prick who thinks I have no business getting between him and his beloved master."

Devon closed the oven and walked back to the sofa. "Did you speak to the Death King, then?"

"Yes," I said. "He seemed to think I was his employee, so I put him straight on that. I don't need that kind of crap in my life. What does he expect me to do about someone turning his liches into roadkill?"

She flung herself back on the sofa and picked up the needle and thread again. "How'd they die, exactly?"

"If I knew that, I'd know how to get the Death King off my back," I said. "Something clawed them to pieces, but from the way their bodies were rotting, it was like they were living humans, not liches."

She blinked. "Someone brought them back to life just to kill them for real?"

"His Deathly Highness doesn't seem to think it's possible," I said. "But he admitted their soul amulets were unaccounted for, too."

"Did he ever catch the guy who betrayed him?" She threaded the needle again. "I know the earth mage was caught…"

"He's in jail," I said. "The Order's jail, not the Death King's. Problem is, all the liches look the same, and I wouldn't be able to pick the traitor out of a crowd."

"Tricky one," she said. "But like you said, the Death King is better equipped to identify the culprit than you are. If you ask me, he's trying to shove away responsibility onto someone else. What did Brant think?"

"He still hates the Death King, of course," I said. "He also stayed behind to check out the market, so I'll have to see if he has any updates when he comes back. Also, Dex is missing. I didn't see him the whole time we were over there."

"Weird," she said. "Did the Death King lock him up again?"

"Not that I'm aware of." I watched the loading screen appear on the TV screen. "Maybe he found someone else to hang out with."

It seemed unlikely. Most people didn't even notice sprites, and they typically didn't associate with humans, either. Dex had only made an exception for me after I'd saved him from a dodgy rogue who'd stuck him in a cage to sell at the market, but we'd worked side by side for years and that ought to merit at least a goodbye, right?

The sofa jerked to the side as a sudden surge of energy rushed through the room, making the hairs on my arms stand on end. At once, the TV turned off, as did the Xbox, and I dropped the controller.

"What the—?"

An alarming crash sounded from the shop, and Devon and I both made for the door at once. I got there first, opening it, and something solid and fleshy collided with my face. Recoiling, I hit out, and sent my attacker crashing into the table. A light snapped on courtesy of Devon, illuminating a decomposing mass that hardly looked alive.

The creature flopped over on the table and leapt at me with its clawed hands flailing. I raised my foot, and a sharp kick sent it flying, landing on the floor a heap of flesh and bone.

"What the hell is that?" Devon pressed a hand to her mouth, gagging. I did likewise. The smell was horrific, and despite the way the heap of flesh kept flailing about, there was no way anything in that stage of decomposition should still be able to move.

"I don't know." Holding my breath, I reached into my pocket and grabbed a coin, tossing it at the fleshy mass. It flopped over, feebly twitching. "Not sure what it *was*, either. If it ever used to be alive."

The image of those liches laid out like the festering corpses of slain animals came to mind, and I choked on bile. The heap of dead *thing* kept twitching, more feebly than beforehand. If it wasn't already dead, it had to be dying, surely. Its stumpy legs twitched, its raw skinless arms pushing as it tried to stand. A ragged breath tore through its body, and a jolt of recognition mingled with my revulsion.

Devon ran from the room, while I circled the beast, wondering how to put it out of its misery. I didn't need to wonder for long. The creature's feeble thrashing faded by the second, until it shuddered to a limp halt.

Devon returned with a mop and bucket I hadn't known we even had. "Is it dead?"

"I think so," I said.

She put down the bucket. "Whatever it is, I'm not keeping it in the house. Where'd it come from?"

"Through the node." I swallowed hard. "I think it used to be a phantom."

Devon lowered the mop. "How'd you figure that one out?"

"A hunch." I didn't particularly want to get too close, but I picked up the bucket while Devon used the mop to transport the monster's body. "You know I saw those decomposing liches earlier? That thing looks pretty similar, but less... substantial. Less human. Like the phantoms would look if they had bodies."

"Well, it's not winning any beauty contests." She lowered the mop and the creature flopped into the bucket.

"No kidding." I adjusted my grip on the bucket, trying not to look at its contents. "I guess we should return it to the Parallel."

I didn't particularly want to go back, but it wouldn't do our business any favours to leave it decomposing in the shop.

"I'll dump it in the bin," she said. "Or bury it in the garden, maybe. It's not gonna do any harm now it's dead."

"I guess not, but if another dead monster lands on my face in the middle of the night, I'm sleeping in the garden." I hefted the bucket over my shoulder and walked out of the shop into the back room.

"Thanks for reminding me," said Devon. "You know

what—fuck it, I'm calling the Order."

"If you're sure, but please don't start an argument with them." I made for the back door into the garden. "Also, if they ask too many questions about the Death King—"

"I'll tell them to check in with His Deadliness themselves if they really want to know what he wanted with you. Trust me, I know how they work."

She dialled, while I took the bucket into the back garden. Burying the dead thing underground would be the best way to avoid it being found by any Order personnel who visited our shop... as long as it didn't rise as a zombie and come shambling into the house.

Great way to avoid nightmares there, Liv.

I unlocked the shed, retrieved a shovel and some thick gloves, then got to work digging a hole. The garden was a tangled mass of weeds—neither of us had the time for gardening—so the odds of someone finding it were low, but I still dug a deepish hole just in case. As a gamer who was better at running than fighting, I wasn't built for manual labour, so my arms ached by the time I straightened upright.

Devon still hadn't come outside to tell me if she'd made any progress with the Order, but I wasn't leaving the dead thing lying around while they decided whether we were worth bothering with or not. Holding my breath, I emptied the bucket's contents into the hole. Then I began to pile earth on top. We'd have to avoid the garden until the smell went away, but this would have to do.

I picked up the empty bucket and spotted something small glinting in the very bottom, underneath where the creature had been. With one gloved hand, I scooped it up. The coin was pale gold in colour and blank on both sides.

Not money, I didn't think, but there were all kinds of weird coins floating around in the Parallel. Might even be worth some cash.

That was a mystery for tomorrow. For now, I intended to thoroughly scrub every inch of myself to get the stink of the dead creature off me.

As I walked back into the house, Devon accosted me. "Bastards didn't care. Told us to call them tomorrow if we thought the creature was a genuine threat. They were bloody accusatory, too, as though we invited the thing in here ourselves."

"I figured," I said. "So did they agree with our plan to bury it in the garden? I don't want them coming over here and demanding to see the evidence, unless they want to dig it up themselves."

"Nope, they just said it must have been an accident that it showed up." She snorted. "In other words, they were implying it was one of us who brought it with them."

"Meaning me." I should have guessed. I was the only one of the two of us who frequented the Parallel on a regular basis, and the one with the reputation as a troublemaker.

If you asked me, the Order should have been a little more concerned given how many nodes were present in the city, but if they refused to see the dead phantom as a potential threat, there was nothing more we could do to convince them.

Never mind the Order: I had yet another reason to regret turning my back on the Death King's offer. The trouble had followed me to my own door after all.

———

That night, I floated out of my body and through the roof of the house. I'd expected a slew of nightmares after last evening's incident, so the ease at which astral projecting came to me was a refreshing change. I wheeled around above the rooftops, admiring the glinting lights of the nodes piercing the city like transparent spires from another world.

I floated into the city centre and above the slew of drunken students staggering out of nightclubs, the sound dulled to a pleasant hum in the background. I was a bit too close to the Order for comfort, so I changed directions—and found myself nose to nose with the shadowy form of the Death King.

"It *was* you." My voice came out steady, belying how his sudden appearance had startled me. "I thought I was dreaming last time."

"If it's easier for you, then you're welcome to think of this as a dream," he said. "What are you doing here?"

"Speak for yourself." I looked around to make sure the Order wasn't within hearing distance, though hell if I knew whether or not anyone could actually see me. "I didn't do it on purpose, but I do live on top of a node. What are you doing wandering around here in the middle of the night?"

"Why are you interested?" he said. "You already walked away from my offer."

I frowned. "Did you astral project all the way over here to berate me while I was sleeping?"

"Is it hard for you to believe the universe doesn't revolve around you?" he said. "I didn't come here to see you."

"Ouch." I pressed a hand to my chest, feeling an

uncanny chill when it passed straight through me. "Forgive me for jumping to that conclusion, considering you just ambushed me when I was minding my own business. Besides, it's not like there's a lot of us wandering around here."

Including the Order's own people. Then again, they were the ones who'd wiped out any surviving spirit mages, either by killing them or by taking away their powers like they'd done to Cobb. As for me, they'd thought taking my memory would be enough... but it wasn't.

He glanced in the direction where the Order's headquarters lay as though the same thought had occurred to him. "Perhaps not, but I would have thought you'd have more caution."

"Coming from the guy who hired me as his private investigator."

"I thought you turned down the job."

"I did," I said. "I still don't understand why you picked me and not the Order, or someone with actual connections and experience in the area."

"I picked you because you've proven to be trustworthy when it comes to matters of utmost secrecy." His matter-of-fact tone startled me, but I managed to keep my expression blank.

I folded my arms—with difficulty, given my transparent state. "Excuse me? Didn't your Air Element attack me because they thought I *didn't* guard your secrets?"

"I told you, I didn't give them permission to do that," he said. "I was merely stating a truth. You chose to return my amulet to me, despite the challenging circumstances."

"You mean despite the fact that you kept trying to have

me killed," I said. "Doesn't mean I understand your reasoning. If you're afraid this beast that's slaughtering your liches is going to target you next—"

"I'm not afraid for myself," he said. "Believe it or not, I value those who serve in my army, and I'd prefer not to lose any more of my people."

Huh. It never would have occurred to me that he was the slightest bit concerned about the fates of his fellow liches.

"Okay," I said. "Well… I value my life, too. And you should know, a decomposing phantom fell through the node in my house a few hours ago and landed in the middle of Devon's shop. Given the state of the body, it fell victim to whatever creature slaughtered your liches."

"Is that so?" he said. "What makes you so certain it was a phantom?"

"It sure as hell didn't look human," I said. "Also, phantoms have followed me through the node before. It was dying, decomposing, the same way those liches were."

"So you're reconsidering my offer," he surmised. "Why would the phantom target you?"

"You tell me," I said. "I didn't send out a Bat Signal asking every half-dead monster in the vicinity to land on my face. Unless you sent it yourself." Wait. Another thought occurred to me. "Whereabouts were those two liches found, exactly?"

He looked at me for a long moment. "Beside the node near the castle."

Well, shit. "The revenants who the creature killed were on top of a node, too."

The nodes couldn't return someone from death to life, but they *were* sources of energy as well as pathways between realms. Was that why all the victims had been found in close proximity to a node?

"Is that so?" he said. "Am I correct in thinking you're reconsidering my offer, then? I will stand by my offer to pay you generously."

"It's not just the cash I need," I said "The Order… well. You know how they think of spirit magic. I can't stop using it even in my sleep, apparently."

"You want me to help you learn."

Yes.

I clamped the voice down before I spoke aloud. "No, I want you to guarantee the Order will never know of any spirit magic I use in the course of this investigation. If I have to use it again, I want to know I won't be punished for it."

"Are you sure?" he said. "I could teach you how to use astral projection consciously to prevent incidents like this."

Damn him. I kept forgetting how much of a master manipulator he was. "First you think of yourself as my employer, now you're trying to be my teacher?"

"The offer stands," he said. "Are you certain you want to help me in this case?"

Not in the slightest. I should know better than to accept, given the trouble that he'd caused me already. On the other hand, I wanted answers. Not just about the phantom, but about the revenants, and Dex's disappearance. If the King of the Dead alone could give me those answers, so be it.

"All right," I told him. "Have it your way. I'll find your killer."

7

Thankfully, no more dead phantoms fell through the ceiling overnight. Instead, I woke to the phone ringing, and blearily grabbed for my mobile and checked the name on the screen. Mum, being a morning person as usual. Yawning, I shoved my glasses on and answered. "Hey."

"Hey, Liv," she said brightly. "Thought I'd call. I haven't seen you for a while."

"I guess not," I said. "I've been busy with work…"

Meaning, I worked hard to keep my family out of my magical life, especially the parts involving liches. Dead or deader-than-dead.

"Should I drop by later?" she said. "I know you're busy with that costume party."

"Cosplay, and uh, it's not a good time right now." Not as long as zombies kept falling from the ceiling, anyway. "I'll drop by in a day or two. We're having… plumbing difficulties."

"Want me to send someone over?"

"Nah, Devon has it sorted. We're fine." *I hope.*

"Are you sure?" she said. "Well, you know best. Is she going to the comic play, too?"

"Comic con." Which was… this weekend. Crap. I hadn't even begun to think about my own costume, what with our own unexpected zombie apocalypse at home.

"Yes, of course," she said. "I know you've been busy with your new boyfriend. You haven't posted any pictures of him online yet. Is he the young man we met before?"

"You…" I broke off. She couldn't seriously mean the *Death King,* could she? "No. Absolutely never in a million years."

For a start, he was about a thousand years older than me. And dead.

"Well, you can hardly blame me for guessing when you never tell me anything about the men in your life," she said.

"Brant doesn't have social media," I evaded. "And he has a busy life, too."

"Where does he live?"

"In town." Well. He lived in *a* town, just not on this side of the nodes. Truth be told, I hadn't visited his house in a while, as we'd mostly met up on this side in the last few weeks. Just my luck that Mum would be in the mood to ask a hundred questions. "It's where he works…"

"I thought you said he drove a delivery van."

"He does." *Thanks for the cover story, Past Liv.* "He delivers things all over the region."

"Well, tell him to deliver himself to our doorstep so Elise and I can meet him," she said, her tone half-teasing. Poor Mum. She hadn't signed up for her only child to get the real-life equivalent of a Hogwarts letter and then make a complete shambles of her life.

"I'll see what I can do," I said. "Gotta go. I need to help Devon with the shop."

I ended the call before she invited herself over to meet Brant and ended up with a zombie phantom as a bonus.

As if on cue, my phone buzzed with a message from Brant asking if I was free. Good timing. Or not, because I still needed to tell him I'd accepted the Death King's offer... while I was sleeping. Which wouldn't sound weird at all.

I replied telling him to give me an hour, so I'd have the chance to shower and get dressed. On my bedside table, I'd left the coin I'd found in the bucket. I'd thoroughly scrubbed it down before handling it with my bare hands, but no marks had come to the surface. Out of any other ideas, I put it into the pouch with my cantrips to take into the Parallel with me. Perhaps Brant would know what it was, or he knew someone who did.

When I got downstairs, it was to find Devon sitting on the sofa, scribbling away in a notebook. "What're you doing?"

"Rolling up stats for ceiling zombies to use in our campaign," said Devon. "Might as well make use of our screwed-up life."

"Yeah, as long as one doesn't fall through the ceiling on D&D night," I added. "That'd derail the campaign, to say the least."

She shuddered. "We'd better find out what's causing this before then."

"No kidding." I went into the kitchen to scrounge for

some breakfast and shoved some bread into the toaster. "It's like a zombie plague in reverse."

"It's got to be a spell," said Devon. "The dead can't turn into the living again. Except… well, Brant did, but he wasn't really dead."

"Good point." I looked up as the doorbell rang. "Speaking of whom."

Brant had only been a lich for a short time before his soul had been returned to his body, so he hadn't succumbed to whatever made the other liches' state irreversible. Time, perhaps. They'd lived for centuries, some of them, after they'd chosen to separate their souls and bodies. There must be a point of no return when it was impossible to reverse the process. The Death King alone knew how it all operated, and whether he shared it with me probably depended on how much I pissed him off. Which was debatable.

I walked into the shop and opened the front door. "Hey, Brant."

"Hey." Brant greeted me with a warm hug and a kiss. "What's the latest?"

"A zombie fell through our ceiling." I gave him the rundown as I munched on my toast, while Devon sewed more of her costume. I opted not to mention last night's midnight excursion—it'd only complicate things, and besides, there was nothing I'd said to the Death King that I couldn't have said in person.

Brant pulled a face. "A phantom? You're saying it just… came through the node by itself? It didn't attack you or anything?"

"It tried, but it fell to pieces first." I hesitated, then

reached for the pouch at my waist and pulled out the coin. "This was left behind. Not sure what it is."

"Huh." He scanned the coin's pale gold surface. "Nope… it can't be a cantrip or anything, it's totally blank. I guess it's worth asking around."

"At the market?" I suggested. "I did clean the coin first, don't worry. We don't need any of us to drop dead of a zombie plague."

"Good," said Devon from behind a ream of fabric. "I was awake half the night expecting that thing to dig itself up and come knocking on our door."

Brant arched a brow. "You buried it in the garden?"

"It absolutely stank. We'd have the neighbours making complaints, let alone the Order." I returned the coin to the pouch. "If this is happening on the other nodes, too, the Order will have to take notice."

The other nodes were located at complete random, from the middle of people's houses to busy roads. If zombies started raining down on the public, I could only imagine the chaos that would ensue. As amusing as the idea of the Order running around like headless chickens to deal with a miniature zombie apocalypse might be, the result would spell bad news for the secrecy of the magical world.

Brant rose to his feet. "I haven't heard any other reports. Maybe it came from the Death Kingdom, and because you've been there recently…"

"It followed me home?" Damn. He might be right, actually. "I don't know if the phantom was definitely killed by the same thing that's murdering liches, but there's something nasty on the loose in the revenants' tunnels, too. It has to be the same monster."

His mouth pressed together. "You're saying you want to work for the Death King after all, then?"

"Devon and I could use the cash," I said. "Did you find out anything more about the COS at the market yesterday?"

"Nothing much," he said. "As far as the regulars describe it, they just set up overnight. About a week after they cleaned up the streets following the battle, they came to the market with boxes full of cantrips and that was that. Oh, and they fixed up the warehouse, too. Got rid of the draughty old walls and stopped the roof from leaking. Some of the regulars were happy, others were disgruntled that the newcomers were making such a blatant attempt to ingratiate themselves with everyone. But most of them thought the place could use a clean-up, so..." He shrugged.

I turned this over in my mind. "A week after the battle... perhaps the fight is what prompted them to kick it into gear."

"Dicks," said Devon. "All of them."

"The Order refused to come here and help with the dead phantom," I explained to Brant. "They implied I was to blame and that it was our problem, not theirs. If a zombie appears inside their headquarters, it'd serve them right."

"Maybe then they'd step up and take notice," he said. "Seems easier than putting yourself in harm's way."

"Hey, I was only trying to play a video game, not call zombies into the house," I said. "Besides, the Death King asked me to help and not the Order. And I'd like to know why."

Brant still wore a wary expression. "Are you certain he's not responsible himself?"

"Why would he kill his fellow liches and then ask me to step in to play detective?" I said. "You know the Death Kingdom. They keep to themselves."

This time, though, he hadn't. And while finding out why the trouble had landed in my house was foremost on my mind, I couldn't let myself forget the reason the Death King had made an exception to the usual rule: the lure of having his very own spirit mage. A Spirit Element to join his army.

"Okay, but I don't think you should use this node to cross over into the Death Kingdom," he said. "Not as long as zombies keep showing up, anyway. We can go through to the market, though, if that's okay."

"Go ahead," said Devon. "I'll put up an umbrella."

"Ha."

I felt for the node, and its familiar rush of energy claimed me. Brant and I crossed over into the Parallel—and landed in the middle of a circle of revenants.

I kicked out, my foot colliding with solid bone and flesh. The revenant flew back into its neighbour, only for Brant's flames to catch it in the face. Orange flames devoured three revenants, but the fourth dodged and leapt at me. I grabbed a cantrip and threw it wildly, but nothing happened. *Oh, damn.*

I dropped to a crouch and the revenant sailed over my head, into the path of Brant's flames. Blinking the haze from my eyes, I realised I'd thrown the blank coin at them, not one of my cantrips. That'd explain why it didn't work. I picked it up and put it back into the pouch.

"That's it," I said, kicking the ashes away. "We have got

to find out what's in those tunnels. If it's freaking out the revenants, the vampires' council will want to know."

"The council doesn't take reports from humans," he said. "Believe me, I've tried."

"Wish they did." The vampires who ruled the city rarely showed their faces in public either. "There's bound to be a local vampire wandering around the market who we can ask. It's where they buy their light-repellent charms."

Since we'd planned to head that way to begin with, we made our way to the warehouse once again. If anything, the flow of foot traffic was even thicker than the previous day. I halted near the entrance, scanning the line of people leaving the warehouse. All vampires had the same odd ageless features as elves did, except with pointed teeth instead of pointed ears, which made them easy to spot.

"Hey there," I said to a passing vampire with long dark hair and dark circles under his eyes as though he was fighting against the vampires' natural instincts to sleep through the day. "I wanted to ask you a question."

"Go away."

Brant blocked his path. "Wrong answer."

"What d'you want?" he muttered. From his lack of manners, he wasn't an ancient vampire, but a new one. That explained why he was wandering around in broad daylight, regardless of how it messed with his natural body clock.

"To know why revenants keep feeding on the nodes aboveground," I said. "That's three times we've been ambushed in two days. You know why?"

"Shit, I dunno," he said. "Maybe they wanted a change of scenery."

"Hilarious," I said. "Something is driving them away from the underground nodes. Haven't the council noticed?"

"Who cares?" He sidestepped Brant with a vampire's natural speed and grace, and between one blink and the next, he was gone.

Dammit. I hadn't a hope of catching him up on foot. True vamps were far above their revenant brethren speed-wise.

"I reckon only the council will know, if anyone," Brant murmured. "Want to go inside?"

I dipped my head. "It's worth checking out our friends at the COS again."

We joined the flow of people heading into the warehouse, letting the crowd's momentum carry us towards the long tables at the back. The dim ceiling lights caught on the rows of golden coins, and a huge volume of people stopped by to admire the display even if they weren't actually buying anything.

"You again?" said the woman at the stall. "Looking to make a purchase this time?"

"Yes," I bluffed, scanning the rows of coins and thinking hard. "I'm looking for…" A spell that wasn't too expensive. The last thing I needed was to fritter away our remaining cash on a dud cantrip.

"I'll pay," Brant said, as though he'd guessed my thoughts. "We'll take two light spells."

She named a price, and my heart dropped into my shoes. No wonder they were undercutting our business. We charged nearly twice that for one cantrip, let alone two.

Brant handed over the cash and she selected two

gleaming golden coins to slide into a paper bag. "Something wrong?"

I took the bag from her. Even the paper bag looked like an import from the world on the other side. "How can you afford to charge so little? Isn't a single cantrip worth several hours of work? The materials alone cost a fortune."

"Ah, we get a bulk discount, being such a large group," she said. "We wanted to make our wares more accessible to the general public."

"A bulk discount?" I echoed. "From whom?"

"Our suppliers," she said.

Weird. Mass-produced spells shouldn't be possible. If they weren't carved by hand, they didn't work right, which was one reason practitioners' arts remained more or less the same as they had for centuries. Why mess with a good thing?

My gaze caught on a box behind the counter. Inside lay several small coins… blank coins. Wait a minute.

I reached into my pouch and pulled out the coin I'd found on the dead phantom. "I have a question. Can you identify this coin?"

"I'm not an antiques dealer," she said, an impatient note entering her tone. "That's a blank cantrip."

So it is. "Okay, thanks."

Gripping the coin in my hand, I walked away from the stall. *What was a dying phantom doing with a blank cantrip?* It was smaller than the ones Devon used, which was why I hadn't twigged to start off with.

"Was she right?" asked Brant. "Give it here, I'll check with someone else."

I passed the coin to him. "If it was a cantrip carved with a spell, it should have disintegrated after being used."

A sudden suspicion gripped me, but before I could voice it, Brant accosted a red-haired mage behind the nearest stall. "Excuse me, can you identify this coin?"

"What?" said the mage. "That's a cantrip base, isn't it?"

"Told you." I took the coin from Brant and slipped it back into my pouch.

He hurried after me. "Where are you going?"

"To test a theory." I walked outside and pulled one of the shiny new light cantrips out of the paper bag.

"What're you doing?" he asked. "Wait—don't use that here."

"I'm not." I walked swiftly until I reached the alley containing the stone staircase we'd been down before.

"Liv!" He hurried after me. "This is not a wise move."

"When did I ever make wise decisions?" If I ever had in the past, that person had died along with two years of my memories.

I descended into the darkness of the tunnel. When my feet touched down on steady ground, I held out the cantrip, took in a breath, and activated it.

A flood of light spun over my hand, lighting up the murky tunnel. Hints of the foul smell from before rushed towards me, and I held my breath, cupping the coin-shaped spell in my hand. Mass-produced or not, it was as faultless as any cantrip Devon had made.

"Hang on." Brant caught me up. "I know what you're thinking, but why not pick a less... grim place to test it out?"

"Too late now." I shone the light on the tunnel walls. "Might as well look around while we're at it."

He conjured a flame to his hand. "Want the other one?"

"We can save it for later," I said. "Or rather, for evidence, if this goes the way I think it will."

I didn't *want* to look in the darkness for more dead revenants, but it looked like the world at large had abandoned the tunnels to rot. Unless they were directly affected, the vampires didn't want to know, and the odds of a nobody like me gaining an audience with the council were zero.

Brant slipped his hand into mine, the other cupping a dancing flame. "If the cantrips didn't work, someone would have chased those COS people out by now. Everyone uses light spells."

"I know." I shone the cantrip's glow on the walls. "Maybe we should have gone to check out the tunnels where the Death King's traitor friend hung out. I wonder if he's still spending his time down there."

"I doubt it, now Vaughn's in jail." Brant's voice tightened at the mention of his earth mage friend, who'd stabbed both of us in the back. "Someone else lives in his old house now, so I doubt they'd appreciate us poking around in the basement, either."

I trod further along the tunnel, holding my breath to mask the stench of slaughtered revenants, whose bodies lay ripped open to expose the rotting organs within. No wonder the others had been avoiding the underground node.

"I don't think we're gonna find anything down here," Brant said, holding his coat over his nose and mouth. "It's abandoned."

"Hmm." More dead revenants blocked our path to the node. At least a dozen. If a predator lurked somewhere in the darkness, why kill them if it didn't plan to consume their bodies? Weird.

The coin's light vanished abruptly, plunging us into darkness. "There it is."

"C'mon." Brant held his flame in one hand, the other taking my arm to help me walk out of the tunnel without tripping over in the darkness. I didn't object, because despite the light going out, the coin was still solid and cold in my hand. It hadn't disintegrated into dust like it should have done. *I knew it.*

I climbed the staircase to the surface and held out my hand to show Brant. As I'd suspected, the coin remained in one piece, except blank, as though the marks had been erased. No... as though it'd never been marked to begin with.

"I guess the only way to see if it's reusable is to get Devon to try turning it into another cantrip." I turned the coin over. "Both sides are blank. It's as good as new."

"Useful."

"Suspicious," I corrected. "The person who made the coin I found when the phantom fell through the node is the same as the one who made these."

"I agree there's a similarity there," he allowed, "but if all the COS's cantrips go blank, anyone might have created the one they used on the phantom. Doesn't have to be the manufacturer."

"I thought there were laws governing the creation of new spells." Set by the vampires' council. The Order might not rule here, but that didn't make the place lawless. "The vampires have restrictions on the trade of magical supplies, too."

"Yes," he said. "They do."

They must know about the COS, but they didn't care about the rest of us losing business. Look at how that vampire had acted when I'd mentioned the revenants.

"How do I make a request to see them?" I said. "It's not like I have contacts who can get me inside their council hall to speak to their undead rulers."

Or did I?

There was one person who might make even the vampires' council sit up and listen… the Death King.

8

———

Brant wasn't convinced. "He's as bad as they are. Worse, if anything. The vampires pretend to be working for the good of everyone in Arcadia. The Death King looks out for himself alone."

"Like most mages are any different." I walked past the warehouse to the empty stretch of ground bordering the swampland. "I'm under no illusions about him. Believe me. But he can help."

I think. The guy had walked into the Order's headquarters giving commands left and right and they'd scrambled to do as he told them. Why should the vampires be any different?

Brant grumbled, but he did walk with me through the swampland all the way to the gates into the Death King's territory. I protested, but he said that while he wouldn't come inside, that didn't mean he'd leave me to walk across the swampland alone. Thankfully, we didn't encounter anything worse than a few phantoms—as dead as they should be, and indifferent to our presence.

I walked towards the gates and the liches parted to let me enter. On the other side, however, I found my way barred by Davies, the Fire Element. He looked me up and down as though I was a zombie who'd fallen through his ceiling. "What d'you want?"

"To talk to your boss." I took a step forwards, but he didn't move aside. "He won't be pleased if you don't let me in."

"Do you think the Death King wants to talk to the likes of you?" He folded his arms. "I don't think so. Do I see that cowardly fire mage of yours lurking outside?"

"Brant isn't a coward." I stepped up so we stood nose to nose. "You should know, your master isn't the only person who can remove someone's soul."

His mouth twisted in a scowl, but he stepped aside to let me pass. "Go ahead, knock yourself out. You wouldn't be the first idiotic mage my master has tricked into turning into one of his unwilling servants."

"What the hell do you mean by that?"

He didn't look back. "Hurry up before I change my mind."

Arse. I suppressed the impulse to flip him off and walked up the stone stairs into the castle, making a mental note to ask Devon to add a bad-tempered Fire Element to the next stage of our D&D campaign.

I crossed the smooth flagstones of the entrance hall over to the dais at the back, where the Death King was in the middle of speaking to the Water Element. She was a curvy black woman who wore her hair in a thick braid, dressed in the same armoured clothing as the others. Her cloak was lined with blue and decorated with the skull-shaped insignia of the Death King surrounded by circles representing each of the elements. Each Elemental Soldier had their respective Element highlighted, which in her case was the blue swirl for water.

The Water Element caught sight of me and gave me a curious look, though not an unfriendly one like Davies had. Then she nodded to the Death King and exited the hall through a side door. The same door we'd gone through to see the dead liches, in fact. The other Elemental Soldiers were presumably up to date on the investigation.

"Olivia," said the Death King. "Do you have anything new to report?"

I told him about the morning's events. He listened in silence to my account of the market, the experiment with the cantrips, and our trip into the tunnels.

"So," I said, "I'm guessing the people making those cantrips are using some kind of new material that doesn't disintegrate—"

"I don't care about that," he interrupted.

"But it's relevant," I pressed. "If someone is using a spell to kill the dead, and they're using those cantrips to do it—"

"No coins were found at the scene of my liches' deaths."

"Maybe they fell through the node, then." If they'd landed on the other side, they'd probably have been picked up by ordinary humans and assumed to be fake money or something. Without the marks of a spell, there was nothing designating them as magical.

"There's no proof," he said. "I understand that this new initiative puts you in a precarious position with regard to your business, but it's not pertinent to our investigation."

Irritation prickled at my skin like an itch. "Fine, then. Let's just ignore the fact that the vampires are acting shifty around the subject of their revenants showing up dead and rotting in the tunnels, and the council seems to be doing nothing about it. I might add that they'd rather negotiate with the revenants than with the likes of me, so—"

"I'm not ignoring the vampires," he said. "I have every intention of making contact with the vampire council myself."

"Oh, good," I said. The vampires must have given the COS permission to operate at the market, but that doesn't make them legit."

"I beg to differ," he said. "Nobody can sell on that scale without the express permission of the council."

"Yeah, I know that," I said. "But if they were legitimate, they wouldn't have been so cagey when it came to answering questions about their suppliers. Brant is going to find out—"

"Then by all means, leave it to the fire mage," he interjected. "I will arrange a meeting with the vampire council to discuss the deaths of their revenants. Is there anything else you wished to tell me?"

"No, I think that's all," I said. "I mean, I did wonder if the lich who betrayed you might still be using those old tunnels as a hideout even with Vaughn in jail. But that's just a guess."

"The earth mage." His voice hummed with anger. "The Order has him in their clutches, or I would question him again myself. The foolish human might not have asked the identity of the traitorous lich he worked with, however. He himself used an alias."

"He did?" I said, disarmed. "But—he and Brant were friends."

"That proves nothing," he said. "There are no limits to which some might practise deceit. If the traitor lich shows his true colours in front of me, I will make him sorry he ever turned his back on my rule."

Chills raced through me, and the temperature of the entire castle seemed to plummet below freezing point. "Right. Okay, that's all I wanted to say."

I gladly left the castle, leaving the chill of the Death King's magic behind. I'd forgotten how damned scary he was. No more human than any of the other monsters I dealt with. Stupid thing to forget, really.

I hurried down the steps and damn near ran into the Fire Element, who stood at the foot of the stairs making a flame dance above his hands. "Whoa."

"Watch where you're going." He put out the flame. "Are you leaving?"

"Of course."

To my annoyance, he tailed me to the gates, where Brant waited outside.

Brant gave me a wave, his expression tightening at the appearance of Davies. "You again."

"Me." The Fire Element looked him up and down. "Too chicken to risk your soul by coming inside?"

Brant stepped right up to the gates. "Wanna insult me when you're not cowering behind your master's fence?"

The Fire Element gave a wolfish smile. "Don't you have the guts to set foot in here? Or have you not forgotten your stint as a lich?"

Brant took a step forward. Dangerous flames danced in his eyes.

"Hey!" I snapped. "Cut it the hell out, the pair of you. If you want to waste your time with childish posturing, feel free, but I'm heading home."

"You don't get to tell me what to do," said the Fire Element.

I grabbed Brant's tensed elbow. "Nope, but you can fuck all the way off for all I care."

Brant dug his heels in for an instant, then seemed to realise that starting a fight in front of the castle belonging to the man who'd ripped out his soul was not a smart move.

"Ignore him." I steered him towards the node. "The Death King's already majorly pissed off."

"Why?" He stalked towards the node, his shoulders tensed.

I quickened my pace. "Because someone betrayed him, of course. He doesn't need an elemental duel on his doorstep as well."

Brant didn't answer, but he unresistingly walked with me to the node, and we crossed over to the other side.

Devon must be in the shop, because the only signs of her in the living room were the piles of fabric beside the sofa. Brant blew out a breath, his eyes still dancing with flames. "That guy just pushes all my buttons."

"Yes, I know he's an arsehole, but he can still vaporise you."

"Let him try." He scowled. "He hasn't the right to look down on the rest of us. He's nothing more than a traitor."

"Because he works for the Death King?" The elemental mages had this weird habit of shunning anyone who submitted to working for someone who wasn't one of them. Hell, to some of them, even working for a mage of a different discipline was frowned upon in certain circles. I'd thought Brant had outgrown that particular phase, but I supposed seeing a fellow fire mage working for someone who he despised was too much for him. "Wouldn't you take the chance to live in a castle if it came up?"

"Not in the land of the dead, I wouldn't," he said.

"You sure?" I put on a teasing tone, hoping to distract him. "They even get to ride horses to work. Dead ones, admittedly, but still."

His brows shot up. "You rode one?"

"Beats trekking through the swamp," I said. "I didn't see Ryan around this time, but not all the Elements are snooty bastards like Davies."

Not that I'd seen much of the Earth Element either. Or had a conversation with the Water Element. Anyone who could handle the Death King in any capacity had far more patience than I did. Maybe that was one of the main qualities he looked for in his soldiers. Aside from uncommon skill at magic, that is.

"I'll believe it when I see it," he said. "What did you and His Deathly Highness talk about, then?"

"We discussed who else might be working against him," I said. "I brought up Vaughn and the traitor lich, but we still don't know who it is or how they're hiding from him. I do wonder if there might be a clue left in Vaughn's old lair, after all. It's worth a look, I think."

"Are you back?" Devon called from the shop. "Come in here and tell me all about it."

Brant pulled me into his arms. His lips traced mine, sparking warmth inside me that quelled the lingering chills of the Court of the Dead. "See you in a bit?"

"Sure," I said. "I'll grab lunch and catch up with Devon, and then we can go on an underground lich hunt."

First things first, I went into the shop and presented Devon with the blank cantrip and the light spell Brant and I hadn't used yet.

"What's this?" she asked.

I explained the theory Brant and I had tested. "The cantrips work, all right, but they don't fall to pieces after being used. They just turn blank instead. Test the second one if you like."

"The COS are selling reusable cantrips?" She took the blank coin from me. "Damn. No wonder they can afford to charge so little. Of course, any practitioner can reuse them, which might hit them in the back when there are suddenly a dozen other practitioners selling cantrips at the market who wouldn't otherwise have been able to afford the materials."

"Fair point," I said. "That one's yours to play with."

"Sure, why not." She flipped the coin and caught it in her palm. "I'll see if I can crack this coin open. There's got to be a downside somewhere."

"Warn me if you're going to blow anything up," I said. "Anyway, Brant's gonna dig around and find out who their suppliers might be. The Death King isn't particularly bothered about the COS, though. He thinks it's irrelevant to the investigation."

"That's nice," she said. "It's only our livelihoods."

"Yeah, well, someone is turning his people into rotting corpses," I said. "Maybe he'll change his mind when he speaks to the vampire council. A brand-new business like that... there's no way they don't know."

Her brows rose. "He's meeting the vampire council?"

"Allegedly." I shrugged. "I tried to snag a vampire to question at the market, but he was downright rude when I brought up the revenants. You'd think the council would be getting more complaints, considering the revenants are running around aboveground, unchecked, while the underground nodes are out of use."

"They might be." She flipped the coin again. "If I were them, I wouldn't make their concerns public."

Hmm. The smell alone was enough to put me off playing detective in the tunnels, let alone the possibility of running into whatever creature had dealt those deadly wounds.

As for the rest? I'd need to wait and see what the Death King said before I started antagonising the vampires.

———

After a lunch break and an hour of watching Devon turn the blank cantrip into a creation of her own, my phone buzzed with a message from Brant. *Meet you on the other side? I'll be there in five.* A smile formed on my face. I hadn't bothered changing out of my Parallel gear, ready to meet him again as soon as he gave the go-ahead.

"What're you grinning at?" asked Devon. "It's going well with fire-boy, is it?"

"Believe it or not… yes, it is." Better than the last time. Though it helped that we weren't holding one another at arm's length. I wasn't, anyway. Brant was… trying. His protective nature became grating sometimes, not to mention his rapid-fire temper, but he was making an active effort to keep me involved in his life. "He must have crossed back over here just to text me. Saves time."

"Only if you don't bring zombies back with you."

Come to think of it, I'd used the node to travel back from the swamplands again earlier, but nothing had followed me that time.

I crossed over through the node and found Brant already waiting on the other side, on the street near the warehouses. "No revenants this time?"

"I already burned them," he said. "I didn't think Devon would appreciate it if I landed in your house, so I figured this was the best way for us to meet."

"Considering the zombie incident, I have to agree," I said. "Devon would, too. So… what have you found out?"

"I asked around to find out who lives in Vaughn's house now," he said. "Apparently a few rogues moved in as soon as the place was vacated. Without permission. They might be willing to let us poke around and see if he left any clues about the traitor lich's identity behind."

"Then it's worth speaking to them." If they'd camped out in an abandoned house, I'd guess they were either mages or desperate practitioners.

We walked the short distance to the house, which blended in with its neighbours by virtue of being dilapidated as hell. The roof stood at a crooked angle, the bricks were charred—most likely from Brant's flames during his enraged battle with his former friend—and the wooden door had been replaced at least once, probably for the same reasons.

Reaching the door, Brant knocked. I put on a false smile which became strained the longer nobody answered.

"Who is it?" said a low, masculine voice from behind the door.

"We're not here to threaten you," Brant said. "We used to know the person who once lived in this house, and we want to ask—"

The door flew open, revealing the vampire I'd accosted at the market. His hood was down this time, revealing a moon-pale face, sharp features, light grey eyes, and long dark hair.

"I told you to go away," said the vampire.

"What are you doing in here?" I said.

"I should be asking you the same question." He frowned, exposing his pointed fangs. "This is private property, this is."

"You started squatting in here after the last owner was arrested by the Order," I said to him. "You don't own this place any more than I do."

The vampire leaned on the door frame, blocking my view of the hallway. "Get out."

"I don't think so." Brant's hands sparked, kindling to flames. "As Liv said, you don't own this place. We could drive you out if we wanted to."

"Really?"

Two more vampires appeared behind the first. I shot Brant an exasperated look. *We came here to find out the identity of the lich traitor, not start a fight with a group of pasty newbie vampires.* They must be new. The older vamps lived in manor houses, not dilapidated shacks which had once housed criminals. But even newbie vampires could be deadly opponents, given their speed and strength advantages over us normal folk.

I reached for the pouch at my waist. "Answer our questions and we'll leave you alone. Did you ever meet the earth mage who once lived in this house?"

One of the vampires vanished. An instant later, a pair of cool hands brushed my neck from behind. "Get out."

Brant swore and threw a flame at the vampire, who released me in an instant. "If you burn us, our sire will hunt you down in the night and rip out your innards."

"That's lovely," I said. "Brant, tone down the flames."

The vampires might be moody bastards, but that didn't mean they were on the side of the enemy. And if they belonged to a more powerful vamp, their sire had the potential to make things really nasty for us, a complication we didn't need.

Brant glared at them. "Deal, but if you touch Liv again, I'll burn you to cinders."

The vampire stepped around me, entered the house, and slammed the door on us. I debated hammering on it until they let me in to confront them, but now I thought about it, the liches and the vampires hated one another. No way would the lich traitor come back to this place now a group of vampires were squatting inside the house.

I rolled my eyes. "Newbie vamps are such drama queens."

Brant grunted. "What now? I doubt the lich traitor is hiding in their basement."

"No, but there's still the other underground lair he used." The place where the earth mage had taken me when I'd ambushed him on the Death King's territory. It wasn't like Vaughn had concentrated his meetings with the lich here in his house, after all. "It's worth looking around."

The two of us walked towards the warehouses once again, this time heading for an abandoned alley. As we drew closer, I found myself missing Dex's presence, even with Brant at my side. The fire sprite was the one who'd brought Brant to rescue me from my underground cage... because I'd tracked him down using spirit magic. Could I find him using astral projection? Maybe. I was a little more practised than I'd been back then, after all.

That would have to wait until after we'd searched Vaughn's old bolt hole. The corridor at the foot of the narrow staircase was lich-free, while the door into the room where I'd been imprisoned lay open. Chills whisked down my arms at the memory of a lich looming over me in the darkness. A terrifying, indomitable foe, or so I'd thought at the time. Not so much now I'd seen two of them flayed open by a beast that defied description.

The lich wasn't here. Mr Cobb was in jail, and so was Vaughn. The place felt empty, and it made me miss Dex like a physical ache in my chest.

"Hey." Brant nudged me. "Something up?"

"I don't understand where Dex went," I whispered. "He's never disappeared for this long before. I even managed to astral project and track him down from inside the cage when I was a prisoner."

Now, even the cage was empty, though the upturned soil within was a reminder of the earth mage's secret tunnel leading under the Death King's territory. I couldn't picture a lich using it as an escape route, though.

"I don't think there's anyone here," muttered Brant. "The lich would have no reason to come here alone, not when this place is known to be on the vampires' watchlist."

"I doubt they keep a close eye on the place." I stepped closer to the cage, trying to put myself back in the mindset I'd been in when I'd astral projected away from a node for the first time. Cold silence filled the background, punctuated by a distant humming sound... not just a sound, but a sensation, too. "Give me a second. I just need to check something."

Silence filtered in as I tuned into the humming sensation. The nearest node lay to the west, I knew, but I didn't need to be on top of a node to astral project. I let the humming sensation spread throughout my body and floated upwards, out of the underground hideout and into the street above.

Hovering on the spot, I searched for any signs of Dex's presence in the skies above Arcadia. He couldn't have just vanished, surely. The nodes stood out like pinpricks against the surrounding world, more of them appearing the higher into the air I ascended.

Brightness pinged on my vision. I turned my head, seeing a shape too small to be a human moving within the node to my left. I floated in that direction, straining my eyes to see inside the glowing light. "Dex?"

I halted, my heart lurching against my ribs. The brightness resolved into a dark shape within the node's current, surrounded by revenants. Piercing screams sounded from the revenants as the dark shape within the node lashed out with viciously sharp claws. The beast was too distorted for me to make out its features. Even when it raised its head and looked directly at me with pitted eyes...

I reeled, floating backwards over the rooftops and back to my body.

I blinked back to alertness to find Brant was shaking me. "Liv?"

"We've got to get to the node."

I took off at a run, though I knew we'd be too late to stop whatever was happening on the other side. I ran out into the corridor, climbed the stairs, and hurtled through the alley towards the bright spark of the node.

I skidded to a halt. Dead revenants lay all over the alley, their bodies flayed open, and on top of them lay the decomposing corpse of the fiend I'd seen within the node. A phantom, like the one that'd attacked our house, lay dying, its clawed hands shrivelling on the spot, its skin peeling off, its organs decaying.

As Brant caught me up, a coin fell out of the air, borne by the current of energy from the node. Brant and I watched it tumble for an instant, then I reached out and caught it in my palm.

"This is proof." My fingers closed on the coin. "The Death King will have to listen this time."

9

By the time we reached the swamp again, I was starting to wish I'd asked Ryan how to call one of those skeletal horses. Trekking back and forth through the swamp was getting old.

"Warn me next time you take off like that," Brant said.

"I didn't think we had much time." And I'd been right. A *phantom* had killed the revenants, then died itself, as though the very force that had returned it to life had taken back what it'd given. It should be impossible, but I knew what I'd seen.

"It's lucky the thing was already dead when we got there," he said. "Those claws could decapitate someone."

"Don't you think it's odd that they only seem to be targeting beings that should already be dead?" I said.

Not only that, the phantom had come through the node when it'd attacked, so for all we knew, there might be more of them waiting to pounce. It made sense to use a node as a power source, because nodes were places of high magical energy, powerful enough to connect the two realms… and, in some cases, powerful enough to breach the boundary between life and death.

Shit, Dex. Where are you? I was outright worried for him now, but I hadn't seen a single sign of him when I'd astral projected out of my body.

I halted mid-step as the skeletal outline of a horse appeared against the mist wreathing the wastelands. "Hey, my ride's here after all. This is Neddie."

"I am *not* riding on that," Brant said flatly.

"You don't have to." I reached out to stroke the beast's head. The horse hissed and snorted when it spotted Brant.

He backed up a step. "What's the problem?"

"Probably thinks you're gonna start a fire," I said. "Maybe I should go and see the Death King alone. He might still be in a temper."

Besides, I didn't need to deal with a brawl between Brant and the Fire Element on top of the carnage I'd already witnessed today.

"Sure, but I have the evening free," he said. "Want me to come over?"

For some reason, he never invited me back to his place and always came over to mine instead. Maybe because of the risk of the Order finding out I'd spent the night in the Parallel. We'd taken that risk countless times during our first shot at a relationship, but the Order had become more stringent since then.

Without warning, the horse's foot shot out, sending Brant face-planting into the swamp.

I turned to the beast. "Oh Elements. What was that for?"

The horse gave another snort. Brant lifted his head,

dripping wet, and I bit the inside of my cheek to avoid laughing.

He shot the horse a furious look, wiping his face with his sleeve. "I'm outta here. Text you later."

"I'll see you this evening," I called after him. My hand steadied the horse before it could give chase. It nudged my arm as though to ask why I wasn't already climbing onto its back. "Fine, but you need to stop picking fights with my boyfriend, mister."

I swung up onto the horse's back, and it set off at a steady rhythm. The thick leather saddle coupled with my knee-length coat meant its bony form didn't hurt my legs —much—but the horses were clearly more used to carrying the dead than the living, and its rocking gait gave me a mild headache. The two liches at the gates gave no reaction to my appearance and stepped aside without a word.

And the intrepid sorceress foolishly enters the Court of the Dead. Again.

I climbed off the horse and hurried up the steps to the castle doors. The Fire Element didn't stand in the way this time, but the instant I opened the doors, I found myself nose to nose with the Death King.

"Whoa." I caught my balance at the edge of the top stair.

"Back so soon?" he said. "What did you learn?"

"I was right." I reached into my pocket and held up the coin. "There was another attack on a node. A phantom was slaughtering revenants, and by the time I reached it, it was already dead."

"You saw a phantom attack the revenants?" he asked in

sceptical tones. "Phantoms have almost no power. What do you mean, by the time you reached it?"

"I saw it while I was astral projecting at first," I explained. "I had to return to my body before I could go there in person, and when I got there, it was already dead."

"Was there a particular reason you left your body behind?" He beckoned me after him into the hall. "Or do you just like exercising your talent?"

"Do I what?" Was he judging me? I really couldn't tell. "I was looking for Dex. He's still missing. And considering the beast seems to be targeting the dead, I don't want to know what it can do to a sprite."

"No, I expect not," he said. "The phantom attacked the revenants and then died itself?"

"So it seems. But this was left behind." I held out the coin, before remembering he couldn't touch it. "It was a cantrip made using the new material the COS use at the market."

"Which proves...?"

"It means this was the work of a spell, not an individual."

"A spell must have a person behind it."

Did he have to argue with every word I said? "If you want to be pedantic. The individual, whoever they are, wasn't anywhere at the scenne. It may be that they're using an intermediary to set off the cantrips in order to avoid getting caught in the act. We need to find who's creating them, and to do that..."

"We need to consult the vampires," he said. "And the council have agreed to speak with us tomorrow."

"Tomorrow?" I frowned. "Wait, did you say 'us'?"

"I believe it would be wise if we were both present for the questioning," he said. "Lord Blackbourne of the vampire council agreed."

The vampires wanted to speak to *me*? That couldn't be good. "They don't know I'm a spirit mage, do they?"

I bloody well hoped not. They vampires' council might be a separate entity to the Order, but that didn't mean they weren't secretly buddies behind the scenes. Just look at the Death King.

"Of course they don't," he answered. "I didn't tell them anything but your name. However, you're a witness to the actions of the beast that's killing my people, and I think two voices will be more beneficial than one."

"If you say so." I drew my arms around myself against the chill sweeping through the castle walls. "I was under the impression they liked the Order almost as much as they liked the Court of the Dead."

Then again, they had the Order to thank for their being able to gain dominance over Arcadia in the aftermath of the war. After the ruling Elemental Council had perished, they'd left a power gap in their place. If the Order had wanted to gain power over the magically inclined, they could have stepped in as the war ended, but they'd chosen to stay on the other side of the nodes and leave the city to the vampires.

"The vampires didn't bring up the Order when I asked to arrange a meeting," he said. "I believe they are aware of the attacks on the local revenants, but I cannot say if they have drawn any conclusions."

"Guess we'll find out during the meeting, then." The vampires. I was going to see the vampire council—in the company of the King of the Dead, no less. To think I'd assumed riding on a skeletal horse would be the most bizarre experience of my week.

"Yes, we will," he said. "And next time you decide to use your spirit magic, do tell me, won't you?"

"Tell *you?*" I said. "Why? What does it matter?"

"It matters because the murderer is targeting spirits," he said. "It may be that the definition includes those who have left their bodies behind to astral project."

"Seriously?" No wonder Brant had been so freaked out. I hadn't seen the person responsible for turning the phantom into a grotesque half-dead monster, and they'd used a cantrip rather than being there in person... but the phantom had wound up as dead as its victims.

"Exactly," he said. "I'd rather you didn't perish before the case is brought to a close."

"And there I was thinking you didn't like me."

Whatever his reply was going to be, I never found out. The door to the castle slammed open with a booming sound which echoed from the high ceiling.

"We're under attack!" shouted the Fire Element. "Another lich is dead."

The Death King moved at once, gliding towards the doors.

"Call the other Elements," he ordered Davies over his shoulder as he vanished outside.

I ran down the stairs behind him, hurrying towards the sparkling light of the node. Even from here, I could see the darkness within it, and below...

The lich lay sprawled in the mud, flayed open, body decaying like a weeks-old corpse. If any coins lay beneath his body, I didn't see them, and I didn't want to lift the rotting corpse to find out.

The node's energy current buzzed beneath the earth, inside my own veins. No signs remained behind of whatever had returned the lich to life and then left them for dead. Their hood had fallen back to expose a face already caving in on itself, bones jutting from between flaps of greying skin.

Footsteps prompted me to turn around. The other three Elements had joined Davies. Ryan looked sickened, as did the Water Element. The Earth Element stood too far back for me to see his expression.

The Death King faced the four Elemental Soldiers. "Remove the body and take it to the same room as the others. Tell nobody else of this."

He didn't wait for a response, instead gliding back up the stairs and through the front doors into the castle. I hurried up behind him, even though all my instincts told me to stay back, and he veered sideways into the hall of souls.

"What're you doing?" My footsteps echoed as I ran to keep up with his bodiless glide.

No reply came when he entered the hall and glided down a row of soul amulets. He reached a shelf and stopped, then began to examine each amulet one by one.

"You're looking for the victim's soul amulet," I concluded. "Might it have been taken recently?"

The longer the connection between soul and body remained severed, the less likely it was that they'd be able to return to life. Most liches had willingly surrendered the physical world in favour of immortality, but I'd never heard of a spell that could turn a lich back into a living, breathing being again.

A phantom can't have done it. They can't have broken in here to steal someone's soul.

The Death King didn't reply. His silent glide continued, which creeped me out more than I'd have been if he'd been yelling obscenities. I got the message and left the castle, finding the Air Element levitating the dead lich's decomposing remains out of the node.

"If I were you, I'd leave," they said.

"I'll just have a quick look around the scene of the crime."

I walked the short distance to the node, the swirling current of energy appearing the same as ever. Crouching down, I scanned the ground beneath the node. Swamp water washed over my boots, while mud sucked at my feet. And beneath the mud lay a coin, half-buried.

With one hand, I lifted it into the air and held it up to the light. Mud darkened its pale gold surface, but I'd bet it was as unmarked as the others.

The question was, who—or what—had used the cantrip on the phantom? And where had they come from? Anything might lie on the other side of the node.

Before I could question my decision, I pocketed the muddy coin and stepped into the path of the node.

A familiar buzzing sensation hummed in my veins, and I pictured the rotting phantom clearly in my mind's eye, willing the node to obey my thoughts. Instead, I remained standing on the spot.

"It didn't come out of thin air," I muttered. "C'mon, do me a favour and take me—"

A pair of claws shot out, narrowly avoiding spearing me in the chest. I pivoted, hovering on the spot, suspended in the current of energy. Shit. I wasn't in my body any longer, instead floating within the current.

"What are you?" I yelled at the phantom. It was half solid where it'd once been transparent, its humanoid form equipped with clawed hands and a round, toothy mouth like some kind of mutated worm.

The phantom gouged its claws at me in answer. I drew on the node's power, feeling it humming inside me, and the beast recoiled away from the torrent of energy. It seemed the third stage of spirit magic—drawing on the node's strength to bolster my own—even worked while I was astral projecting.

Yeah, about that. I need to find my body.

I focused hard on passing through the node, and I landed in the living room to find Devon crouching over my body. "What the hell did you do this time? I thought you were having a seizure."

I slid back into my body. "I think I astral projected in the middle of a jump."

She shook her head at me. "Your timing might have been better. The Order has been harassing me again. They want to see you at their office two hours ago."

I had zero patience for taking the bus after my near-death experience, so I used the node to hop into the Parallel and then crossed back over, coming out of the node on the road opposite the Order. Judith startled at the sight of me, so badly that she nearly dropped the box she was carrying.

"Hey," I said, in falsely warm tones. "What does the Order want?"

"How—what?" she said. "You're not supposed to be in the Parallel."

"I'm working on a case." Well, it was true. Did the Order want to know about my mission? If they expected me to share all the private details of the liches' murders I'd discovered in the last couple of days, they could forget it. "Who wants to see me?"

"Mrs Carlisle." She watched me leave with a bemused expression on her face.

The head of the retrieval unit. What did she want with me?

It was only after I left Judith behind that I realised that the logo on the box she carried was the mark of the COS. So she was in on it, too. I made a mental note to question her further at the next opportunity, then I showed my ID to the guards outside the Order's headquarters. The phantom attack had left me so frazzled that I barely noticed their usual raised eyebrows at the black mark on my record.

When they'd let me in, I crossed the reception area and made my way down to the basement. Mrs Carlisle occupied the same chair she had previously, a bored expression on her face, and didn't acknowledge my presence.

I halted in front of the desk. "You wanted to talk to me."

"Yes," she said. "I did. You are working on a case in the Parallel?"

"I am," I said. "With the Death King," I added, in case she got it into her head to start asking unwanted questions.

"Yes." Her mouth pinched with distaste. "I am aware of the unusual circumstances of your meeting, but the fact of the matter is that I cannot allow you to continue to be involved with a case which is not within the constraints of your role at the Order."

"Excuse me?" I said. "There's no rule against me taking other jobs."

"On the contrary, this case of yours runs counter to your position as a retriever," she said. "The Death King is a rival authority. You cannot work for both of us."

"I'm not working for him," I said. "I'm working *with* him. Major difference there."

What the hell? What'd brought this on? The Order had better not be involved with whoever was murdering the liches. That was all I needed: another traitor with my name on their hit list.

"I don't see the difference," she said. "The Order requests that you cease to work on this case, immediately."

"I don't think so." The rebellious words came out before I could reel them in, and I pulled the muddy coin from my pocket. "I found this at the scene of the crime I'm investigating. Does it look familiar to you?"

Her gaze passed over the coin. "That's a cantrip."

"It was." I held it up to the light. "Your new cantrips from the market are all designed to go blank when their spell is used up. Whatever spell was cast on this one turned a phantom into a living creature and a lich into a rotting corpse. Someone is using the Order's cantrips to commit murder."

When her brows rose, I realised, too late, what I'd given away.

"A lich?" she said. "I see why the Death King would find that concerning, but my point still stands. I insist that you cease to work on this case immediately."

Anger surged within me. "Is there any work you want to give me, then? Because if I don't get some cash on my hands soon, I'll be forced to reconsider my employment prospects."

"There's a case in here with your name on it." She scrolled down the computer screen.

That did not sound promising. I wanted to argue the point, but the link to the COS was tentative at best, and anyone might have purchased a cantrip to reuse without the Order needing to be involved. Maybe the vampires could shed some light on who might be responsible. I wasn't skipping my meeting with the council, no matter what the Order said.

Mrs Carlisle tapped a few keys on the computer. "There have been reports of some dangerous spells which have fallen into the hands of a group of newly created vampires. They were seen near the market. I have the address here."

I groaned inwardly. "No need. I think I know exactly which vampires you're talking about."

10

Either Brant had some hitherto-unknown psychic abilities, or he'd had an inkling the Order would be on my back, because I found him waiting outside when I left the building.

"Devon told me," he said, dispelling both options. "When I went back to your place. Sorry I took off earlier."

"Sorry I laughed when the horse kicked you." I fell into step with him as we walked towards the node. "In my defence, it was hilarious."

"I guess it probably was," he said. "What did the Order want?"

"I have to go back to deal with those vampires we found in Vaughn's old house tomorrow," I said. "Apparently, they have some illegal spells they're using on civilians to knock them out cold so they can feed on them."

"I can go and look," he said.

"The Order will find out if I don't do it myself," I said. "I can't risk pissing them off. Besides, I need the money."

"What about the case, though?" he said. "I mean, I

won't be disappointed if you turn your back, but I thought you were keen to stay on the Death King's good side."

"I am," I said. "Kind of. I don't have any more clues, but I guess I can ask when I meet with the vampires tomorrow night."

"Meet with *which* vampires?" His eyes rounded. "Not the vampire council?"

Oops. After my outburst at the Order, I couldn't seem to stop running my mouth off, it seemed.

"The Death King got himself a meeting with them to discuss the murders," I said. "I got invited along, too, for some reason."

"Don't go," he said. "I mean it, Liv. The vampires are bad news. The Order won't like it either."

"They don't own me," I said, irked. "Neither do you, for that matter. I'm not meeting them alone. The Death King—"

"Is no more likely to spare you than they are," he said. "You're nothing to them, no more than a tool."

"Oh, thanks," I said. "A tool, am I? What am I supposed to do to stay totally unsullied, strike out alone in the human world? I might not have grown up like you did, but that doesn't mean you need to treat me like I'm made of glass."

His face reddened. "Look, I don't mean to order you around, but the vampire council aren't interested in meeting civilians for no reason. They want something from you."

"Maybe they do," I relented. "It's been a long day, and I'm tired and pissed off. You don't have to remind me these people are dangerous. I know."

"I know you do." He exhaled in a sigh. "The truth is, I'm scared for you."

My mouth parted in surprise at his admission. I knew it must have cost him to admit to fear.

"Of what?" I asked. "Of being killed by a half-dead phantom reanimated by a spell?"

"No," he said. "The Order already tried to destroy you once before. You're strong, but the vampires, the Death King... they don't play to win, they play to obliterate the competition. They're both vying for control of the Parallel. And they'll destroy anyone who stands between them if they have to."

I gaped at him. The Death King hadn't said anything about wanting to control the Parallel, but then again, who was to say that wasn't his eventual goal? He must want something other than to rule over the Court of the Dead for the entirety of his endless life. As for the vampires, they were equally reclusive. Equally dangerous.

But I had to go through with this. For Dex's sake, if nobody else's.

I wound my hand into his. "Let's not talk about this tonight. I'll order takeout and you can watch me get killed by a dragon in Skyrim again, okay?"

———

"Haven't got none," said the vampire, leaning on the door frame to block my view inside the hallway.

I couldn't say I was surprised. The three vampires had reacted exactly as I'd anticipated to my request that they turn over the illegal knockout spells the Order had sent me to retrieve. Why they wanted to knock out civilians when they already had all the perks of being vamps was a total mystery to me, but the Order had decreed they hand over the spells immediately, and as their retriever, that meant I had to stay here until they complied.

I remained in front of the door, despite the warning flash of fangs, cursing the Order inwardly for landing me in this crap. With my upcoming meeting with the vampire council tonight, I didn't want to push my luck by skipping out on this job. "That's not what the Order's report says."

"Fuck the Order."

"Nice sentiment, but I'm going to stay here until you hand over the spells, or else I'm coming in to get them. I have a warrant which says I'm allowed to stay here until you give them to me."

I didn't have a warrant, but I was damned if I left without what I'd come for.

"Oh, hey, Liv," said a voice.

I glanced over my shoulder. Trix appeared behind me, a cheerful smile on his face as though we were exchanging pleasantries in the middle of a sunny park rather than on a vampire's doorstep.

"Hey," I said, fervently glad of the elf's timing. "Would you be able to help me persuade these gentlemen to hand over their illegally acquired knockout spells?"

"It's not illegal!" the vampire protested. "I got 'em from Flare."

"You got them from who?" I said. "Who's Flare?"

"No-one. None of your business."

"You're not very bright, are you?" I said. "You just said you got your spells from Flare. Who's that, your supplier? Was it stolen, by any chance?"

"Bugger off. I didn't break any laws."

"You're squatting in a house which belonged to a criminal who tried to kill me," I told them. "Let's just say you look about as reputable as Smaug the Magnificent sitting on a mountain of gold. Besides, using knockout spells to snag people to feed on is illegal."

"Please give us the spells." Trix glided over. "I'll have to come inside, otherwise Liv will get herself hurt, and I don't want that to happen."

The lead vampire sidestepped the elf and lunged at me. My fist came up, colliding with the vampire's chin. Pain splintered my knuckles. Ow. When would I learn not to punch vampires?

Trix hit out, as fast as a vampire himself, his fists whirling. Punches hit in quick succession as all three vampires tried to engage him at once, but getting a hit on the elf was like trying to grab a bar of soap. He spun and danced among them, giving me the chance to slip between them and into the house.

Inside, they hadn't even properly unpacked their bags, and a sack of cantrips lay on the carpet like a bag of cash from a heist movie. I'd have preferred to confiscate the lot, but following the Order's instructions to the letter was my best bet at this stage. I turned over cantrip over cantrip, looking for the right one.

Once again, I felt the twinge of Dex's absence. I'd tried looking around for him again when I'd crossed over into the Parallel, but no signs of his smirking face had appeared. It was enough to make me want to ask the Death King if he knew how to get him back, but he would hardly care for the life of a simple fire sprite who didn't belong to his Court. As for the Order, they didn't even know he existed, and they'd probably take my friendship with him as proof of my criminal nature.

Giving up on finding the right cantrips among the haul, I grabbed the whole bag and slung it over my shoulder. Sometimes working around criminals was more trouble than it was worth.

Outside, I found Trix standing over the bodies of the dazed-looking vampires. "Thanks for the help."

"Anytime," he said. "Should I hit them some more?"

"Uh…" I looked down at their unconscious bodies. "I think that'll do. The Order wanted me to get their illegal haul, not kill them." More's the pity. My hand was really starting to throb by now, so it was probably for the best that I didn't stick around until they woke up.

"What did they steal?" asked Trix.

"Spells, apparently from someone called Flare." I held up the bag. "Does the name sound familiar to you?"

"I know an elf called Fallellorax."

"Er… not quite." I was fairly sure no elves were involved with the illegal cantrip trade. Their own magic made ours look like a party trick by comparison. "Thanks for the help, anyway."

I walked away, my hand throbbing. Brant was off on some other mission, which was more of a relief than I'd admit aloud. We might have made up after yesterday's argument, but that didn't mean I wanted to give him another shot at convincing me not to meet with the vampire lords tonight.

Instead, I went home, directly via the node. The more often I used the node to travel into my own house and then to the Order, the less I could be bothered with getting the bus. Devon barely glanced at me when I landed in the shop. "Got what you went for?"

"Uh-huh." My hand gave another throb. "Got a healing cantrip? I punched a vampire again."

"What are you like?" She tossed a cantrip at me, then returned to sewing a button onto her costume. "By the way, I'm working on a set of costumes based on our D&D campaign. I figured you were too busy to make your own."

"Right… the comic con," I said. "I should have asked Trix if he was going. He just helped me kick the shit out of the vampires."

"Nice," she said. "Also, I tested the cantrip, and it worked."

"Which one?"

She lifted a coin—the one which had been blank. "This one. I've reused it four times and it's reset every time it's run out. If it has a limit, I haven't seen it."

"Damn." I'd known the cantrip worked the same as a regular one despite the recycled material, but I would have assumed it'd wear out at some point.

"Exactly," she said. "I want in on these suppliers, whoever they are."

"Maybe the people at the COS's store in the market would give me more details if I told them I want to get some for myself."

"Not if they think you're threatening to steal their customers." A calculating look passed over her face. "But I guess they must be trading with people on this side, if they're supplying the Order. Maybe I'll ask the Order to let me have some of their fancy new supplies. The worst they can do is say no."

I raised an eyebrow. "You sure about that?"

"They're not going to wipe my memory over an innocent request for more materials," she said. "I'll ask the Order the next time they come here."

"If you're sure." It wasn't my job to tell her what to do, but given the Order's refusal to budge on the issue of me working with the Death King, I doubted they'd give in on this one, either. "I'd better head over to the Order before they start pestering me again."

I stepped through the node, landing in the usual spot down the road from the Order's HQ. Whatever the general public thought of a dishevelled woman carrying a sack of what looked like pirate treasure through the city centre, they'd probably seen weirder, because nobody gave me a second glance.

I entered the Order's HQ and made straight for the retrieval unit. Mrs Carlisle wasn't in, but stacks of cardboard boxes filled the rest of the office, all marked with the COS logo. They must have bought enough supplies to last several months if they were dropping them off in the retrieval unit of all places. We were the lowest rung on the ladder and didn't even get suitable clothing, let alone protective charms for dangerous missions. I wondered what the odds were that I'd get caught if I sneaked a few cantrips into my pockets.

Footsteps sounded on the stairs, and I wheeled around as Mrs Carlisle entered the office.

"What are you doing?" she said, eyeing the sack of cantrips over my shoulder.

"Returning the illegal cantrips you asked me to bring in." I planted the sack onto the desk. "Speaking of cantrips, why do you need so many? There aren't that many staff in the retrieval unit."

"Yes, I'm aware," she said. "These cantrips are held here in preparation for events like the tragedy a few weeks ago. They'll also prove useful for routine missions, too."

"I thought survival packs for retrievers were an unnecessary expense."

Or so I'd heard, anyway. Her mouth pressed together. "I would have thought you'd be pleased to no longer have to depend on your friend Devon's charity to provide you with basic safety cantrips."

"It isn't charity. We're business partners." I did her paperwork for the Order, while she gave me enough free cantrips not to have to buy them out of my meagre earnings. We'd both be in equal trouble if we were forced to shut down. Her family had kicked her out at eighteen and refused to let her back in when she'd failed her exams at the academy. She had nowhere else to go, least of all in the Parallel, and was as dependent on me as I was on her.

Yet the Order was willing to destroy her life because of how much they despised me. My hands shook with anger, and I clenched my fists at my sides. "I got those cantrips from the vampires, as requested. They claimed to have bought their haul from someone known as 'Flare'. Know the name?"

"I'm not familiar with the illicit dealings of the Parallel's underworld," she said. "Your mission is done, so there'll be no more deviations today. Clear?"

"Crystal." A meeting with the vampire council didn't count as a deviation, technically, since I was officially off the clock. Not that the Order would accept that as an excuse, but refusing the vampire council struck me as riskier than turning up to a meeting with them. They hadn't made any threats, but invitations to meet the council who ruled the city didn't come along every day.

How much did they really know about the current developments at the market, and the force sneaking through the nodes, killing the undead? As for the COS's mysterious suppliers, did *they* know someone was buying up their spells and using them to kill the dead by turning them back into the living again?

11

Early that evening, I set out for my meeting with the vampires. It took me an hour of dithering to pick an outfit, but in the end, I opted for my usual Parallel gear: durable coat, trousers and boots, plus my pouch of cantrips and my lucky dice. Just in case. I paced in circles around the living room until I couldn't delay any longer. Drawing in a breath, I stepped into the node's path.

As I passed through the current of energy, a sharp pain pierced my neck. A clawed creature appeared from nowhere and clung to my side, biting and tearing. The foul stench of the dead filled my nostrils. Coughing and gagging, I hit out, dislodging my attacker as we landed in the swampland on the other side.

Cold swamp water splashed my boots, and the clawed beast crumpled into a decaying heap. I caught the coin before it hit the ground, but it was already blank on both sides.

Not again.

"Ow." I gingerly touched my neck, and my fingers came away damp with blood. I needed to fix the damage before I went to see the vampire lord. They might wear a civilised veneer, but I'd bet a bleeding human wandering into their midst would be too much to resist.

The swampland was dark, the castle cast in even more shadow than usual. I trod through the marshy earth, glad I'd worn my boots, my neck throbbing with each step. *Maybe Brant was right—this is a seriously bad idea.*

The Death King stood waiting for me outside the castle, a darker shadow etched against the blackness. "There you are."

"I got attacked by another phantom on the way." I showed him my bleeding neck. "Got anywhere I can clean up? I don't want to leave a trail of blood on the vampires' floor."

"Ryan will take you inside."

The Air Element appeared from the darkness, so sudden they startled me. Even more so when a skeletal horse appeared behind them like a demonic hellhound. I pressed a hand to my thumping heart. "At this rate I'm gonna drop dead of fright before I set foot in the vampires' place.'

The horse cantered forward and nudged my hand with its bone-white head. I recognised it as Neddie, the same horse I'd ridden before... and who'd kicked Brant head-first into the mud.

"He likes you," Ryan observed. "C'mon, this way. The horses get weird around blood."

"So do the vampires." I pulled back my collar from my neck, hoping I hadn't already got blood on the dark fabric. "Do you have any healing cantrips, then?"

"Of course." They led the way around the castle and through a side door. A corridor waited ahead, and I counted six wooden doors, three on each side. The Air Element unlocked one of them and led the way into a wide room.

I stared around in surprise. The room was the size of a large studio flat, with a modern kitchen at one end and a door leading into a bedroom at the other. The main living room contained a massive TV and gaming system in front of a large plush sofa.

"I see what you mean about the Death King letting you live in luxury." I followed them through the darkened room, where they opened a cabinet in the kitchen and handed me a healing cantrip. "Thanks. Is it okay if I wash off the blood?"

"Go ahead."

After using the healing cantrip, I ran the kitchen tap and dabbed at my neck with a damp cloth. "I didn't know you Elements played video games in your spare time. Is there even electricity or internet here?"

"We can play offline," they said. "The whole castle has its own electricity supply. Cal, the Earth Element's doing —he's a genius with electronics."

"I can't imagine the Death King has much use for it." I found myself grinning at the mental image of His Deathliness with an Xbox controller in his hand.

"You'd be surprised," they said. "Sometimes I go back into the other realm to play with my friends back there, but I dropped out of touch with a lot of them when I was hired as the Air Element."

Because most people were too scared of the Death King. I didn't blame them, but it was a shame Ryan was stuck with only three actual human people for company, one of whom was a complete arse. "That's cool."

A chill breeze swept through the room, and the Death King stepped straight through the door as though it wasn't there. "I wouldn't advise you to be late to meet with the vampires."

I put the cloth down. "Does he do that all the time? Whatever happened to privacy?"

The Death King frowned. It was at that point that I noticed he wore his human guise. Why did he need to play human to meet with the vampires? They knew who he was. "If you're done, we'll leave now."

"All right, keep your wig on." I caught sight of Ryan wearing a scandalised expression and made a mental note to hold my tongue once we reached the vampire council. It'd been a long, hard day, and my nerves were high enough that for some reason, the Death King no longer registered as a threat. *Calm it, Liv.*

The Death King didn't speak a word as he led the way out of the castle and into the murky grounds.

"I didn't have to dress up, did I?" I asked.

"No," he said. "Given your propensity to attract danger, it wouldn't have been worth the effort. What did you do to draw your attacker's attention?"

"Nothing whatsoever." I buried my hands in my pockets, doubly cold with the damp water on my neck. "It jumped me when I came through the node."

I hoped I hadn't accidentally let anything into the house. Devon wouldn't be amused if I'd sent another zombie phantom in her direction.

"And have you found anything new?" he asked.

"Another one of these." I showed him the coin. "Same

spell as before, I'll bet, but it didn't leave any traces behind. The Order doesn't seem to give a shit, so the vampires better have something good to say."

There was a long pause. "What did you tell the Order?"

Ah. I'd accidentally let slip that his fellow liches were being killed. "I showed them the coin, but they refused to see a link with the COS's suppliers."

"You showed them the coin?" He turned to me, his human face shadowed so it looked as scary as his masked one. "If I wanted to hire someone from the Order, I'd have gone to them, not you."

"The Order dragged me in," I said ineffectually. "I had to give them a reason for all my trips into the Parallel. They're using the COS's cantrips themselves, you know, and I thought if I prompted them to look into it, they might take me seriously."

"And did they?"

My shoulders slumped. "No, but they can't say I didn't try to warn them. Also, they want me to stop working with you."

"Yet you still came here."

"I did," I said. "This isn't work. We're meeting the vampires at their own request."

Instead of replying, he glided across the swampland, forcing me to run to keep up with him. I'd have preferred to ride a horse, but I didn't much fancy arguing with him in such a tetchy mood. So much for being a united front against the vampires.

The same icy silence pursued us as we crossed the swampland, and if he could hear my chattering teeth, he didn't comment. I'd usually been careful about keeping secrets, but the fact that everyone at the Order seemed to be ignoring the potential issues with the COS and their operation rubbed me up the wrong way. The Order was usually the first to throw the book at people, after all.

My shoulders tensed as the warehouses came into view. I'd wondered if anyone would recognise the Death King in his human form, but not many people were out on the streets at this time. Most had the sense not to stay out after dark, with vampires and other creatures of the night on the prowl. Curtains were drawn in the windows, doors were barred, and the more affluent had used magical means to seal their houses closed against potential threats.

The Death King's silent glide continued until we'd left the warehouses behind and entered the main road leading into the city's heart. Despite the scarred streets and collapsed buildings remaining from the war, the vampires had kept their meeting point close to the Citadel of the Elements, formerly home to the council which had ruled the city of Arcadia before the war.

On the far side of the main square, an empty black tower stood etched against the night sky. The magic that had once sustained the citadel was long gone, but somehow it remained standing. Not that anyone went inside if they had any sense. Like the other places the Elements had vacated, they said so many phantoms haunted the tower that none dared to enter for fear of succumbing to madness. Shivers danced down my spine at the sight of its gleaming walls, engraved with the symbol of the Elements—five circles surrounding a sixth combining all five. I wondered if the Death King had borrowed his own design from theirs, replacing the central symbol with a skull.

The Death King veered sideways towards a squat building on our left with narrow windows curtained in black. The vampires didn't actually live there most of the time, but their council met at night, and despite the darkness, movement stirred behind the velvet curtains.

Doubts entered my mind, spurred by the haunting shape of the abandoned citadel. What if the vampires *did* know I was a spirit mage? Was I endangering everyone I knew by coming here to meet with them? It was too late to turn back now, so I held my head high as the Death King greeted the pale young man standing at the door. He was unmistakeably human, his throat peppered with needle-sharp bites.

Bracing myself, I walked after the Death King through the polished oak doors. The red-carpeted hallway was lit by old-fashioned lanterns, igniting the path through a door on our right.

We entered a wood-panelled room containing a long table lined with chairs of dark wood and plush red upholstery. A smartly dressed vampire sat at the head of the table, gesturing to us to sit near him. Pale as milk, he had features that indicated Asian heritage, slick black hair, and a complexion that made him appear several centuries younger than his likely actual age.

"Grey," said the vampire, with the hints of an accent. "It's an honour to meet with you."

Grey? Was that the Death King's real name?

"Lord Blackbourne," he said. "The honour is mine, I'm sure. This is Olivia Cartwright."

The vampire lord's pale eyes flickered over me. "So this is she."

Okay... "Hello, Lord Blackbourne," I said carefully. "I'm

Olivia. The Death King and I are temporarily working together."

"Why, pray tell, did you ask for an audience with me?"

"We—" I cleared my throat, my heart hammering against my ribcage. "We wanted to speak to you about some recent unusual deaths here in the city. The revenants are being driven out of the tunnels, hunted by something that's killing them in a brutal fashion. Something dead."

The vampire lord drummed his elegant fingers on the table. "And why is this supposed to be of concern to me?"

"It's not just the revenants it's affecting," I went on, when the Death King didn't deign to speak up and confirm my story. "Phantoms have been attacking anyone who goes near the nodes, including the revenants. They're afflicted by some kind of spell which turns them into clawed monsters—*living* monsters. You must have seen the bodies. They're decaying, as though they came back to life only to be killed again."

"Is that so?" He gave the Death King a glance. "Is there any particular reason you picked this human to help you in this case? You must know she's in a precarious position, being a spirit mage."

Shock punched the air from my lungs. "Excuse me? I'm not—"

"Please spare me the lies." The vampire rubbed his temples with his long fingers. "They give me a headache. I knew you for a spirit mage the instant you stepped into this room."

Shit. This isn't good. It's not good at all. If he told the Order, I was dead.

"Are you reading my mind?" Even the vampires

weren't capable of such a feat, but there were rumours of their perceptive nature. I should never have come here to speak to one of their lords.

"No, but it's harder for your kind to hide what you are than you might think." He smiled, revealing pointed fangs. "Your very nature is altered by the magic you wield. The more you use it, the more it shows, to those of us who know what to look for."

I gave the Death King an alarmed look, but his expression was impassive. "Do all vampires know? I mean, can they all tell in the same way?"

"Not all," said Lord Blackbourne. "It depends on how observant they are."

"Are you—?" I swallowed against my dry throat. "Are you going to tell anyone else?"

"Only if I have reason to."

Translation: only if I pissed him off. Good to know.

The Death King stepped in. "We would like to know if you have observed the effects of this phenomenon affecting the undead beings in the city. We believe it is being caused by an illegal usage of magic."

I reached into my pocket and held up the coin from earlier. "I've found a blank cantrip like this one at the site of each attack. It's one of those new cantrips from the market which turns blank after being used."

"Interesting." He didn't take the coin from me. "Unless you can give me a cantrip which is intact and in full working order, I will not be able to divine its nature, much less who is responsible for creating it."

Dammit. I should have known. "Aren't you worried someone is stealing supplies from the COS at the market to turn into illegal cantrips? I take it you approved their new operation?"

"Of course I did," he said. "The COS has been in the works for a long time. It's going to save a lot of money and hassle for the practitioners of the city."

"Not just the legal practitioners, though," I said. "If anyone can now create an infinite number of illegal spells, they can make some real problems for everyone else here, including the vampires."

"Infinite?" he echoed. "I doubt that will be the case. If this individual is acting alone, they would only be able to act as fast as their skills allow. For a complex spell, a considerable time investment would need to be made."

"It can't only be one person." But who would know how to create an illegal spell like that? "Besides, it's targeting the dead specifically. Aren't you concerned for your fellow vampires?"

I felt the Death King's disapproving stare on me, but I didn't acknowledge him. I wanted to hear it from the vampire himself.

The vampire lord gave a thin-lipped smile. "If a spell exists which we cannot outrun, then perhaps we deserve what we get."

My hands clenched. "The person doing this is using the nodes in some way, too. All the bodies have been found on top of the nodes. I guess it's because the spell requires a surge of energy…"

"So do most of the commonly used cantrips out there," he said. "What did you hope to gain from speaking to me? Unless I used the Order's method of banning everything that disagrees with them, there's nothing I can do to control what others do with their magic."

"Do you have any ideas as to who might be responsible, then?" I asked.

The vampire looked directly at the Death King. "Look at your own first, I would advise."

"What does that mean?" I stole a glance at my companion, but his expression was impassive. Bloody secretive immortals.

"I will take that under advisement," he said. "Is there anything else you wish to tell me?"

"I thought this might be of interest," said the vampire, reaching into his pocket. He pulled out an object and slid it across the table. A round medallion with a skull engraved on the surface.

A soul amulet.

The Death King stilled beside me. "Where did you find this?"

"One of my people found it in the tunnels underneath the city," he said.

"I see." The Death King's icy tone sent shivers through my entire body. "And its owner?"

"I assume you already found them." The vampire rose to his feet with an elegant bow. "I think that's all for now."

A clear dismissal, clear enough to prove the vampire had known there had been lich victims without either of us mentioning the killings. Because the killer had left the soul amulet lying here in the city, miles from the scene of the lich's death.

A frosty silence hung around the Death King as he walked out of the vampires' house, making my nerves jangle. Finally, I gave up on my attempts to suppress my curiosity.

"Grey?" I said. "Is that your name? Or should that be

was?" It made sense that he'd have been called something different back when he'd been human, but I'd had little cause to think on the matter. Aside from the heart-stopping instant when he'd been on the brink of death after losing his soul amulet, he seemed endless, as though he'd never been anything other than the King of the Dead.

He didn't look back at me when he answered. "A nickname. Lord Blackbourne finds it amusing. He and I have known one another since before I was King."

The thought disarmed me. A world without the Death King in it—or without this particular Death King on the throne—seemed as alien as the idea of the spirit mages walking among us.

As though sensing I wasn't out of questions, he quickened his pace, his feet hardly seeming to touch the ground.

"What did he mean?" I hurried to keep up with him. "When he said *look to your own,* he meant one of your liches stole the amulets before killing your people, right?"

He didn't answer, continuing to silently advance through the dark streets. While I normally had a healthy wariness of what might be lurking in the shadows of the city at night, I feared the man in front of me more. Yet not enough to run away, not even when we entered the swampland, nor when we crossed its shadowy paths towards the castle.

"Aren't you leaving?" He glanced sideways at me as we finally reached the gate. "You should go home."

Yes. I should. But I couldn't get the vampire lord's words out of my head. *He knew I was a spirit mage.* Unless I avoided contact with all vampires from now on, word would make it back to the Order sooner or later.

And the man in front of me might be the only person who stood a chance of teaching me how to hide it.

"I—" I broke off. "I know the lich traitor is probably the one who stole the amulets, but I didn't want to bring them up in front of Lord Blackbourne. Was I right to do that?"

"I suspected he knew." He turned to face me for the first time since we'd left the vampires' meeting place. "There's little the vampire lords are unaware of when it comes to the movements of their equals."

"And—me?" I buried my freezing hands in my pockets. "I'm not exactly on an equal footing with them." To say the least.

"You're concerned that they will tell the Order what you are."

"No shit." Oops. I probably shouldn't forget I was speaking to someone equally capable of spilling my secrets—but my fear from the vampire's revelation had momentarily knocked aside my common sense. "Who wouldn't?"

The Death King's brows rose. "The vampire lords have better things to do than to turn the Order against their own employees."

"It would only take one slip-up." Fear constricted my chest. "One wrong word to the wrong person. How do I stop myself from giving off this… whatever it is that gives me away as a spirit mage?"

"You can't."

My hands curled into my fists. "That's it?"

"We cannot change our natures." He indicated the gates, where two liches parted to allow us through. "None of us. Vampire, Element… spirit mage. The Order knows that."

I screwed up my forehead. "They didn't take away my magic, so they must have known that I'd still register as a spirit mage to anyone with the ability to tell. Right?"

"You just answered your own question." He remained still for an instant, his shadowy form etched against the night sky. "But if you wanted to know whether using spirit magic would make your signature more prominent, you were right."

My heart sank. "So I have to stop using it?"

"That's not what I said." He turned to me, the moonlight animating his human face in a disconcertingly lifelike manner. "Your nature is impossible to hide, strong or not."

"The Order knows." I spoke more to reassure myself than anything else. "They already want to kick Devon and me out into the Parallel. They'll have even more of an incentive if they find out I disobeyed their command to stop working with you. Hell if I know why they're so set on me turning down your offer of work. Unless they think you're going to turn me against them."

His brow arched. "If I were perceived as a threat to the Order, I wouldn't be in this position. Do you think the Order would allow an independent ruler to establish dominance without making sure they weren't a threat to their own rule?"

My mouth parted. "Does that include the vampires, too?"

"Yes, it does," he said. "It isn't in my interests to start a conflict with those who work to protect the magical community in either realm. I have no desire to see my Court consumed in another conflict."

"The Order isn't in charge here," I said. "Isn't that why you wanted to recruit me to begin with?"

"I overestimated your commitment," he said. "Understandably, no doubt. You have no desire to embrace your identity as a spirit mage, and until you take a side, people like Lord Blackbourne will be poised to take advantage."

"Aren't committed?" His words stung more than they had the right to. "I'm sorry I didn't take you up on your offer of a job, but there's too much at stake for me to risk pissing the Order off. And I don't want to live here in the Parallel."

"Then what do you want?" he asked.

My memories back. To learn spirit magic.

No. I couldn't go that far… not if I wanted to retain any chance at walking away from this alive.

But what about Dex? And the other liches, falling victim to the killer? Even the Death King, whoever he'd been in his previous existence?

"Information," I finally answered. "If I'm to find out how the liches are being killed, I need to know more about spirit magic."

"If that's the case," he said, "you'll need to come with me."

Apprehension dug its heels in, but if he thought me uncommitted, I'd have to go ahead and prove him wrong.

I walked up the steps to the castle, ignoring my fatigue and wariness. He glided ahead of me, through the door and into the entrance hall. Then, I followed him around the corner and into the hall of souls.

12

T he hall of souls stretched out in front of us,
filled with long shelves lined with amulets. Old-
fashioned lanterns hung at intervals on the
walls, casting long shadows over the shelves, and I startled
when I realised we weren't alone.

Several liches gathered around the room, pockets of
shadow in the shape of people. I backed up to the Death
King's side, only to find his human guise had slipped away
in the last few seconds, leaving him as masked and terrifying as ever.

"Do you have anything to report?" he asked the assembled liches.

As the liches moved closer, I retreated another few
steps, sensing I wasn't supposed to eavesdrop. My breath
frosted the chill air beside a pillar formed of interlocking
bones. I decided not to look closely enough to determine
if they were human bones or not.

After a minute of whispered conversation, the liches
departed. None of them bothered to open the door before

exiting in a sweep of shadows. Now alone, the Death King reached into a pocket of his coat and removed the amulet the vampire had given him.

I cleared my throat. "If you don't mind telling me… that amulet—whose is it? I mean, whose was it?"

"That's what I'm here to find out." He faced the shelves of amulets once again.

I inched closer, rubbing my hands together for warmth. "Are they arranged in any particular order?"

Did he have to pick up and examine every single amulet if he wanted to find the identity of the missing one's owner? It seemed a hell of an inefficient method, but as far as I knew, until the recent events, nobody had ever stolen anything from here.

"They're roughly organised by the date the individual turned lich," he said, "but if one went missing, even its owner might not notice at first."

Like he hadn't noticed his own soul amulet had ended up in my hands, at least at first. I looked more closely at the amulet he held, noting the faded lines on the edges. It might be bigger than a typical cantrip, but a spell had bound the soul into place. "How could a spell so complex be undone?"

"Because no spell lasts forever." He didn't turn around. "There are always weak spots, if you know where to find them."

I turned this over in my mind. "You mean the lich traitor undid the binding spell himself? If that's the case, what's to stop any of the liches doing the same to anyone who annoys them?"

"Few liches have the capacity for such magic," he said. "Removing a soul is one thing. Binding it to a vessel is another entirely, as you know well. And undoing such a binding? Rarely heard of."

A shiver curled down my spine at the memory of cupping his life essence in my hands, and the accompanying shock and surprise that someone so indomitable could seem so vulnerable.

"But you do know a way?" I sucked in a sharp breath when he turned around, his faceless mask blending into the darkness.

He held up the amulet. "To create a true lich, one's soul must be separated at the moment of death."

My heart climbed into my throat. Everyone said the liches had made some kind of deal with death, voluntarily detaching their souls from their bodies in order to live forever, but I'd never heard it confirmed from one of them directly before.

Yet the corpses we'd discovered had been decomposing as though they'd been slaughtered recently, and like the ritual that had turned them into liches had been reversed. What spell could possibly accomplish such a feat?

Nothing of concern to the vampire council, apparently. But then again, it wasn't Lord Blackbourne's people who were dying. The vampires didn't have any claim on the revenants, seeing them as lesser beings. Kind of like the liches saw phantoms and the like. Phantoms hadn't even been human, if their clawed forms when they returned to life were any indication, so the vampires would need to feel directly threatened to do anything about them. I hadn't thought Lord Blackbourne had seemed like he might be working against us, but he sure as hell wasn't on our side, either.

"What did phantoms used to be when they were alive?" I asked the Death King. "I mean, did they always look like... those clawed monsters?"

"You just answered your own question." He lowered the amulet, his tone heavy with annoyance at me for changing the subject. "The spell returns the dead to life, but it seems to have a time limit on it. They start decaying swiftly."

"Hang on." I screwed up my forehead. "If the same spell which is bringing the phantoms back to life is doing the same to the liches, can it really be your lich traitor who's behind this? And... are you sure the intention is to commit murder? Because bringing the dead back to life isn't exactly a typical method."

Was the traitor lich truly out to murder his fellow liches, or might he have another motive entirely?

"The result is the same," the Death King said, his voice clipped. "This murderer may have brought my liches back to life, in a way, but it was with the intention of leaving them dead. The theft of their soul amulets proves that."

"All right." The subject bothered him, evidently, but I didn't really blame the guy. He'd spent the last Elements knew how many years thinking he was going to live forever, and it seemed his fate might be to end up a rotting corpse after all.

I watched him carry the soul amulet to the shelf, and then something else occurred to me.

"Wait," I said. "The soul amulet is still intact even though there's no soul inside it. Can they be reused? Like..."

Like the COS's new cantrips?

The Death King's spine stiffened. "It would be a great insult to the previous owner."

"I didn't mean—" I broke off. "I just wanted to know if it was possible. Where do you get them from? I mean, do you carve a new one for each new lich?"

He walked in silence for a long moment. "We have a large collection of soul amulets from our time among the living."

"They can't be destroyed, then?"

"Not by any natural force," he said.

"Who carved them?" I asked. "You?"

His whole manner chilled. Literally. Frost formed on the shelves, and my fingers numbed. I buried my hands in my pockets, my heartbeat kicking into gear. *Quiet, Liv. Stop poking him when he's already in a bad mood.*

"Some of them, yes," he said.

He'd done the same to Brant to teach him a lesson, but he'd reversed the process and brought him back. If he'd been left with his soul detached for too long, though, the spell would have been irreversible. Like the others. They'd been without living bodies for so long that now the best they could do was conjure up an illusion of their former selves, and only the Death King seemed to be able to do that.

"Can you turn down the air con?" I said through frosted lips.

He stepped away from me, and some of the chill faded a little. "I forget how human you are."

"Yeah, we can't all be immortal death lords." My teeth chattered. "I know it's obviously a sore subject with you, but I'm struggling to understand what any lich would have to gain from murdering his fellow liches using a spell that returns them to life."

"He wanted the Order's traitor to take my place," he said. "Perhaps he fancies himself the next Death King."

"If you're immortal, then how does leadership pass from one Death King to the next?" I asked before I could help myself.

"How do you think?"

"The last one dies," I concluded. "You knew you wanted to become king when you turned?"

His reply was short, terse. "What makes you think I chose this?"

My mouth parted. He'd turned at the moment of death. He'd *died* for this… or so I'd thought. Had he really not chosen this fate?

From the way the temperature plummeted again, I had an inkling I was treading on dangerous ground, and if I didn't steer the topic into less treacherous waters, he'd kick me out and we'd undo all the progress we'd made. I hadn't come here to ask him personal questions, however potent my curiosity might be.

"Then how do you go about selecting the next leader?" I asked. "Do you get a say at all?

"I have a few liches selected as my potential successors," he said. "It's in my interests to prepare for any possibility."

I imagined he did, especially after how close he'd come to losing his title recently. "So if the traitor wants to take your place, is there a reason he targeted those particular liches?"

"No." An impatient bite entered his words. "None of

the victims so far have been liches I work with personally."

"Maybe he's building up to it," I said. "I mean, reversing death magic strikes me as experimental at best. The revenants might have been a test run. And the phantoms, too."

"Perhaps." His stare seemed to bore into me even with his eyes hidden by the mask. "There are many corners of the spirit arts which are little-known even to us."

"Spirit magic." Lord Blackbourne's face appeared in my mind's eye. *Look to your own...* and he'd known me for a spirit mage right off. "Are... I mean, were *you* a spirit mage? When you were alive?"

A heartbeat passed. "I was."

"And..." The words stuck in my throat. "That's why you can create other liches, isn't it? You're more powerful than the others..."

Because he'd been like me. Before he'd died.

"Yes," he said. "Nobody but a spirit mage can turn another person into a lich, and even then, they run the risk of making the change permanent."

"I think I'll pass, thanks," I responded.

I'd rather stay alive. The perks of being undead didn't outweigh the obvious downsides to entering an eternal existence as a walking corpse. But it explained a lot about his knowledge of spirit magic. He'd used it himself when he'd been alive as well as afterwards.

And a spirit mage must be responsible for the spell turning liches into fresh corpses. Mr Cobb might have been arrested, but it seemed he wasn't the only rogue here in the Parallel.

"I expected as much," he said. "However, this particular

spell strikes me as experimental. There are ways to return the dead to life, for a short time, but not into living, breathing beings."

The image of Dex reforming in mid-air filled my mind's eye. When I'd brought him back from the brink of death. *For a short time. No... that can't be true.*

The Death King tilted his head. "Yes? What is it?"

My conflicted emotions must have shown on my face. "Dex has been missing for days now. He can't... I mean, I brought him back to life, and now he's gone. Is it because of what I did?"

"What would give you that idea?"

I shrugged, my skin pebbled with goose bumps. "He's never vanished like this before. I tried astral projecting and looking around the nodes, but the phantom interrupted me."

If he'd been on top of a node at the wrong time, whatever I'd done to pull him together after his death might not be enough to save him this time.

"You haven't tried since?"

Was there a challenge in his voice? "I want to find him, but I don't want to invite even more trouble. Either he doesn't want to be found, or..."

Or he was gone. A cold pit opened in my stomach. What kind of a friend was I, leaving him alone to face whatever dark force was hunting the dead?

"If you astral project, a sprite shouldn't be able to hide from you," he said.

I tried before. He wasn't there. But had I really? I hadn't searched everywhere, just one node. Perhaps if I persisted —and if I ran the risk of running into another half-dead phantom—I might be able to find him. If I couldn't find him in the physical world, the spirit world was all that was left. "Can I do that from in here?"

"Can you?" he said. "Yes, it's perfectly safe."

"I take it the liches won't draw on my face while I'm out of my body?" In response to his raised eyebrow, I added, "That's what my friends did to me the other day."

"Yet you trust I won't do the same?"

I blinked at him. Could I picture the Death King drawing on my face? Nope. But then again, I hadn't expected him to let me use his castle as a base to go hunting for Dex, either. Given the number of times he'd scared the shit out of me, I should be worried he'd do worse than draw on my face, but I had a friend to rescue. I'd wonder why I'd come to trust the Death King later.

I slipped out of my body, reaching out with my senses to track down the nearby nodes. The one closest to the castle blazed on my vision, but I flew past it this time, towards the shadowy outline of the gates.

"Dex?" I called.

He wasn't in the lands of the dead, not if I hadn't seen any signs of him in my last few visits. Where else might've he gone? Surely not underground, not with faceless beasts slaughtering revenants. He must have found somewhere else to rest, somewhere he wouldn't be disturbed by the living or the dead.

I floated to the swamp's edge, and halted beside the tree which I used to store my props in. A spark of light pinged on my vision. *Aha.*

"Dex?" I called, peering inside the jagged hole in the tree bark.

The light brightened into a transparent humanoid figure crouched inside the tree. "Get away from me!"

I jerked back, flipping over in mid-air. "Dex, you're alive!"

"No thanks to you," he said. "You just gave away my hiding spot. Now everyone will know where I am."

"You disappeared!" I said. "I thought you were dead, dammit. What are you hiding in here for?"

"I don't know!" he said. "Something is causing the phantoms to lose their *minds*. I know they don't have minds, but I saw some *weird* shit out here and I want no part of it, thanks."

"I think I know exactly what you saw." I hovered above the marshy ground, glimpsing his pale shaking form inside the hollow of the tree. "Look, just stop panicking for one second, Dex. That won't help either of us. I'm hunting down those phantoms myself, or at least trying to track down whatever's causing them to go apeshit, and I'll help you, too."

He made a noise of protest, then froze mid-motion. I never would have thought I'd see a fire sprite grow pale with fear, but every speck of colour vanished from his fiery form. His wide eyes were fixed on a spot somewhere over my shoulder.

I turned around, dread clutching me with sharp fingers. A hunched fleshy shape hovered in the air with its clawed hands outstretched. Dex shrank back, while I remained still, unwilling to leave the phantom a path to reach the fire sprite. It shouldn't be able to harm me while I was astral projecting, so maybe I could figure out what was driving it.

"Hey," I said to the creature. "What did that to you?"

"Don't *talk* to it," Dex hissed from inside the tree. "Make it go away."

The creature didn't look capable of moving in a straight line. Its legs were spindly and thin, hardly able to support its body. Pinkish-grey flesh covered its bones, while its clawed hands were disintegrating with each passing second. A pair of grey bat-like wings flapped weakly behind its shoulders.

"Dex, do you see a coin anywhere?"

"No—get *away!*"

The phantom lashed out with a claw, and sharp hooks dug into my arm, piercing me in places it shouldn't be able to touch. Alarm blared through my nerves, and I grabbed for the nearest node's power.

Magic surged into me, pushing the phantom back and numbing the pain in my arm. Its form turned more solid by the instant, decaying as it did so, its clawed hands drooping. The glow brightened, the life force spiralling out of the phantom and into the node's path.

The phantom gave a final lunge and disintegrated, its fleshy remains crashing to the marshy earth.

Dex shuddered. "Creeps. They get one good punch in before they die—but if they get their hooks in you, you're dead. If you're like me, anyway. You're fine. You have a living body. I don't. Blazes and tides…"

"I'll bring you with me." I extended a hand into the tree. "Come on, I won't let anything happen to you."

Dex crawled up my arm like a warm and transparent spider monkey. I withdrew from the tree, scanning the swampland for more phantoms, but the path was clear. I floated back towards the dark shape of the castle with him clinging to my shoulder.

"You'll have to let go of me when I'm back in my body,

or else you might cause me to catch on fire," I said to him as we ascended the stone stairs.

"Where *is* your body?" he said. "You're in… no. You're *inside* the castle?"

"Yep." I floated through the oak doors into the entry-way, and towards the hall of souls. Dex's grip tightened at the sight of the endless rows of shelves.

"Damn." He whistled. "Who'd have thought all this would be in here? Who're they, then? Liches?"

"Dex, don't touch anything." I winced when he let go of me and floated above the shelves with an eager expression on his face. "Dex! Do you *want* to get locked up again?"

He skidded to a halt when we came within sight of the Death King—and my body, standing nearby. I shot him a warning look, then slid back into my body. My eyes opened, taking in the sight of the Death King speaking to his Elemental Soldiers. He'd invited them in to speak to him while I'd been out of my body, and they crowded around their master among the darkened shelves.

"Are you sure he's the one whose body you found?" the Death King was saying. "This amulet is his?"

"Yes," said the Air Element, their voice low. "I'm sorry, Sir."

The Fire Element's eyes narrowed when he caught sight of Dex clinging to my shoulder. Heedless of my warnings, he'd moved close enough that my coat was uncomfortably warm on one side.

"What is that?" Ryan spotted the fire sprite, eyeing Dex with an expression of mild fascination.

"A fire sprite," I said. "Dex, let go of me. There aren't any phantoms in here."

"You found him." The Death King turned to me. "Olivia, you and the sprite should leave."

That was it? The impulse seized me to argue, but from the Elements' sombre manner, he'd just found out the name of the lich who the amulet had belonged to. Besides, the way Dex was trembling wasn't lost on me.

"All right." I turned away. "I'm heading out."

I left the hall of souls, walking the short distance to the doors out of the castle. Dex rode on my shoulder down the stone steps. "You're going through the node?"

"Not like I have another way home." It was too dark to safely wander around the swampland outside the gates of the Death King's territory. Even here, I kept thinking every shadow was a phantom, ready to pounce.

"Well." Dex exhaled in a sigh. "If that's the case, I will find another hole to hide in."

"What's the issue?" I twisted my head to look down at him. "You've never been scared before. Not like this."

He shuddered. "Those phantoms aren't like other magical beings. They're corrupted."

"By spirit magic," I said. "Don't forget I used something similar to bring you back to life."

He let go of me, his expression stricken, and darted away. "As if I could ever forget it."

"What's that supposed to mean?" I ran after him, my feet splashing in the marshy ground. "Look, if you won't tell me what's wrong—"

"I *died,* okay?" he all but bellowed in my face. "I died, and I'd rather it didn't happen again."

My mouth parted, all words fleeing. He'd tasted his own mortality, and he never wanted to experience it again. Could I really blame him for that?

"You could always come back with me," I said to Dex. "To my house, that is. I can't pretend a phantom won't show up anyway, but it's safer than here. You can lie low until I find out who's responsible for the spell affecting the phantoms."

He flew down to my shoulder. "If I were you, I'd stay out of it."

"Yeah, slight problem," I said. "I'm pretty sure whichever lich was working with Vaughn is involved, and as long as that remains the case, the whole of the Court of the Dead might be vulnerable."

"So?" he said. "You didn't care if the Death King lived or died before."

"I didn't risk life and limb to get his soul back only for him to fall victim to a phantom." I reached the node, which surged through the air in a torrent of light. "I'm going home. You're welcome to come with me. Take it or leave it."

The fire sprite sighed. "Fine, but I expect special treatment."

"Only if Devon agrees."

Devon would not be thrilled, but it was the only solution I could think of to avoid losing him again. I stepped into the node's path with Dex clinging to my coat. As I did so, I saw the Air Element exit the castle and turn in my direction as though to watch me leave, and then we were gone.

"You did what?" asked Devon.

Dex flew around the living room, forcing Devon to lift her pile of fabric out of the way of the fire sprite's path.

"I had to bring him back," I said. "He was terrified of being the next to die. With good reason, if the person responsible for unleashing those spells knows the Death King and I are on their tail."

Dex zipped overhead. "I'm free!"

"At this rate, it'll be the Order who locks him up," she said. "Or I'll bury him in the garden along with that dead phantom first."

Dex flew above the dining table, which was set up for this week's game night. "I cannot be contained!"

If Dex had been solid, I'd have cuffed him on the back of the head. "Cut it the hell out. We're doing you a favour, and the least you can do is not get us into trouble with the Order."

Devon blew out a breath. "You do realise we're going

to comic con this weekend? He can't come with us."

"Don't give him ideas," I said. "I know it's not ideal, but if I'd left him over there in the Parallel, he'd either have to hide in a tree or risk getting caught by whatever's turning phantoms into piles of dead flesh. This was my last choice."

"The vampire council didn't have any ideas about the undead killer, then?" she asked.

"Only that the lich traitor is probably involved, but nobody knows who it is." The Death King had to figure that one out himself, but until then, I could at least keep Dex safely out of the way of the killer. "The vampire handed us an amulet belonging to one of the victims, which confirmed the traitor stole the amulets out of the hall of souls before killing their owners."

"So a lich is behind this?" she said. "For sure?"

"Not alone." I hesitated, knowing the Death King wouldn't want me blabbing his secrets to all my friends. "Most liches don't have enough power to remove another person's soul. I think it's a spirit mage again. A spirit mage doubling as a mad scientist with a grudge against the liches. I can't think who else might have the talent."

Dex skidded to a halt in mid-air. "No mage has that kind of power, either."

"The spirit mages did." Before they'd died out, anyway. Died out... or lived beyond death.

What makes you think I chose this?

The Death King's words reverberated in my mind, sending a fresh wave of chills racing down my spine. Only a spirit mage could turn another person into a permanent lich. If he'd done it to the others, who'd been the one to bind *his* soul? Was there truth to the rumour that the liches as a whole had become the way they were due to some dark bargain with death itself? If so, then how had the Death King been turned against his will?

The vampire had said *look to your own* to find the killer, but maybe it'd been a warning to me as much as to the Death King. If I was turned into a lich, I'd be equally vulnerable to the spell myself. There'd be no turning back.

Perhaps it wasn't the Death King the vampire had been trying to warn after all.

———

I didn't sleep much that night. Dex zipped around the house for hours, revelling in the freedom of no longer being confined to a tree, but even when he quietened down, my mind refused to rest. Especially when I found myself wanting to astral project and find the Death King so we could continue our conversation from earlier.

Now was not the time for my curiosity about spirit magic to reawaken. I couldn't afford to get distracted from my mission... but what if the truth about the deadly spell lay in my memories, like last time? Inevitably, I then found my mind wandering back to Dirk Alban. He hadn't taught me how to detach a soul and place it in a vessel... at least, I thought not. But then I remembered how naturally it'd come to me when I'd been pressured to move the Death King's soul to another amulet, as though I'd been working from experience as well as instinct. And when I'd saved Dex's life. Miracle or not, carrying that power in one's hands was the very definition of unnatural, but it wasn't like I could turn back the clocks and erase the decisions that had led to that moment.

In the end, I fell into restless and uneasy dreams, and woke when my phone started ringing. I saw Brant's blurry name on the screen as I accepted the call. "Hey."

"Hey, Liv," he said. "You sound even grumpier than you usually do in the morning."

"Uh, I kinda have Dex with me," I admitted. "He's been in a hyper mood all night."

"You found him? When?" A moment's pause. "You went to see the vampires, didn't you?"

From his tone, he was gearing up for a lecture and a half. "Look, I just woke up five seconds ago. Dex is here because he's been hiding in a tree for the last few days, scared the monster who killed the revenants will come after him, so I need to play nice with the Order so they don't find him hiding in my house. Can I meet you after I check in at the Order's HQ?"

"I'd love to, but I have a job in the Parallel," he said. "It can't wait, unfortunately. See you tonight?"

"If you wanna come and join us at D&D night, sure."

Unless the Order dumped some other tedious mission on me, I'd get the weekend off, so I just had to see what they wanted me to deal with today and then I'd be free for tonight's marathon gaming session. Not even a mysterious killer or a displaced fire sprite with entirely too much energy would take that away from me.

I hung up, checking my messages. Mum had sent me another text asking if I was free. I replied truthfully that I'd be at the comic con this weekend, relieved not to have to lie to her again. Every time I thought I had a handle on balancing my two lives, another rogue spirit mage just had to come along and ruin my day.

When I went downstairs, it was to find Devon sitting

in the living room, holding one of the cantrip coins I'd brought her between her fingertips and wearing a head torch as though she was about to go inside a dark tunnel.

"What're you doing with that?"

She looked up, accidentally blinding me with the brightness of the head torch. "I'm trying to uncover the marks of the previous spell. This is the cantrip from the undead monster who attacked you yesterday. If I can find the marks, I might be able to figure out how the spell was put together."

"But… there's no traces of the spell left on the coin. I looked." I averted my gaze until she'd switched off the torch, black splotches dotting my vision. "Is there a way you can uncover what the spell was, then?"

If anyone could, it was Devon. Blinking the glare from my eyes, I peered over her shoulder at the pale gold of the cantrip's surface. The lines could as easily be from wear and tear as evidence of a spell, but she was more of an expert than I was, and with reusable cantrips, each would surely leave a mark behind.

"Oh yeah, I have something else for you." She reached into her pocket for another cantrip. "Since you seem to be making a habit of running around behind the Order's backs again, I thought you might have need of this."

"Invisibility cantrip." I took it from her. "Thanks. I owe you one."

"You're running around doing extra jobs to keep us from going under. Don't deny it," she added, as I made a noise of protest. "Take the weekend off. And don't let the Order's nonsense get between you and D&D night. Got it?"

"I'll try not to." I slipped the new cantrip into my

pouch. "All right, let's see what ridiculous quest the Order has for me today."

With luck, they wouldn't have found out about my excursion with the Death King last night.

"We're going to the Order?" Dex zoomed around my head while I went upstairs and grabbed my Parallel bag.

"Only if you agree not to draw attention." I rolled my eyes at him, my heart lifting despite myself at the notion of having my partner back. "You're free to do whatever you like in the Parallel, but don't forget half the Order is looking for excuses to have me smacked with a disciplinary warning."

Dex made a rude noise. "They can't discipline *me.*"

"Do you really want to chance that?" I walked downstairs and shrugged into my coat, then put on my new boots. "Don't forget an Order member *was* the last rogue spirit mage. They're far from disconnected with this crap."

Dex refused to ride the node and I didn't want to tempt fate either, so I took the bus into town and tried to ignore him zipping past the windows, a bright spot above the traffic. A least it was a distraction from the constant out-of-tune singing from the old woman on the seat next to me. After I'd escaped public transport hell, I walked up to the Order's headquarters and instructed Dex to stay put outside before entering. Despite my knowledge that the last spirit mage had come from within this very building, I didn't believe someone inside the Order was directly responsible for creating the spells turning liches into rotting corpses. Even Mr Cobb had been acting through others out of necessity due to the Order stripping his own spirit magic. But the lack of overt spirit mages within the Order didn't mean their less scrupulous members didn't have contacts on the other side who knew about the latest scheme.

Once again, Mrs Carlisle occupied the desk in the retrieval unit.

"Olivia," she said, upon seeing me enter. "I have a new mission for you."

"Oh?" I said warily.

"We have word of an illegal cosmetic spell in the hands of a practitioner," she said. "This is the address."

She handed me a slip of paper. The Order seemed none the wiser about my excursion yesterday evening, so I risked removing one of the blank cantrips from my pocket. "By the way, what should I do with the used cantrips I was given yesterday? Is there some kind of recycling bin?"

"Put them in there." She rattled a box at me.

I put the coin into the box. "Where do they end up?"

"The delivery unit takes care of them." She handed me another pack of cantrips without another word.

Takes them back to the Parallel, you mean. Another question came to mind, but if I pushed too far, she might get suspicious. Besides, now I had Dex with me, I had another way to track their destination.

As I exited the building, two delivery unit staff walked in, carrying a box between them. Good timing. The staff were responsible for carrying deliveries through the nodes, between the Parallel and here, and while I'd never paid them close attention until now, I'd bet my lucky dice those boxes contained cantrips from the market.

Dex flitted over to my shoulder. "What're you scheming?"

"Did you see those guys?" I whispered. "I bet they came here to deliver more boxes of those cantrips."

I'd attempted to fill him in on the situation at the market last night, but I wasn't sure how much of it he'd taken in.

"Want me to light that box on fire and see if it burns?" he asked.

"No, just follow them," I said. "See what's in the box they're carrying. The delivery area is around the back of the building and it's out of bounds to anyone else."

I wouldn't be allowed out the back exit without drawing suspicion, but nobody would spot the fire sprite. I could have used the invisibility spell, but I'd save that for after Dex confirmed the box's contents were what I thought.

The fire sprite returned a couple of minutes later. "The box was full of cantrips, and they exchanged it for another one. Now they're on their way to the node."

"Then we'll go with them." I reached for the pouch at my waist. "Calm down, and please stay quiet. The invisibility cantrip won't work on you."

I watched the door, and when the same two men emerged, I turned on the invisibility cantrip. Unseen, I tailed the pair of them until they reached the crossing-over point. They walked slower, encumbered by the box they held between them, though it didn't look heavy.

In an instant, they vanished into the node's path. I stepped after them, landing in a street near the market. One of them glanced up at Dex, but he flitted out of sight before his appearance could register.

I remained very still, waiting for them to move. The

box's lid shifted, and I glimpsed coins within. Blank ones. *Thought so.*

They were returning the used cantrips to the people responsible for carving them, and I had every intention of finding the heart of the operation. We weren't far from the warehouses, and sure enough, my steps halted when the two men stopped outside a narrow building crammed between two warehouses and spoke to a uniformed woman dressed in grey. Sooty marks lined her face, which bore the pockmarked visage of someone who'd spent too many years in the Parallel's magic-damaged atmosphere. I tried to eavesdrop on them, but the general noise of people on the streets drowned out their muttered conversation. I got the gist, though: this was the place.

When the two men slipped through the door, Dex and I followed, unseen. Inside the building lay identical boxes piled in neat stacks. A storeroom, then. But this wasn't where the cantrips were carved with the runes which gave them life. I looked around the small space, and my gaze snagged on a narrow wooden door behind the boxes, from which a clamour of voices issued. I trod that way, easing the door open.

A torrent of human noise crashed over me in a wave. I stared around, momentarily stunned at the sight of the sheer number of people crammed into the large warehouse adjoining the storeroom. Rows and rows of uniformed workers stood behind long tables, each carving a single coin at a time. A pile of unused coins lay on each one's left hand side, while a smaller pile of coins covered with symbols lay on their right. There had to be a few hundred people in here. All practitioners. *Where did they come from?*

I could hazard a guess. The Order must have shifted half their practitioner employees over here to carve cantrips for public use. Not just those from the Birmingham branch, but others from up and down the country and still more from within the Parallel itself.

If the Order wanted to hire their own practitioners, though, why not make them work inside their own headquarters? It wasn't like there was no space. I walked down the row, looking from left to right. The practitioners worked on their feet, without pause, and a creeping suspicion took hold of me. Here in the Parallel, the supervisors didn't have to abide by any laws. Their bosses could have them carving away at the cantrips for hours and they'd have no choice but to obey if they wanted to keep their jobs. An operation of this size would have been difficult to hide back home, but here in the city, nobody gave it a second glance.

If I'd had any magical talent, I might have ended up forced to join the endless rows of workers carving runes onto the cantrips as well. Was this what they were trying to push Devon into doing? Being forced to work in an environment like this would kill her. I didn't doubt that for an instant. Worse, I could see why the vampires hadn't intervened. After all, they weren't breaking Arcadia's laws, and who was to complain about a cheap source of new cantrips? Ones that actually worked as intended, no less?

The clamouring noise coupled with the hypnotic motion of the practitioners at work was making me dizzy, so I continued to walk without looking too closely at the workers. Among them stood other uniformed people dressed in dark grey like the woman outside the doors. Supervisors, I assumed. Either from the Order or from here in the Parallel, it didn't matter. Because they answered to the same people.

I retraced my steps to the door leading into the storeroom, wondering what in hell I was supposed to do now. I was certain the person targeting the dead was at least obtaining the coins they used from this very place, but I wouldn't know where to begin searching. Every person in the warehouse was under the close watch of a supervisor, but maybe one of them had gone rogue. Hell, it might be someone in charge who'd done so. Given the Order's history, it wouldn't surprise me.

As I pushed open the door into the storeroom, a spark of warmth against my shoulder made me jerk back. Dex leaned forward and pinched my ear. "Don't wander off like that," he admonished me. "I found something you'll want to look at."

"What is it?" I kept my voice low.

"Here." He flew ahead, his slight spark of light illuminating a clipboard which lay atop a pile of boxes near the door. A scrawled list of names was pinned to the clipboard.

I peered at the list, and shock jolted through my nerves. Among the names listed of the supervisors was Mr Barrett Cobb. He'd been involved in the planning phase of this operation, and it seemed someone had neglected to remove his name from the list after his attempted coup and murder spree.

I crept out of the storeroom and into the street, my heart sinking with finality. To get to the truth, it seemed I might have to rip open old wounds, and speak to the man who'd come close to costing me everything I had left.

14

Once my invisibility cantrip wore off, I had no choice but to get on with my hunt for whatever illegal cantrip the Order had sent me after this time. Following the directions the Order had given me, I made my way to a district of winding streets wreathed in the smell of burning wood and herbs.

Dex flew alongside me. "What're we after?"

"Some illegal cosmetic spell," I said. "Seems a practitioner is up to no good."

"Do I get to throw fire around?"

"If they're naughty, yes," I said. "Get it all out of your system. If you wreck tonight's D&D game, Devon will kick you out."

"Me? Never." He flew ahead, and I let him, safe in the knowledge that he wasn't as uncommon a sight here as back home. Sprites might be rare, but magic in general was much less likely to draw unwanted attention. I reached the run-down house where our ne'er-do-well mage was hanging out, knocked, and a stoned-looking practitioner with greasy hair answered the door.

"Here to get some illegal cosmetic spells." I wedged my foot in the door when he tried to close it. "I'm from the Order."

"Get fucked," he growled.

"I have a permit." He didn't look capable of hitting me back, so I had a reasonable shot at getting in and out without any further conflict. A swift paralysing cantrip left him frozen in his own doorway, and I left Dex to watch him while I squeezed past into the house.

The practitioner unfroze as I was going through the cabinets in the kitchen. "What're you doing?" he called over his shoulder. "Get outta my house."

"Looking for illegal cosmetic spells." I opened a drawer and found a handful of coins. Harmless spells, really, but the Order's word was final. "I'll be taking these."

He caught my arm as I walked out the front door with my haul, but Dex flew into his eyes, sending sparks dancing down the narrow hallway. The practitioner retreated with a muffled curse, closing the door on us.

Dex spiralled away from the door and hovered in front of me. "You didn't even need my help."

"That was an easy job compared to the last one." I held up the coin to the light. "This looks like the same type of coin as the ones being carved at the warehouse."

"So it is," he said. "You want me to set *that* on fire?"

"No!" I said. "Don't you think it's suspicious that illegal spells are getting a resurgence? I reckon someone's smuggling blank coins out of the warehouses on the side. I wouldn't have thought it was one of the people who actually work there. Not someone who's dependent on the job to keep a roof over their head, anyway."

The guy I'd taken the cosmetic spells from hadn't been particularly dangerous, just desperate, but if there'd been an uptick of crimes on the side since the warehouse had opened, the Order needed to know. Even if they might deny it was any of their business.

"Don't ask me," he said. "What does this prove?"

"It proves there *are* people using the reusable coins to commit crimes on the side," I said. "Maybe it's someone from within the Order's own forces. Again."

But the idea of reporting the people in that warehouse didn't sit right with me. Most of them plainly had had no choice but to comply with the rules, as it seemed nearly every independent practitioner with any measurable skill had been forced to take on a job there.

"Dex, can you sneak around the warehouse and keep an eye out for trouble over there?" I said. "I'll speak directly to a supervisor myself. Ask some questions."

"I suppose I will." He bowed in mid-air. "Your wish is my command."

We retraced our steps—visible this time—and I waited outside the narrow storeroom sandwiched between two warehouses, looking for someone authoritative to speak to. A stocky man in uniform walked out, and I waylaid him.

"Excuse me," I said. "When do the workers get out for the day?"

"Who wants to know?" He lit a cigarette and puffed out a billowing cloud of smoke. "Interested in working with them?"

"Ah, no, I work for the Order," I said. "But my friend

might have to come and work here soon, so I promised I'd scout for her. She doesn't live in the Parallel, so she doesn't have a permit yet."

"That's unfortunate," he said. "I'll be blunt… your friend would be better off taking an ordinary job on Earth instead."

"It might not be an option." Not without giving up her magic. "Why do you work here, then?"

"If you're with the Order, you'll understand how it is," he said. "We do what we can to survive."

Not exploit others. Even if they'd come willingly, those workers might not have had alternatives. But mentioning that wouldn't bring me any closer to answers about the person using their cantrips to commit crimes.

"Haven't you heard the rumours?" I bluffed.

"Rumours?" He frowned, the cigarette drooping from his mouth.

"Of cantrips being smuggled out of the warehouses," I went on, as though I knew what I was talking about. "There's been an upsurge of illegal spells appearing ever since the warehouse opened, I heard."

"It's reached the Order's attention?" His eyes widened a fraction. "We've been doing everything we can to find the culprit."

Damn. I'd actually guessed right… except it'd been up in the air as to whether the authorities were aware of the problem until now.

"Really?" I arched a brow. "From what I hear, it's not getting any better. I was just sent to retrieve some illegal spells from a rogue. That's twice this week."

"You're a retriever?" He lowered his cigarette. "We're keeping an eye out for any signs of trouble. It'll be some hard-up practitioner trying to make some extra cash, I don't doubt."

"Maybe," I said. "And Cobb? Wasn't he supposed to be involved?"

His eyes bulged. "Who told you that?"

I shrugged. "Heard it mentioned. I was there for his arrest, so..."

"Yes." He gave a nervous glance over his shoulder. "That's supposed to be classified. You won't mention his name to anyone else, will you? If we're seen to be associated with that sort, the vamps will shut us down."

"I won't say a word." I stepped aside as Dex flew out of the warehouse. I'd found out everything I could ask about without drawing suspicion, and what I'd learnt had given me enough to ponder on.

The supervisors knew someone was stealing their cantrips, but not who. The Order doubtless knew, too, but they didn't want word getting out, either.

As for Mr Cobb's involvement? I didn't *want* to speak to him again. The Order would never let me, but if I told the Death King about his potential involvement, I didn't see him dismissing me this time around.

"Hey!" Dex pinched my ear. "You're spacing out. Learn anything useful?"

"Yeah, you might say that." I exhaled, falling into step with him. "What about you? You weren't spotted, were you?"

"Nah, but the supervisors thought someone was throwing sparks around when I went past, so I figured I'd better leave."

"Wise idea," I said. "Turns out the supervisors know someone is working behind their back, and I'm pretty sure the Order does, too. They didn't *tell* me, but I bet someone with more influence would be able to convince them."

"Like who?" He groaned. "Not the bloody Death King again."

"Believe me, I'm not enthused either."

"Could have fooled me," he grumbled. "Anyone would think you were an aspiring lich."

"I already said no," I told him. "Not that he was offering to turn me. I reckon he needs a living spirit mage on backup in case his soul ends up in the wrong vessel again."

"Why's that?" He swooped overhead. "Oh. *Oh.* You're the only one who can reverse it."

"The only spirit mage willing to," I corrected. "There must be others hiding here in the Parallel. Like the person responsible for killing the dead, for instance."

How many other spirit mages might be at large? If I'd ever known, the truth was lost along with my memories. And once again, I was faced with the same decision... trust in the Order, or trust in the King of the Dead.

———

Dex and I parted ways at the node, at which point he went home to annoy Devon and I went on through the swamp-land to annoy His Deathly Highness.

At the gate to the Death King's castle, however, the Fire Element barred my way. "He's not in."

"What do you mean, he's not in?" I said. "I didn't even say why I was here."

"You're here to waste my master's time, what else?"

said Davies. "He has better things to do than to associate with Order lackeys like yourself."

Great. Just when the Air Element had started treating me like an actual person, another dickhead had stepped up to take their place.

"Look, it's important," I said. "It's to do with solving the murders of the Death King's people."

"In what way?" He narrowed his eyes. "I don't know why you think you deserve special treatment, but the Elemental Soldiers are working with our King on this case, too, and he trusts us above all else. If you refuse to tell me why you're here, then I can only assume you're working against him."

"Don't be absurd." I glared at him. "I'll have you know your boss offered me a job to work alongside the four of you, so he trusts me as much as he does you."

"He did *what?*" said the Fire Element. "No. That's not possible."

Maybe I shouldn't have told him that. But the Order would never let me speak to Mr Cobb alone. If he'd been involved in the COS's inception, he *must* know who was working behind the supervisors' backs, right? I'd have suspected the man himself if he hadn't been in jail.

"Ask your master and he'll confirm we're working together."

"If it's not important enough to tell me, then it's not worth disturbing him, either," he said. "Besides, I told you the truth. He's not in the castle, and I don't know when he'll be back. You're wasting your time."

Bastard. "I'll be back later, then."

I walked through the swampland as slowly as I dared. Maybe I'd run into the Death King while I was out and about. Yeah, and maybe he'd declare himself my BFF for life. The Fire Element's comments grated on my nerves. What the hell was his problem? Maybe he didn't trust me not to turn on his master, too, but you'd think the Elemental Soldiers would want to hear what I had to say.

And now I had to go back to the Order, who'd sooner promote me to manager and give me a free goody bag than let me speak to one of their most highly guarded prisoners.

———

Upon my return to the Order, Mrs Carlisle kept me filling out paperwork for so long that I ended up stuck on the bus in rush-hour traffic. I arrived late for D&D, but the game hadn't started yet. Devon and the others sat in the living room, chatting around the table with their dice at the ready. Takeout containers littered the table around the game board.

"Hey." I pulled out a chair and picked up a bag of Indian takeout. "Why're you late starting? You didn't have to wait for me."

"Trix isn't here, either," Devon said. "I wondered if you two might have run into one another."

"No," I said. "That's weird. He's usually the first here."

"Who's that?" Red, our elven cleric, pointed at Dex, who flew in circles around the ceiling. "Hey... is that a *sprite?*"

"Meet Dex," I said, resigned. "He's a fire sprite who's staying here with Devon and me for a bit."

"Damn right." He flew down above Devon's shoulder. "Can I play an NPC?"

Devon gave me an exasperated look. "Will you behave if I say yes?"

"Of course!" He hovered above the game board. "Your wish is my command."

I picked up my tiefling rogue character and waited for Devon to resume our campaign. In the gaming world, I got to steal far more interesting things than illegal cosmetic spells and rarely got caught. When the dice cooperated, anyway. Across the table sat Craig and Carla He, both of whom worked in admin at the Order. In the game, Craig played a wizard gunslinger gnome while his sister played a half-elf warlock with questionable demonic ties. Red, who seemed to have taken a shine to Dex, played an elven cleric and the group's healer, while Trix was usually the head of the fighting contingent in the group. Maybe he'd got himself tied up in the Parallel.

Despite my reservations, Dex was actually pretty good at playing along. He took on the role of a snarling fire demon guarding a mountain of treasure, and by the end, the others were asking if he'd be a regular player.

"Maybe, if he's still here next week," I said. "There's the Order's rules, you know."

"We won't say a word." Red put a finger to her lips. "Right, Craig?"

"Course not," he said, nodding to his sister. Carla, who was in the middle of helping Devon clear up the takeout containers, nodded. They were on the same level within the Order as I was, while Red had left the magical world to become a computer scientist. Somehow, our group had managed to hold together for the last couple of years, and I was reasonably confident the others wouldn't give Dex away to the Order. *I hope not, anyway.*

The others left, and Devon and I got to work cleaning up the game board.

"Weird of Trix not to show." I handed Devon some of her prep sheets which had fallen under the table.

"When did you last see him?" she asked.

"When he helped me beat up those vampires the Order sent me after." I took a step back from the table, spotting Dex flying out of the kitchen. "He knocked out three of them at once."

"You weren't dealing with vampires today, were you?"

I sat down on the sofa. "Nope, but I may have followed an Order delivery of those cantrips before I went on the mission."

I told her about the warehouses I'd sneaked into and the operation I'd found set up inside them, including my half-bluffed conversation with the supervisor.

"Damn," she said. "How'd they move that many people over?"

"Through the nodes," I said. "That's what I gathered. Also, they know someone is smuggling some of their cantrips out on the side and using them to commit crimes. Now I've got them worried the Order is looking into it, but they might not be. The missions Mrs Carlisle has been giving me are listed as standard and if she knows what's going on over there, she hasn't breathed a word to me."

"Dicks," she said. "So the Order is moving into the Parallel? Who's supposed to enforce the laws here?"

"It's just their spellcraft they seem to be outsourcing at the moment," I said. "I wouldn't have thought they'd ditch this realm entirely. They've worked too hard to maintain their power. But get this—Cobb's name was on the list of people involved in the planning stages of the operation. He was involved in the cantrip business from its start."

Her brows shot up. "Did you ask the Order?"

"I wasn't supposed to see his name," I said. "I was going to ask the Death King to use his persuasive influence to get answers from the Order, but he wasn't around, and his Fire Element sent me packing. I wonder if he has any idea who's smuggling the coins out on the side and handing them to a rogue practitioner. I doubt he does, though."

Not just any rogue, but a rogue practitioner with skill at spirit magic.

Damn. I was in way over my head with this one.

A sudden flash of light engulfed the room. Dex exclaimed in a panic, while I swore and jumped to my feet. An instant later, a heavy body dropped onto the sofa like a stone.

"What the hell—?" I broke off, alarm blaring through my nerves. "Brant. Are you okay?"

Brant half-lay on the sofa, unmoving. His eyes were closed, his body still and sprawling.

"Help!" I looked wildly at Devon, who stood frozen by the game table.

"Oh, damn." She ran through the door into the shop, and there came the sound of several cantrips falling off a shelf. "I can get a cantrip to heal him. Hang on."

Carefully, I turned Brant onto his back. Deep wounds lacerated his chest, as though he'd walked headlong into a set of sharp claws.

"What did you do?" I whispered.

No response came. Devon ran back into the room a moment later, dropping cantrips everywhere. A healing cantrip slid into my hand and I placed it onto Brant's chest, over the wounds. Despite how deep they looked, there was no blood, and they didn't seal underneath the cantrip's touch.

"What's wrong with him?" said Devon. "Want me to call an ambulance? You'd need a hell of a cover story, but if the cantrip's not working…"

"I'm not sure a regular hospital can handle this." I traced the wounds with my fingertips, and a faint spasm shook my fingers. He wasn't bleeding—not visibly—but the sensation of energy brushing my palm drew me to peer closer at the wounds. Swirling currents of energy, of life force, spiralled from the lacerations in his chest, drawn into the node. His life force was bleeding out through a wound that wasn't physical at all. *Oh, Elements.*

As I'd feared, no human doctor could help him, but where could he safely go? Trix was missing, and the Order wouldn't lift a finger to help a non-member.

There was only one option left.

15

I astral projected and floated through the node, emerging onto the Death King's territory. I hardly took note of my surroundings as I floated up to the castle door, but once again, the Fire Element blocked my way.

"Back *again?*" he said. "What do you want this time?"

"I need help." I was as far from in an argumentative mood as it was possible to get, but I refused to let this dickhead get in my way. "My boyfriend was injured by some kind of monster. I need the Death King's assistance."

"What makes you think anyone here will ever help you?" He gave me a cold look. "You should leave."

"Get out the way," I warned. "My boyfriend is dying, and I swear to the fucking Elements, I will end you if you don't get out of my way."

Behind him, the castle doors flew wide. The Death King stood there, a dark shadowy form masking the doorway. "What is it?"

"I need your help." I ignored the Fire Element's scoff of

disbelief. "Brant was attacked by the same phantoms that killed your liches, and he's dying. His spirit—it's torn open, somehow, and I don't know how to fix him."

"No ordinary healer will be able to help him," he said. "And nor will I."

My heart plunged. "I can't just let him die."

The Death King called over his shoulder, "Ryan?"

The Air Element stepped into view. "Yes?"

"Go through the node to find Olivia's... friend. Bring him back here. Immediately."

Thank the gods. He's willing to help. Brant wouldn't be thrilled at the prospect of coming back to the Death King's domain, but I had no choice.

Ryan walked alongside me to the node. "Whatever attacked him was under the same spell as the beasts that killed our people?"

"The wounds looked the same, except not physical." If Brant had seen anything more, I'd need to wait until he recovered to ask.

"That's why you came to my master," said the Air Element. "I will help you, but he'll have to leave the castle as soon as he recovers."

"That's fine." As long as he recovered. *Please let him be okay.*

Ryan and I crossed through the node into the living room, where they lifted Brant over their shoulders. I was more than a little impressed. I wouldn't have a hope of carrying him single-handedly.

Devon watched me, wide-eyed. "Can the Death King help him?"

"I hope so," I said. "I'll see you tomorrow. I'll try to make it to the comic con—"

"His life is more important," she insisted. "Don't worry about it."

"Cheers." I blinked back tears. "Give me a shout if you need me."

I stepped through the node, hurrying after Ryan as they carried Brant towards the side entrance to the castle.

"Where're you taking him?" I asked.

"The Elements' quarters," they said. "It's not perfect, and the others won't be pleased with me for bringing a stranger into our home. On the plus side, Davies won't kick up a fuss until he comes back, and he spends all his time guarding the castle these days."

"Yes, and stopping me from getting inside." I caught up to the Air Element at the door. "Overprotective, isn't he?"

"Can you blame him? We've all been shaken by these recent attacks." They walked ahead of me into the same apartment as before. Inside the living room, the Air Element laid Brant down on the sofa carefully. With his eyes closed, he looked peaceful, except for the wounds lacerating his skin. No... his *spirit*. Images of him turning lich permanently infiltrated my mind, and fear clamped a vice over my chest.

A cold breeze whispered into the room as the Death King entered.

"He was attacked?" he asked, his tone as cold as the breeze.

I clenched my numb hands. "I think there's something wrong with him beyond the physical injuries."

"I see." He glided over to the sofa, extending a hand over Brant's chest. "Yes... his spirit is badly damaged. The killer was attempting to sever his soul."

My stomach lurched. "Is it... fixable?"

"For you?" he said. "Yes, it is."

I trod to his side and held out both hands over the wounds lacerating Brant's spirit. "But I don't know how."

Didn't I? I'd brought Dex back from death. Maybe I could do the same with Brant.

"You do," said the Death King. "Look."

The strength of the nearby node flooded into my veins, and I concentrated hard, directing that energy at the wounds ripping through Brant's chest. Demanding they knit together. At first, nothing happened, but I held my hands still, focusing on channelling the node's power through my own hands. A shimmering light overlaid the holes in his chest… and they began to fade at the edges.

Minutes blurred together, but I didn't dare move. Energy continued to flow through my body into Brant's, until the rippling wounds merged, the lines becoming one once again. Not a single trace remained.

"It is done." The Death King hadn't spoken a word while I'd worked, and I couldn't say whether his presence was a comfort or not.

My entire body trembled as I raised my hands, and the energy rushed out of me. I caught my balance against the sofa, suppressing the overwhelming need to sink to the floor and close my eyes. "Will that be enough? He still isn't waking up."

"Leave him here overnight," said the Death King.

Ryan shifted on their feet, frowning. "What about Olivia?"

"What about me?" I said.

"I assume you wanted to sleep at some point," said Ryan. "And your boyfriend is on my sofa. Unless you don't mind sleeping on the floor, I'd suggest you go home. I'll let you know if anything changes with Brant."

"All right, if you promise nobody will attack him during the night." Meaning, Davies. "I want to talk to the Death King first. Then I'll go home."

Immortal death lords didn't need to sleep, after all. He didn't look surprised at my comment. "If you so desire."

The pair of us walked out of the room and down the corridor, through another door into the castle's main hall.

The Death King halted beside the dais. "What did you wish to talk to me about, Olivia?"

"The COS." I rubbed my eyes, exhaustion setting in. "They're employing hundreds of people to carve spells into blank cantrips in the warehouses, and they're working directly with the Order. They also know someone's smuggling coins out on the side and using them illegally, but they don't seem to think it's serious enough to warrant telling the vampires. That, or they're afraid it'll get them into trouble."

I told him about my recent missions from the Order, and my conclusion that the COS's new initiative had accidentally revitalised the market for illegal spells.

"So you think a spirit mage is taking advantage of this new operation," he said. "If anybody in the COS was registered as a spirit mage, the vampires would know."

"Mr Cobb was supposed to work there." I let the words linger between us. "He was involved in the initial planning. He wouldn't have shown up on the records as a spirit mage."

"He is a spirit mage no longer," said the Death King. "This is not his work, but that of someone whose talents remain intact."

Which brought us back to where we'd started. I'd have to wait until Brant woke up for him to tell me how he'd ended up attacked by one of the beasts under the effects of the spell... but he'd survived. I'd managed to save him.

"He's staying *here?*" The Fire Element barged into the hall, his expression livid. "No way. He's an outsider. So is she."

The Death King regarded him for a moment. "The circumstances are less than ideal, but that young man might be able to help us find the cause of the attacks."

I jerked my head at Davies. "If he hurts Brant, I won't be responsible if he ends up with a skull jammed up his rear."

"I will take that under advisement," he said. "Go home, Olivia."

Davies scoffed. "Yeah, Olivia. Go home and stop bothering us."

I was too tired to rise to his bait. Healing Brant had drained me, and while there'd be hell to pay later, I had to get home before I passed out cold. I was thoroughly worn out, as though channelling the node to save Brant's life had taken all the energy out of me, and my health bar was depleted.

Despite the thoughts whirling in my mind, I stumbled through the node and barely made it to the sofa before I collapsed.

I woke hours later when Devon trod through the living room. "You slept down here?"

"I was tired," I mumbled into the cushions. "Brant… he's okay, but I had to heal him."

"You managed to save him?" she said.

"Yeah." I lifted my head, seeing she wore half a set of armoured clothing and carried a wig under one arm. "Shit. The comic con—"

"I told you, you don't have to come. I'm not leaving for another couple of hours, anyway."

"All right." I pushed upright. "I need to check on Brant first. I can look for Trix while I'm at it."

If he wasn't awake yet, I'd start by speaking to those vampires. Brant had been there the first time I'd confronted them, while Trix had beat them up. It was a tenuous link, but I wouldn't let the attack go unpunished.

Devon shot me a concerned look. "Are you sure you're okay? How badly was he hurt?"

I slumped against the cushions. "The attacker tore open Brant's soul. If I hadn't been a spirit mage, I wouldn't have been able to save him."

Her eyes rounded. "It was a phantom? I didn't think they packed that much power."

"We'll see what he says when he wakes up." I trailed upstairs to my room, where I found Dex flying above my bed.

"Good morning!" Dex said.

"He's been sleeping in your bed," said Devon. "Thought you ought to know."

"You'd better not have burned anything." I opened the wardrobe. "When I'm ready, do you want to come with me to threaten some vampires?"

"I wouldn't miss it." He flew downstairs, no doubt to

hassle Devon, and I grabbed some clothes and made for the bathroom.

A long shower revived me somewhat. Brant had had a damn close call, and now I was awake, I felt bad about leaving him alone overnight in the Death King's home. Ryan might be trustworthy, but Brant didn't know that. He hated the place, and this was the second time he'd nearly died in the castle. I hoped he hadn't woken up yet, for all our sakes.

I got dressed, put in my contacts, and grabbed my Parallel bag before hopping through the node into the castle courtyard. It was weird how quickly it'd become familiar to me. I might have turned down the Death King's offer of a job, but I spent so much time here lately that I might as well build my own little hut in the swamp myself.

I made my way around the back of the castle to the Elements' quarters and knocked on Ryan's door. It opened a moment later, revealing the Air Element already dressed in full armour, their green-lined cloak swirling behind them.

"He's not awake yet," they said before I could open my mouth. "Don't worry, he probably needs the rest after what he went through."

"Yeah," I said. "To be honest, I'm kinda glad he didn't wake up. He'd have been seriously panicked to wake up in a stranger's room without me there. Let alone the Death King's castle."

For all I knew, he might have freaked out and set the place on fire. But what else could I have done? Trix was missing, and besides, only a spirit mage could have healed the damage to his soul. Just thinking about what might have happened if he hadn't made it to my house in time brought a chill colder than the Court of the Dead.

A mass of conflicted emotions clogged my throat as I walked into the room and over to the sofa where Brant lay. I leaned over him and brushed a strand of hair from his forehead. He gave a faint groan. "Ow."

"You're alive." My voice cracked.

"Where am I?" he whispered.

"You're…" I hesitated. "Don't panic, but you're in Ryan's room. It was the only way I could save you."

"Who…?" His eyes flew open. "Not… not the Court of the Dead?"

"Nobody's going to hurt you, Brant."

"No." He sat bolt upright and almost fell off the sofa. "No. I can't be."

"I had no choice, Brant. You were dying." I caught his arm before he did himself an injury. "You already nearly died once. Just lie down. Please."

He grumbled something uncomplimentary, managing to prop himself against the back of the sofa. "I can't be here. It's not safe for you."

"I'm a damn sight safer than you are at the moment," I said. "What the hell attacked you? Your soul was in tatters, Brant."

He slumped back against the cushions. "Shit. He's gonna kill me…"

"Who?" I asked.

"The Death King."

"Oh, for the Elements' sakes," I snapped, more irritated than I had the right to be. "He's the one who helped me to save your life. He doesn't want either of us dead. Can you tell me who did this to you?"

He closed his eyes. "A phantom. Shit, Liv. You shouldn't have... come..." His words trailed off, his body going limp as he fell into unconsciousness again.

Ryan stepped in behind me. "I'll let him stay here for the day, but I can't watch him all the time. If he causes any fire damage to my property, he's out."

"Fair." I supposed I could ask Ryan to help me carry Brant to his bolt hole in the city, but what if he ended up in a bad way again when he was alone and still recovering? I couldn't risk it.

Angry tears burned my eyes. I understood his panic; I'd brought him into the home of his enemy, after all. But he could at least be the slightest bit grateful that I'd saved him.

I swallowed down my emotions and turned to Ryan. It was nice to have an ally around, even one who was reluctant at best to have my boyfriend sleeping on their sofa.

"Thanks for letting him stay," I said.

"No worries," they responded. "What're you doing now?"

"Want to come and help me beat up some vampires?"

16

Ryan and I entered the city of Arcadia and walked past the warehouses. I should be at comic con, but I didn't feel right going home with Brant in such a state. Besides, after the night's action, I needed to blow off steam, and the idea of heading into a sweaty, packed room was unappealing.

Beating up a bunch of vampires, on the other hand, was right up my alley.

I led the way to Vaughn's old house with Ryan one step behind me. "There are three of them, but they shouldn't be a match for both of us together. Trix beat the shit out of them once already."

I halted in front of the house. To knock or not to knock? Given how polite they'd been beforehand…

Warmth brushed my neck from behind, and Dex popped up at my shoulder. Ryan gave me a questioning look, and I nodded.

The Air Element raised their hands and a blast of air smashed into the door, knocking it open. Dex flew ahead of us into the living room, and the vampires exclaimed when the two of us entered behind the fire sprite.

"What are you doing?" one of them yelped. "You can't come in here."

My gaze snagged on the table in front of them. An open bag of cantrips lay gleaming on the surface. They'd replenished their stock, apparently.

A hoarse shout came from elsewhere in the house. I knew that voice. *Trix.*

"You just made a major mistake, matey," I said to the nearest vampire. I knew better than to punch him this time around, so I settled for flinging a paralysing cantrip into his face.

A whirling gale swept from Ryan's hands, sending all three vampires flying into the wall with a crash that caused cracks to splinter across the plaster. The problem with vampires' skin being so damned hard was that Ryan's attack had done more damage to the house than to the vampires.

"Get out of my house!" shrieked the leading vampire, landing on his feet.

I jabbed a finger at the bag of cantrips. "Where'd you get this?"

"None of your business."

Another scream sounded from below our feet. Definitely Trix. What the hell had they done to him?

"Keep them in here," I said to Ryan and Dex, and followed the direction of the noise. I'd thought Vaughn had collapsed the tunnels under the house, but perhaps they'd remained intact. If I were a vampire fleeing justice, I'd pick a house with a basement to hide in, too. *Scumbags.*

A trapdoor at the back of the hall led down into a

cellar. I descended the ladder quickly, hearing muffled crashes from the living room which I hoped meant Ryan was winning the fight with the vampires. "Trix, are you in here?"

My feet touched down on solid ground. At the back of the cellar, Trix stood against the wall, his ankles and wrists bound with ropes.

"Hello, Liv," he said, in his usual cheery manner as though he hadn't been tied up for a day or more.

"Why did you come back here?" I moved over to him, squinting in the dim light filtering through from the open trapdoor.

"I saw some of their stolen goods," he explained. "I know the Order only told you to confiscate the one cantrip, but they had more bags of illegal spells, so I thought I'd come back to take them off their hands before someone else got hurt."

"And they didn't take kindly to that." I tugged at the bonds on his wrists. Damn, those things were tight. "How'd they manage to tie you up? You beat the shit out of them before."

"They used a spell," he said. "Knocked me out."

The guy was the most casual hostage ever. I dug in my bag for my pocketknife and used it to sever the ropes around his wrists. From the crashing noises upstairs, Ryan was giving the vamps a hard time. "What were you thinking, coming here alone?"

"I thought I saw your boyfriend in here." Trix's hands broke free of the ropes, and he stretched his wrists.

"Brant?" That couldn't be right. "You mean yesterday? He's been unconscious all night after he was attacked."

"Ah… yesterday." He took the knife from me and

hacked away at the ropes on his ankles. "I lost track of time in here. How'd you know where to find me?"

"A hunch." Another resounding crash came from above. "I left Ryan in charge of the vampires. I'd better make sure they haven't knocked the roof off."

I climbed the ladder and emerged in time to see Ryan rise to their feet, having collided with the wall.

Ryan rubbed the back of their head. "The bastards hit me with a spell. Turned my powers against me."

"Oh, hell." I ran into the living room, only for a vampire to fling a cantrip into my face. I ducked, and the cantrip hit the wall, sending a torrent of smoke billowing out. A solid force slammed into me, and I flew backwards into the hallway. Ryan's magic steadied me before I hit the wall, and I breathed out a relieved thanks. Then I spotted one of the vampires fleeing through the open door, carrying a bag of cantrips over his shoulder.

"Shit!" All three vampires were on the run, complete with their contraband. Even at my fastest, I'd stand no chance of catching up to them.

Ryan ran out of the door, propelled by their air magic. I sprinted alongside them, but even the added speed wasn't enough for us to catch up. We reached the nearest node, in time to see the last of the three vampires vanish from sight.

"They escaped onto Earth." I skidded to a halt, my lungs burning. "The Order will haul them in the instant they see that illegal crap they're carrying, assuming they catch them in time."

If anything, it was within the limits of my permit to hunt them down on the Order's behalf—if you ignored the fact that I wasn't supposed to be in the Parallel today, that is. One wrong move and I'd be the one arrested.

Ryan crossed the short distance to the node. "I think that fire sprite of yours might have gone with them. I saw him chasing one of them out of the house."

"He what?" Shit. Dex hadn't been in the hall when the vampires had escaped, but they'd all moved too damn fast for me to see.

"Did they escape?" Trix caught up to me, his expression thoughtful. "There aren't many places for them to hide among humans. I think we can catch them."

Guess I'm outvoted.

Crossing my fingers that the Order wasn't waiting on the other side, I stepped into the current of energy after Ryan. Our group landed in the middle of a long corridor lined with posters advertising musicals and theatrical performances, concerts and other events. I looked around in utter confusion, then panic set in, several seconds too late, when it hit me that we were right out in the open in a public setting. And Trix had his elf countenance on full display, Ryan wore a suit of armour, and Dex was... well, Dex.

"What," said Ryan, "is this supposed to be?"

Only then did I see the people walking around us were dressed in costumes equally as conspicuous as our absurd ensemble. Two Jedi knights walked behind a group of Disney princesses, while an array of characters from anime and video games crossed paths with a group of people dressed as what looked like zombies from the Walking Dead. Not a single one of them gave us a second glance.

"Oh, *hell*." I rotated on my heel. "The comic con's happening right now. *That's* the vampires' escape route?"

"Of course," said Ryan. "Humans wouldn't know those coins were illegal spells, would they?"

"No, but I think they'd have questions if the vamps put on their full speed." I walked down the corridor, following the tide of people heading towards the comic con. The closer we drew, the more notice people took of our group.

"Nice armour," someone said to Ryan.

"Are those ears real?" a little girl asked Trix.

So much for not drawing attention. At least I was reasonably confident no Order members would be seen dead in here, but Devon was somewhere inside the main hall, not knowing three real-life bloodsuckers were on the loose.

Ryan took the lead and marched ahead, their boots and armoured clothing ensuring the crowd parted to let us through. Everyone assumed it was just the costume, not the subtle breeze and the aura of intimidation that came as part of being one of the Death King's Elemental Soldiers. Trix and I followed close behind, veering away from the crowd.

Then I spotted the vampires standing in a huddle outside, surrounded by unsuspecting cosplayers. *There they are.*

The wind began to pick up, and I grabbed Ryan's arm. "You can't use your elemental magic here."

"Like hell I can't." They lifted their hands and stalked out of the doors.

Cursing under my breath, I followed. The vampires looked up as a current of air blasted towards them. Cosplayers grabbed hats and props and ducked against the unexpected storm, some of them running indoors. While most people would assume the weather was acting up and not that a pissed-off air mage was among them, the vampires zeroed in on us right away.

Great one, Ryan. The vampires legged it, at speed, and were gone in an instant. I skidded to a halt, out of breath, scanning the groups of dishevelled cosplayers. Where in hell were the vampires planning to run off to? Nobody lived out here. The only possible escape route was the airport…

No way. They weren't planning to flee the country, were they?

I headed for the door back into the building, where Dex flew down into my path, pointing back down the corridor. "I saw them run that way."

"Dammit," I said. "I think they might be on their way to the airport."

"Why?" said Ryan, a baffled expression on their face.

"It's that or they have a secret passion for Star Trek." I walked down the corridor, mentally mapping my way to the exit. "Dex, can you follow them and try to distract their attention? *Only* if you don't let any humans see you."

"What do you take me for?" He zoomed ahead of us and out of sight. I should have known the long corridors would be right up his alley. He'd be having the time of his life in here if not for the crowds.

To get to the airport, the vamps must be getting the monorail. Or running on foot, if they wanted to risk being spotted moving around at vampire speed. They didn't seem the brightest group of newbie vampires I'd ever met, and if they planned to sneak out of the country carrying a bunch of dangerous artefacts, the Order would surely stop them first.

My phone buzzed, on cue. Devon had messaged me. *I can see you.*

I looked around, spying her waving at me in her armoured costume. I nodded to the others to go ahead and ran to catch up with her. "You came? What—?"

"Vampires," I said. "Those three dickheads from the Parallel attacked Trix, they're working with the enemy, and they're about to flee the country with a bag of contraband. We'll try to catch them, but if they get on a plane..."

She swore. "I'll call the Order and ask them to send in a team."

"Hope they get here in time."

Leaving Devon to make the call, I hurried to catch up with the others. Trix moved on elf speed, while Ryan had used their air magic to quicken their pace, until we halted at the monorail leading to the airport.

"They must have gone this way." I boarded the train, and so did the others, though the Air Element didn't look happy at having to take mundane transport.

"Now I remember why I left this realm," they muttered.

"Hey, we can't all live in a castle." I looked out the window and my heart dropped. The vampires were visible even from here, running full-tilt across the car park towards the departures entrance to the airport. We'd never catch them.

The instant the train stopped, we climbed off and wove our way through crowds of disgruntled passengers. At least they assumed our odd appearance was due to our being at the comic con.

Ryan's magic kicked in again and they all but flew ahead of me, into the airport and towards the baggage drop-off.

"Yeah, it's not like there are human witnesses around or anything," I muttered. Bloody vampires. They had to slow down once they reached security, surely—and just what cover story had they come up with to explain why they were carrying a sack of weird coins in their hand luggage?

A commotion drew my attention to the exit, which blew wide open as a torrent of air blasted through, carrying two vampires along with it.

Dex flew above the bewildered humans queuing at the baggage drop-off, while I ran through the automatic doors. Trix ran up to the vampires and snagged one of them by the scruff of his neck, while I accosted the other. "What the hell do you think you're playing at?"

"What else? We're getting out of here."

"Oh, no, you don't." I blasted a paralysing cantrip into his face, and Trix moved in with a length of rope in his hands. The vampire he'd grabbed was already trussed up in a heap.

"I grabbed the rope from their cellar," he said in explanation, grabbing the second vampire by the wrists.

"Good thinking." Even a vampire couldn't run with their legs tied together. But that was only two vampires accounted for. The third vampire must still be inside the airport.

I retreated through the automatic doors again, halting at a disgruntled look from a security guard. The last thing I needed was to be arrested by airport security for getting into a fight with a vampire, so I forced myself to move at a normal pace as I scanned the crowd. Then I spotted the third vampire, arguing with a woman at the information desk. Hiding a smile, I sauntered up behind him.

"No," said the woman. "I can't get you onto this flight. It's already fully booked."

"Isn't that a pity?" I murmured in the vampire's ear, catching his arm. "C'mon, let's go outside."

I tried to drag him by the elbow, but it was like shifting a steel post. I leaned closer to him. "You didn't even book a flight? Amateur."

"Get away from me," he said through gritted teeth.

"The Order is already here." I gripped the sack of coins hanging from his shoulder. "There's no use in running."

He swore and tried to twist out of my grip. I let go when I spotted two security guards staring at the pair of us, and he took the opportunity to slip out of the doors.

Ryan's attack hit him before he could run any further. He tripped over and landed on his face on the concrete, where Trix was ready with the rope. As for me, I ran to retrieve the bag of coins, scooping it up in my hand.

"What're you planning to do with this lot?" I rattled the bag at him.

"Sell them, what else?" said the vampire, his nose bloody. "You're wasting your time arresting us."

"Where'd you get them from?" I prodded him with my foot. "You'll have to answer to the Order soon enough. You might as well give us answers."

"Fuck you," he said. "We'd have made a fortune with these."

"So you're involved with the people smuggling cantrips out of the COS's warehouses, aren't you?" I said. "Who's turning them into illegal spells, then?"

"Ask that mage of yours."

The screech of brakes rang out before I could ask what the hell he meant. Devon hurried over, breathless, as a van screamed to a halt beside us, and a dozen Order guards poured out.

I rose to my feet, slowly, as the Order guards surrounded the three vampires and hauled their captives into the van.

As they did so, the Order's supervisor approached me. "Olivia Cartwright. Would you mind telling me how you ended up here?"

"We were at comic con," I said.

She cocked a brow. "And you happened to run into three rogue vampires?"

"I recognised their faces from when the Order sent me to confiscate some illegal contraband from them earlier this week," I lied. "They were carrying a sack of cantrips around in public, so I figured they were up to no good."

"Do you normally travel with an elf, a practitioner, and one of the Death King's Elemental Soldiers?" asked the blond supervisor in sceptical tones.

"Yep," I said, figuring I might as well commit to the cover story. "We're part of the same D&D group."

"We'll take these," said another Order employee, hauling up the bag of cantrips. "These three will be taken back to the Order for questioning. Olivia…"

"I'm part of an event at comic con," I said, before they could rope me into coming with them. The last thing I wanted was to wind up stuck in the Order all day with Brant still unconscious in the Death King's castle. "I'd better head back in before we miss it."

To my intense relief, they didn't argue. They piled into

the van along with their captives and left us in the car park. Dex hid from sight behind a parked car, but he resurfaced when the van drove off.

Ryan shook their head when they finally disappeared from sight. "There's a node near here if you want to go back into the Parallel."

"Good, because I need to talk to someone about this shit." I held up one of the vampires' cantrips, which I'd swiped before the Order had taken the bag and confiscated everything inside it. "We need to find whoever gave them to the vampires—and who created them."

17

Devon parted ways with the rest of us, as she alone wore an actual costume unsuitable for running around the Parallel.

"I'll let you know if the Order comes back and starts giving me grief," she said. "Bloody vampires. Are you sure you're okay to go back?"

"Brant is still in the Court of the Dead, so I have to head there and pick him up," I said. "Trix, did the vampires mention his name when you were there?"

"No. I was tied up in their basement at the time."

That figured. "All right. I don't think the Death King will let you into his castle, but with the vampires gone, you should be okay to go back to the Parallel. Just avoid anything dead."

"Actually…" He eyed Devon's costume. "I've always wanted to go to a comic con."

"Go ahead." I wished I could do the same, but my mind was in a scramble and I needed to talk to Brant before he flipped out at being confined to the castle and started a fight with the Fire Elemental again. I was starting to regret leaving him there alone, but he'd have been no safer at my house, considering the node lay right on top of it.

Ryan was already heading for the corridor, so I joined them, pursued by Dex.

"That was fun," said the fire sprite. "I'd like to go to comic con, too."

"Don't get used to it," I said. "We'd better hope no witness reports come along later from anyone in the airport who saw us. Otherwise, we'll find ourselves banned from international flights."

Not that I could afford one anyway. Ryan strode ahead, not speaking, and we walked through the node and came out directly in front of the Death King's castle.

"I'll pick Brant up, if he's awake," I said to Ryan.

"Go ahead," they said. "I won't pretend I'm sorry to see the back of him."

"I can't say I don't understand your position, but he's really not…" I trailed off, noticing who stood on the steps of the castle. "Not him again."

Davies stood waiting for us near the castle, a smirk on his face.

"He's not in," said the Fire Element, when I approached him. "Your boyfriend just left."

"What the hell do you mean?" My fists clenched. "He wouldn't have just left. He could barely walk."

He shrugged. "I know what I saw."

"A likely story." If he'd driven Brant off while he was injured, I'd make sure he'd regret it.

Ryan stepped in. "You'd better not be lying, Davies."

"What would give you that impression?" said the Fire Element. "He left through the gates about an hour ago.

You shouldn't have left him here alone if you wanted him to stay put. He hates this place."

"Maybe it's all the dickheads hanging around," I said pointedly. "Fine. I'll find him myself. And if I don't, I'll come back here and see if I can loosen your tongue."

Ryan gave me an apologetic look. "I have to get back to my master. I'll tell him where you are."

"Thanks." I hurried towards the gates, cursing the Fire Element. Where might Brant have gone? His hideout in the city wasn't that far away from here, but he'd been unconscious when I'd left him, and I hadn't thought he was in any fit state to walk on his own.

"That guy's trouble," Dex commented.

"I know." I quickened my pace. "I bet he chased Brant off and then lied about it."

"Doubt he needed to," Dex flew above my head. "If you ask me, fire-boy legged it as soon as he could. I'd have done the same."

I walked on, while Dex hovered so close to the back of my neck it was like wearing a transparent scarf. Given the number of phantoms drifting around, it was understandable that he was on edge, but we gave the nodes a wide berth and made it to the warehouses without being challenged.

There, I turned towards the street leading to Brant's hideout. "He must be there. I can't think of anywhere else except home, and he's too much of a gentleman to cross over into my house without asking." *Unless he's been attacked again.*

Brant's main apartment was on the other side of the city and I didn't see him walking there on foot while he was still recovering from nearly losing his soul. That he'd made it this far seemed improbable, but I hadn't seen any sign of him in the swamp.

I made my way to the right house and knocked on the door. Nobody answered. I knocked louder. "Brant, it's me."

Dex flew past the window, peering through the glass. "I don't think he's at home."

"You sure?" I moved to the window, and a shadow passed over the glass. "Someone's in there."

Friend or foe, there was only one way to find out. I reared back and gave the door a firm kick, knocking it inwards.

A musty, unused smell filled the room inside, which appeared even more dark and uninhabited than usual. I trod inside, an inexplicable current of dread raising the hairs on my arms like I'd trodden on a live wire.

Dex flew overhead, his sparking light providing enough illumination to see the surrounding room. It was sparsely furnished, but the one new feature was a fresh stack of boxes containing Brant's cantrip supply. The lid lay off one of the boxes, and I peered inside.

Every single coin was unmarked. Blank cantrips filled the space within the box, too many to count. "What is he doing with these?"

Brant was no practitioner. He bought his own cantrips via a supplier or from Devon, but I'd assumed he'd found out about the operation at the market at the same time as I had. How, then, had he got his hands on all these unused cantrips?

Heart in my throat, I moved to the next box. More blank gold coins gleamed within. What the hell could a non-practitioner want with so many worthless cantrips?

Unless he planned to sell them for a side income, but it made no sense for him not to ask for my help. Or at least tell me.

Dex hissed out a warning. I rose to my feet, a fresh chill washing down my spine at the sight of a shadow moving against the wall. The shadow detached itself from the darkness, forming into the shape of a lich.

"Olivia Cartwright." I knew the voice. This was the lich who'd betrayed his king, who'd worked with Vaughn. And now…

My hands fisted. "What did you do to Brant?"

"Nothing he didn't sign up for." The lich glided closer. "You'll be joining him soon."

No way. I reached for the nearest node, willing its power to bolster my own, but his words unbalanced me. The current of energy slipped through my fingers, too far away to grasp.

The lich reached for me with a shadowy hand. Cold tingles spread from my fingers throughout my whole body. This same lich had nearly killed me once before, and without a node, I had no other weapons to fight with.

Dex flew headlong into the lich, who staggered backwards in surprise. My own surprise doubled at the sight of the lich's robes smoking at the edges. Dex's whole transparent body was glowing, and more sparks flew from his fingertips. He must be terrified out of his mind, and yet he was still fighting.

But I wouldn't let him take the fall for me this time around, and I refused to watch him die again. "Dex, get out!"

I reached for the node, drawing strength into me.

Bright energy blasted from my hand, pushing the lich back.

The lich made a hissing noise of displeasure. "You shouldn't have done that."

"I'll do worse, arsehole." My hands glowed, illuminating the boxes at my feet. An idea sprang to mind.

The lich reached for me, and I leapt over the boxes, kicking one of them over. Cantrips spilled, and I scanned for one which might help me pin this fucker down long enough to hand him over to the Death King.

The lich caught my arm, his grip startlingly solid. *Shit. That's new.*

His cold breath frosted my neck as he leaned closer, his icy hand freezing my skin. Power rippled around his shadowy edges. He'd drawn in the node's strength himself. "Don't you know, Olivia, that the closer you grow to the spirit world, the more vulnerable you become?"

My breath fogged the air. "Why are you turning on your fellow liches? What's in it for you?"

"They follow a false king," he breathed. "A murderer and a traitor."

"Speak for yourself." He'd totally iced me over. I couldn't move an inch. "You're involved with whoever's creating these illegal spells, aren't you? Cobb put you up to this before he died."

But he couldn't be carving the spells himself. However solid he might seem at the moment, liches weren't human, weren't alive.

"You should know that what is illegal is not always deserving of that title," the lich breathed. "You have toyed with the notion yourself, haven't you?"

I jerked away from his icy touch. "I've never considered creating a spell which can turn a spirit into a rotting corpse, you evil piece of shit."

"A spell that can reverse life and death," said the lich. "A spell that can free us from enslavement to the false king. Is that truly so heinous a notion?"

My hands numbed, my body locking to the spot. I forced out the words through chattering teeth. "He's not... enslaving you. You... what did you do with Brant?"

A different kind of chill bloomed in my chest. There was no good reason for his house to be used as a store-room for the same kinds of coins produced in the ware-houses. *What is he wrapped up in? Is he still alive?*

The lich didn't answer. He wasn't even touching me anymore, but my limbs remained frozen, my body trapped mid-motion as though a coating of invisible ice covered my entire body. I spotted Dex in the corner of my eye, but I couldn't shake my head to warn him.

The lich glided through the closed door, leaving me in the cold. Dex descended, the warmth of his elemental magic making me shiver even more. "Get closer," I croaked. "I need warmth."

"Fire-boy's in trouble, isn't he?"

"So am I." My numb lips stumbled on the words.

Dex flew closer to me and yelped when he landed on my shoulder. "You're sucking the warmth straight out of me."

"Don't be melodramatic," I said through chattering teeth. "Did you see... where the lich went?"

I already knew. He intended to turn on his master, and I still wouldn't be able to pick him out of a crowd. *Fucking liches.*

Dex's warmth helped, and sensation came back into

my body, inch by inch. Too slow. I needed something warmer. Like a fire mage. Or a spell.

I stumbled forward, grabbing for the box of spilled cantrips. It took a few painful minutes of fumbling around before I found what I needed.

As I activated the cantrip, a light flared up, and warmth flooded me. I sighed in relief, my eyes stinging with the release of the pain. I rose to my feet, my limbs restored to normal. *Now he's in for it.* I crossed the room to the door, but of course the lich was gone. He was on his way back to the castle to blend in with the other liches, without anyone knowing he was a traitor.

"Dex, can you fly ahead and warn the Death King?" I pushed open the door and walked out into the street. "Or any of his people?"

"Too late," he said. "I can see liches all over the place over in the swamp. They wouldn't know him from their own neighbour."

"They really need to wear nametags." I retraced my steps to the swampland, impatience prickling at me. In an imitation of Ryan, I let out a low whistle.

"What're you doing?" asked Dex.

The skeletal shape of Neddie the horse appeared a moment later, cantering up to me.

Dex floated above my head. "You're gonna *ride* that thing?"

"You bet." I swung up onto the horse's back. "Let's go."

We'd almost reached the gate when a blast went off somewhere outside the castle, a torrent of light surging up to the sky.

Shit. We're already too late.

I tightened my grip on Neddie's reins, urging him

through the gates. The liches on guard had scattered, and inside the grounds, chaos reigned. Patches of fire engulfed the few plants growing in the swampland, while several wight foot-soldiers lay in the dirt, their bony forms scorched around the edges.

A gasp escaped my lips. No. Brant couldn't have done it. He wasn't here.

"It's that Fire Element," I said. "I should have known he was up to no good. His behaviour should have clued me in from day one." I'd assumed the Death King trusted him, but who else could have set the swamp ablaze?

"Where's he run off to?" asked Dex.

"Inside." I leapt clear of the horse's back and ran up the steps to the castle, bracing myself. The doors slammed open, and sure enough, a man with blazing hands stood in the way of the door to the hall of souls.

Except it wasn't the Fire Element, but Brant, his hands afire and an expression of righteousness on his face. It turned to shock when he saw me. "Liv?"

"I thought you ran off." I said. "What are you doing in here?"

He lowered his hands. "Nothing. I'm back on my feet, but you weren't around, so—"

"Does it have to do with the store of illegal spells in your bolthole?" I took a step closer, surreptitiously glancing around for the Death King. *Where is he? And where are his Elemental Soldiers?*

Brant paled. "What?"

"I found a lich in there, too," I added. "He froze me out and left me for dead. Anything you wanna say about that?"

"You what?" His eyes grew wide. "A lich was in my house?"

"Yes, along with the illegal spells." I emphasised each word. "He seemed to think you wanted him to be there, in fact. Before he tried to *kill me.*"

"I can explain."

At his words, my last hope that there'd been a huge mistake evaporated like smoke. I clenched my hands, my body trembling, dread swirling inside me. "This better be good. Go on."

Before Brant could speak, Ryan appeared in the doorway, a current of air rising from their hands.

Brant spun around, too late, and the attack blasted him off his feet. He hit the wall, a dazed expression on his face. "What the—?"

"I knew you were up to no good." Ryan stalked over to him. "You planned to steal from the hall of souls, didn't you? Don't deny it."

Brant rubbed the back of his head, which came away damp with blood. "You should have stayed down."

My heart contracted, and so did my throat. In the end, all I could say was, "Why?"

Ryan closed in on him, as did I. Brant drew in a breath. "I didn't—look, you know the Parallel is a shithole, and none of us has a chance of making a living back home as long as the Order has a stranglehold on the magical trade laws."

"So your friends want to change that," I said, the words hollow. "Is this what you meant? Murdering liches, working with someone who tried to kill me and who allied with illegal spirit mages—were you in on Cobb's plan, too?"

He flinched. "I—"

"You were," Ryan interjected. "You didn't intend for Olivia to get involved, but I knew my boss never should have let you go when he turned you into a lich. He only spared you because he wanted to give you a second chance."

Each word hit my heart like a blow. "You were involved with *Cobb.* You *wanted* him to kill the Death King and get me locked up or worse?"

"Never," Brant insisted. "I wanted you to stay out of it."

"But you were all too willing to take advantage when you realised Liv might give you a shot at getting into the hall of souls," added Ryan. "You went as far as to fake an attack to get in here."

"You *faked* that attack?" I stared at him. "Who are you working for?"

His shoulders slumped. "I…"

"Get on with it." Davies stepped up to Brant's side. "Come on, you cowardly little shithead. Let's burn the spirit mage."

Fire blazed from his hands, joining the flames in Brant's own palms, and the inferno surged towards us.

18

Brant's attack veered away at the last instant. Davies's didn't, but the Air Element's hands lit up, and a blast of air slammed into me, sending me out of the way of the flames. I rolled over on the ground, breathless, but mercifully unhurt. Ryan wasn't so lucky. They took the fire attack head-on and hit the wall, their armour smoking around the edges.

"You bastard!" I screamed, calling on the node's power.

Magic roared through my fingertips and blasted both fire mages off their feet before they could unleash another double assault. Ryan slid to the ground, bruised and burned. Then a second bolt of spirit energy ripped through the room, raising the hairs on my arms. The Death King stood in the doorway, a swirling current of power surrounding him like the current of a node.

The two fire mages tried to run, but the Death King's attack caught them first. Brant got the full blast of it, flying into the air before crashing into a heap on the floor.

The Fire Element dodged to the side, vaulting over Brant's body and out through the castle doors.

I gave chase, running through the doors and down the stairs. "Get back here!"

I hit the ground running at the foot of the steps, closing the distance between us, but he spun around and flames burst from his hands. In an instant, the ground was ablaze, a scorching torrent that seared my skin even from a distance. I stumbled back as the Fire Element put on a burst of speed and disappeared into the node.

"Shit!" I turned back, seeing two liches carrying Brant down the stairs between them, his face as pale as ice in front of the Death King's presence.

"Take him to the jail," he told the liches. "I'll deal with him later."

I didn't move to intercede when the liches carried Brant past me towards the blocky building outside the castle. The ground felt unsteady beneath my feet, as though the universe had shifted on its axis and left me stranded several miles to the left of where I'd been beforehand.

Brant, a traitor. Brant, working with the Fire Element against the Death King. Against me.

The Death King beckoned to another lich. "Take Ryan to the other Elements. They need a healing cantrip."

Ryan. They were injured… because of Brant and the Fire Element.

"I can help," I said. "My friend Devon keeps a collection of healing cantrips. She's not at home, but she always has some in stock."

"We can handle it here," said the Death King.

Was he dismissing me? I wouldn't blame him, since I

was the one who'd brought Brant into his home, but my fragile countenance was beginning to crack at the edges, and if I didn't find an outlet soon, I'd explode. "And Davies? Do you know—do you know where he might have gone?"

"To his allies, I don't doubt." The Death King turned to the other two Elements, who hurried out of the castle, speaking in urgent whispers.

"What now?" Dex hovered above my head. "Want me to fire sparks at the traitorous little goblin?"

"Do whatever you like." I couldn't stay here. Not with the smell of burning and Brant's betrayal leaving cascading emotions in its wake. "I need to regroup. You... you'll be safe here, if you want to stay."

Safer than with Brant. I never thought I'd say that.

Elements above, what a mess.

I made for the node. I'd hoped to find the house empty so I could scream into a pillow for a while, but instead, I found Devon waiting on the other side.

"I thought you'd be out until tonight," I said.

"The Order kept calling me," she said. "They wanted to know where you were. I knew they'd probably send someone to snoop around until they figured out that you'd given them the slip, and besides, I wasn't in the mood to stay for long. I was worried about you. Did you find the vampires' master?"

"Not exactly." I wrapped my arms around myself, my throat closing up. Why was it so hard to voice the words aloud, even to my best friend?

Devon peered at me. "Shit. What happened?"

"Brant." I swallowed hard. "He—he's with them. Somehow..."

I told her. Silent tears fell down my face while I spoke, and I made a half-hearted attempt to rub them away.

After I'd finished speaking, Devon was quiet for a long moment, her hands clenched so tightly her knuckles had gone white. "I am going to kill him."

"I think the Death King might get there first." I wiped my eyes with my sleeve. "Brant's in jail, but the Fire Element escaped through the node. He attacked his fellow Element and just left them there."

"I don't—" Devon broke off. "I don't understand why Brant wanted to break into the Death King's hall of souls of all places. If the Fire Element's a traitor, too, why didn't he steal the amulets himself?"

"He probably did steal the first few, but Brant couldn't resist taking advantage of me bringing him there." I gave a short, bitter laugh. "He probably feigned unconsciousness so that I'd leave him behind at the castle. How could I have trusted him?"

"Don't blame yourself for this, Liv," Devon said. "Never."

Another humourless laugh escaped. "He's the one who told me I needed to learn to trust him again. How fucked-up is that?"

She took my arm and gave it a comforting squeeze. "*He's* fucked-up. Majorly. He made a bad mistake in siding with the lich traitor. Is that who's pulling the strings?"

"Not just him." I swallowed hard. "He can't be the person actually carving those cantrips. I think Brant and the three vampires were working together, using their homes as storerooms for the stolen blank cantrips, but as for who he's supposed to be handing them to... I guess we'll find out when the Death King interrogates him."

And the soul amulets? I could guess whose he'd been told to steal. Brant's ruse had almost taken him close enough to the hall of souls to ruin everything I'd risked my life for.

"I know." Devon bit her lip. "I also know the last thing you want to do is talk to him again, but did you say the Fire Element is somewhere here? In this realm?"

"Maybe he left the country like those vampires planned to." I scrubbed my eyes again. "I honestly don't give a shit where he's gone."

But Davies had passed the Death King's stringent testing process to gain his position. For how long had he been planning to betray his master? What was in it for him? The lich, I could sort of understand. Brant, too, to some degree. But the Fire Element had one of the most important jobs in the Parallel. As far as mages went, he was set for life. Why had he thrown it all away?

On the other hand, the lich traitor was still out there, hidden among the Death King's people. I wished there was some way I could identify who it was. Brant might know. Like he knew who was pulling the strings. He'd never volunteer that information to the Death King without force, but perhaps he'd tell me if he thought I was alone. He knew he owed me the truth.

I pushed to my feet, sucking in a deep breath. "You're right… I have to talk to him."

"Are you sure?" Her expression pinched with concern. "He's going to know he can manipulate you. It's what he's been doing all along."

Fresh tears pricked my eyes. "Maybe I'm just reluctant to believe he's all bad, but he seemed genuinely conflicted. He certainly didn't want *me* to become a target, but what did he expect? This is a spirit mage's doing."

"All right." Devon got up. "At least take some of my fresh cantrips with you."

"That was the plan." I was bone-tired, but my anger burned like a fire sprite's spark inside me. "I'll make him regret this."

"During our next D&D game, Brant will be forever immortalised as a slimy troll," Devon added.

"That's an insult to trolls, if you ask me."

I stocked up on cantrips, but still felt more vulnerable than I had in a long time when I passed through the node into the castle grounds. The scorch marks were gone, all signs of the Fire Element's attack cleared away, and two new liches guarded the castle.

I narrowed my eyes, looking at them, wishing I could make out any signs that they might be the betrayer. The Death King must be able to tell them apart, surely.

"What are you looking at?" one of them asked in a light, feminine voice.

I shrugged. "I need an escort to the jail. I want to speak to your prisoner."

"No," the lich said. "My master said—"

"She's the spirit mage, isn't she?" The lich at her side looked me over. "You brought him here."

"I didn't know..." I broke off, seeing the Water Element walking back from the jail. I crossed the grounds and met her halfway. "Is Ryan okay?"

"They will live." Her tone was weary. "The fire mage is asking for you."

My chest constricted. "I know helping me is probably the last thing you want to do, but I need to talk to him, and I don't think he's willing to confess the name of the person he's working for to anyone else aside from me."

The Water Element looked me over, her mouth pressed together. "If he tries to escape—"

"Feel free to fill his lungs with water for all I care." The venom in my voice almost masked the sob hidden beneath, but not quite. "He won't be getting any help from me."

The Water Element escorted me the short distance to the brick building which housed the Death King's jail. I found my steps slowing with each passing second. Elements, this was going to be hard, but nobody could do this but me.

I walked into the jail, a shiver of fear trailing down my spine when I felt the familiar horrible chill I'd grown used to during my captivity. My hands curled into fists at the sight of Brant sitting on a bench inside the cell opposite the one I'd spent several days in myself. His head lifted when I walked in.

I indicated to the Water Element to stay in the shadows, so he wouldn't realise we weren't alone. Then I approached his cell.

"I should have guessed he'd send you to do the questioning," said Brant.

"I'm not here on his account," I said, knowing he meant the Death King. "I'm here on my own. It's me who deserves an explanation, not him."

He winced. "Look, I can't—you can't tell him. He wouldn't understand."

"To be honest, I don't understand you, either," I said. "Who are you working for? Who's your employer? I know it's not Mr Cobb, though it used to be. This was his backup plan, in case his first quest to take the Death King's place didn't pan out."

"He… calls himself the Crow." He looked at the floor. "I swear I wouldn't do this if I thought I had a choice in the matter. But I don't."

"The Crow," I said. "What is he—lich or human?"

He shook his head. "I can't… you have no idea what he's capable of."

I thought of those dead liches. "I think I have a pretty good idea. Did you really fake that attack?"

"No," he said. "The monsters he captures to test the spells on aren't contained. They sometimes break free."

Bile rose in the back of my throat. "He's been catching people—and creatures—to test the spell on? As practise for what, using it on the Death King?"

But to use it on him, they'd need his soul amulet. If I hadn't caught Brant before he'd broken into the hall of souls…

Was he lying to me even now? He'd been living a double life for at least half the time we'd been together. No wonder he'd been reluctant to let me know about his hideout in the city, if he'd always planned to use it to store stolen cantrips in.

"He's too powerful," he said. "It's not right for one person to have control over so many armies."

"And it's okay to kill people?" I arched a brow.

"They aren't people," he said. "Revenants and phantoms are less than human. As for the liches…"

"You used to be one yourself, if you've forgotten," I said sharply. "If the Death King hadn't pitied you and undid the spell for my sake, you might have fallen victim to the same spell yourself. Or worse."

"You can't trust him," he said, in a tremulous voice. "The Death King, I mean. He let me go because it was convenient to him, not you."

"Funny," I said. "I seem to remember you being fixated on constantly reminding me how I could trust *you*. And you know, I think part of me always knew you were a rat."

It was easy to tell myself that, but the reality was, I hadn't suspected. Not until the last minute. That's what hurt the most.

He closed his eyes. "I didn't have—"

"A choice? There's always a choice," I said. "So who is it who's smuggling the coins out of the warehouse? The staff, or the supervisors?"

His voice was quiet. "Does it matter? They have no more choice than I do."

"The Order is onto your little operation," I told him. "That's why they sent me after the vampires' haul. Were you planning to tell me before they sent me after you, too?"

"They wouldn't have." His words sounded hollow, as though he didn't believe what he said.

"The vampires kidnapped Trix and held him hostage in their cellar," I added. "That's the kind of scum you're associating with."

"No," he said. "I don't know them that well at all. I didn't even know they were living in Vaughn's old house until we found them there. Did you go back there? Were you hurt?"

I ignored the concern in his voice, unable to tell if it was just an act to buy my sympathy in return. "The Order has hauled all three of them off to jail. I think they're better off than you are, considering. The Death King isn't going to show you mercy this time."

"He'll turn you, too, Liv." He looked up at me, his expression stark with urgency. "You must know how he became king. He turned his fellow liches into his willing servants, and that'll be your fate as well."

I stepped away from his intense stare. "You *wanted* me to learn spirit magic. I guess you thought I might be a useful ally. All that crap about owing someone your soul... I suppose you made that up, too."

He shook his head. "No. I didn't lie. It's true, Liv... and it's why I didn't have a choice."

Lie or not, he'd hidden the truth often enough that I couldn't trust a word he said. Not about the Death King, nor about my fate as a spirit mage. When he'd asked me to learn spirit magic, I'd once snapped at him that he only wanted me to save his own soul. My accusation had come from fear rather than a rational basis, but in the end, I'd been right.

I had nothing more to say to him. If the Death King wanted to question him further, he was welcome to, but a suspicion had seized me. Back when Brant confessed to me that he owed someone his soul, someone who had a hold over him, he'd claimed the person responsible was a vampire.

Was *that* the person behind this operation, the so-called Crow?

There was one way to find out for sure: ask the vampires myself.

19

———

I left the jail and found the Death King waiting outside. He stood there, tall and imposing, and an irrational surge of anger jolted up my spine. His traitor lich had left me for dead, but he and I had both made the wrong call when it came to Brant.

"I thought I'd find you here," he said.

"You thought I'd go running back to him, is that it?" Furious tears stung my eyes, ready to join the ones which had fallen without my noticing.

"No, I thought you'd want to speak to him alone," he said. "Did you gain what you needed to know?"

"The person behind this calls himself the Crow," I said. "I think he's a vampire, and the three rogue vamps the Order has in custody might know where to find him."

"I see," he said. "Do you wish to go to the Order?"

I blinked furiously, cursing the emotions clogging my throat. "It's that or ask the vampires on the council for another appointment with Lord Blackbourne, but I can't

218

rely on them to step up to help us. They don't get how urgent this is."

"The Order doesn't either," he said.

"They have Cobb, too," I reminded him. "I don't know if they'd let even you see *him,* but he knows this Crow person if the vampires don't. Brant is… he's too used to lying. I can't trust a word he says."

"In that case," he said, his tone as impassive as always, "I will come to the Order. I'll leave my other Elemental Soldiers in charge here."

"Are you sure?" I asked. "I know the Order won't let me go and see them alone, but if it's dangerous for you to leave your castle unattended—"

"No more than usual," he said. "After we speak to the vampires, I intend to find where my traitorous Fire Element is hiding."

"All right." In truth, I'd rather cut off my hand than go to the Order. The notion of telling them about Brant's betrayal made me ill. I'd worked so hard to save his soul, yet in the end, he'd ended up losing it anyway.

The Death King's masked face was turned towards me. I couldn't read his expression, as usual, but I was pretty sure he could read mine. I broke my gaze away. "Where's Dex, by the way?"

"Last I saw, he was in Ryan's company."

"Oh. At least he's safe." I'd lost too many allies already. "Are you sure the Fire Element won't come back while we're gone?"

"I have my people ready to watch the node. They'll make him suffer if he returns." His tone dripped icicles down my spine. "Afterwards, I suppose I will be in need of a new Fire Element."

"And I'll be in need of a new boyfriend." I didn't manage a laugh. It was too absurd to think of Brant as a traitor. I'd always known he worked with people on the wrong side of the law, but it wasn't my place to judge what others did when it was impossible to take a step without running up against the Order's boundaries. Here in the Parallel, the laws were lax, and Brant had still steamrollered over them. He'd helped in the capture of innocents. He'd worked with people who'd tried to kill me. And the scumbag had still tried to pursue a relationship with me while acting as though nothing was wrong.

Could I really have been happy with him in the longterm? I'd wanted certainty and stability and I'd thought I'd found it with him, but if I'd let him take me into his inner circle, I'd have spent the rest of my life looking away while he did things that he deemed necessary to survive. Things that hurt other people.

Besides, stability wasn't in the cards for me, not anymore.

The Death King and I left the castle behind and crossed through the node. We landed in the main road near the Order, and when I turned back to my companion, he had his human disguise on. Between one blink and the next, he turned from remote and terrifying into someone who you might pass on the street every day. Certainly not someone who could claim your soul and turn you into a monster, as Brant claimed. He was talking shit, I knew, but the Death King carried his own arsenal of secrets. As for the Order…

My heart plummeted as the sound of screaming drifted over from the street ahead. Smoke billowed out from the rooftops. *Dammit. Please tell me it isn't Brant's allies.*

I broke into a run, catching up to one of the Order employees fleeing the building. "Hey! What's going on?"

"There's been an attack," she said. "A fire mage—"

"Dammit." The Fire Element must have come straight to the Order. I heard a voice yelling after me, but I was already running towards the building, where the Order employees were fleeing en masse. Members of the public were out in the street, too, thinking it was an ordinary fire and not an act of arson by a power-crazed mage.

"Olivia." The Death King caught up to me with ease. "I can go in there, but you—"

"I have a breathing spell." I scrambled for the pouch at my waist. "It's supposed to be for breathing underwater, but it'll work here. I have to check if he's still in there."

I turned on the cantrip and a bubble of air appeared around my head. The Death King didn't argue further. He glided through the doors into the building, and I moved in behind him.

In the lobby, people ran left and right, fleeing the smoke billowing down the stairs. The fire must have started on one of the floors above, but the prisoners were on the lowest level below the basement, sealed in protected cells. Protected against elemental fire, I would have thought, but Davies had come here with a purpose.

The Death King glided across the lobby, and I halted at his side, my stomach lurching. Blood splattered the floor by the back doors leading to the delivery drop-off.

"Shit." I ran outside, ignoring the sign saying, 'No Exit', and saw several Order personnel lying bleeding on the ground. The nearest man stirred as I drew closer. Blood pulsed from two holes in his neck.

"The vampires." I turned to the Death King. "They were in the lockup but not in the main jail. That's why Davies came here—to help them escape."

There was only one way they could have gone from here, so I took off in that direction, vaulting the wall and running down the alley at the back. Sure enough, three figures appeared at the alley's end, drawing closer to the node by the second.

One of them spotted me and shouted a warning to his fellow vamps. A paralysing cantrip flew from my hand, but as I caught up to the vampires, another spell went off like a firecracker. An explosion of some kind of web-like substance covered me from head to toe, and my body locked up as though superglue had fixed me to the spot. He must have grabbed some of the Order's cantrips on the way out. If I hadn't been wearing the water-breathing spell, I'd have been much worse off, but all I could do was watch them run.

Cursing at the alley wall, I tugged at the webbing until I managed to free myself. Pulling a handful of it from my hair, I turned back to the Order's HQ. The smoke had died down a little, suggesting someone had put out the fire. The Order must have at least a few mages on staff, surely, unless they'd moved them all to the Parallel.

The water-breathing spell was still active, so I ran through the back doors into the Order's HQ to find the place almost deserted. I made for the stairs and found the Death King heading towards me.

"He's gone." He didn't stop walking. "He escaped through an upstairs window."

"Dammit." I must have just missed him, too. He'd come here to free the vampires and had had no intention of sticking around. "He—didn't reach Cobb, did he?"

"We'd know if he had." He halted beside me. "What's that on your face?"

"The vampires must have grabbed some spells on their way out," I said. "They got through the node. We'd better go…"

The doors opened, and my heart sank. The last thing I needed was an interrogation from the Order about why I'd shown up right as the place caught on fire.

The Death King apparently thought the same. He reached for my arm, and I startled at the sudden contact. "What are you—?"

The world vanished in a flood of light, and in the next instant, we landed outside the castle.

"How'd you do that?" I jerked away from him in shock, my head spinning. "We weren't anywhere near a node."

"Lich trick." He still wore his human face, and rage suffused his features. "I expect those vampires came back here to warn their supervisor."

"Sire." I clapped a hand to my mouth. "The person behind this is a vampire, and the vamps threatened to send their sire to attack me the first time I paid them a visit. I bet he's the one. This Crow person."

The Death King looked at the castle, his expression so unreadable that he might as well have been wearing his mask. "I think it's time I questioned our prisoner."

As we approached the jail, the Water Element ran up to meet us. "He's gone. A lich used his power on me and broke him out."

"Shit!" I jabbed my foot into the marshy ground,

wanting to scream with frustration. "He and the Fire Element had this planned from the start."

Even their animosity might well have been for show, for all I knew.

The Death King moved towards the castle doors, accompanied by the Water Element. I hesitated for an instant, and the click of a cantrip buzzed near my ear.

"What the—?" I rotated on my heel, the hairs on the back of my neck standing up.

Brant appeared, half visible, at my side. "I'm sorry, Liv."

Then blackness crashed over my head and drew me under.

20

I came to alertness what felt like several seconds later. Cold stone cushioned the back of my head, which gave a dull throb. The Death King was standing over me, still wearing his human face.

"Dammit." I sat up, my head spinning. "Did he—"

"He ran," he said. "Not before taking a detour into my hall of souls, it seems."

No. "Did he take any souls?"

"Mine." His tone was calm, too calm. "One of my people already told me."

"You *what?* What're you standing here for?"

His brows rose. "As flattered as I am for your concern, the fire mage merely *thinks* he took my soul. Did you think I would leave it in the same place after its recent disappearance?"

My mouth fell open. "You used a substitute?"

"A real soul amulet, but not mine," he said. "Another lich volunteered to leave their soul in my place, one who knew the risks."

Damn. He might not have lost his soul, but now the lich traitor, Brant, the Fire Element and the three vampires were all ready to join their master. "How'd he get away from you so fast?"

"I let him," said the Death King. "I expect his master will be displeased with him for bringing the wrong soul amulet. Felicity, did he go through the node?"

"He did," the Water Element said, looking exasperated but not outright surprised at the Death King's ruse. "I doubt he'll stay on Earth for long. He and the vampires are on the Order's wanted list several times over."

"Then they must have a base in town." I climbed to my feet. My balance was a little wobbly, but I was in one piece. Brant hadn't killed me. He'd just knocked me out, using a cantrip. I didn't want to examine that thought too closely. After all, I didn't know what I'd do to him when we next saw one another face to face. Especially if he took the enemy's side openly again.

Dex flew into the main hall and up to my side. "Did fire-boy make a run for it?"

"Not before he knocked me out with a cantrip," I said. "He went to deliver the Death King's soul to his master. Or what he *thinks* is his soul, anyway."

"You used a fake?" Dex whooped with laughter. "That'll show the bastard."

"Doesn't mean we know where he is." I gave the Death King a significant look. "Clever move, but couldn't you have found out whereabouts this Crow person is hiding before you let Brant give you the slip?"

"I already know where he is," he said. "There are strict rules on who can sire new vampires and when, and I assume this Crow was in compliance with the rules if he hasn't drawn the council's attention. That means he's one of a small group of vampires, all of whom live in the same district."

"You might have told me that earlier." Then again, we hadn't known it was a vampire running the show until now. "I'm going after them. But we need backup."

"I'm with you," Dex said. "I wanna see fire-boy burn."

"As do I." Ryan entered the hall, and relief flooded me at seeing them back on their feet. "Whoever you need me to fight, I'll gladly do it as long as it means I get to take Davies down myself."

"You're on." I gave them a grim smile. "Let's go and nail the bastards to the wall."

We made a weird team, that was for sure. Ryan walked in the lead, using their air magic to quicken their speed. The Death King kept up his usual light-footed glide, still wearing his human face for some reason. When I gave him a questioning look, he said, "I'm supposed to be in dire peril at the castle, as far as our foes are aware. Most of them won't recognise me like this."

"Fair enough," I said. "I didn't know the vampires had such strict rules on creating new vamps. Is that why there are so many revenants and so few newly born vampires?"

"Yes, it is," he said. "The vampire leaders might not care what becomes of their fellow magical neighbours, but they are stringent at enforcing the rules that govern their own kind. There are limits on the number of new vampires which can be created, while no council members are allowed to create new vampires while they serve their terms. It's not a perfect system, but it works."

"Oh." Something else hit me. "You know, if this spell *can* affect vampires, perhaps the Crow is eventually planning to use it on himself. Once he's got rid of the side effects."

If so, then perhaps the Death King wasn't the only leader he planned to depose. The vampires might not be my favourite people, but their leadership more or less kept everyone in Arcadia from eating one another alive. If they disappeared as suddenly as the Elemental Council had, they'd leave chaos in their wake.

"Perhaps," he said. "Some liches would be lured into such a scheme, I don't doubt."

"Yeah." The traitor had hinted as much. And Brant… he'd implied the Death King had intended to turn *me* into a lich, too. Yet he hadn't, not even when I'd been at his mercy. "I—I'm sorry I brought Brant into your castle." I couldn't quite meet his eyes, not now he wore his human face.

The Death King didn't reply for a long moment. "It seems I am not the only one of the pair of us who overlooked a traitor at my side."

The Fire Element *and* the lich. How many more might be working against him? I still worried about leaving the castle, but this was likely our last shot to stop the vampire, whatever his endgame was.

The glow of a nearby node caught my eye as we neared the swampland's edge. Then a phantom lunged out of the node, rushing towards us with sharp claws poised to attack. Not just one phantom, but two, three—

"Watch out!" I shouted at the others.

The node brightened as both the Death King and I drew on its power. I ran closer, dodging a phantom's claws, and blasted it into its neighbour. The node darkened, its currents thick with clawed beasts, but I found myself moving into its orbit. Drawing on its strength.

Power roared to life inside me, blasting the phantoms away. The nearest phantom reeled back, its body crumbling. They might outnumber us, but each phantom still had a limited time to strike before they fell to pieces, eaten alive by their own source of power.

The node's current drew me in, even as the phantoms pinned me on all sides, trapping me in the centre. Too many to fight all at once—but the node gave me strength. It had to be enough to beat them.

A sudden cold pair of sharp points brushed against my neck.

"Hello again," purred the long-haired vampire.

I slammed my elbow back, greeted by an explosion of pain. Someday I'd learn not to punch vampires, but today wasn't that day, apparently. With a curse, I pivoted away from the vampire and grabbed onto the node's power. Magic ripped from my palms, and the vampires cringed away from the light. I spotted the Death King and the Air Element fighting back to back, holding the phantoms at bay—but two more people stepped out of the node. Vampires, wearing identical grins.

"Enough games," said a voice. "Hand the spirit mage over to me."

A tall figure appeared within the current of light, moving with impossible grace and speed. His sharp-edged face glowed with the node's power, his hair gleamed like night, and a memory tickled the inside of my mind. I'd seen his face before, somewhere...

Fighting the sudden rush of déjà-vu, I pulled the

node's power into my hands, but felt clumsy, disconnected. The vampire moved with blinding speed. Cold, hard arms wrenched mine behind my back, and pain screamed through my shoulders. I gritted my teeth, fighting for control.

Then the world was rushing away—I closed my eyes against an onslaught of dizziness—and then at once, everything ground to a halt.

The vampire held me in his grip, inside the doorway of a house. Wooden panelling ran on either side of me like the décor of the council house, but the dark, winding hall was unfamiliar to me.

The painful tightness on my arms vanished and my body pitched forwards as a wave of dizziness crashed over me. I caught my balance on the wall, my eyes squinting against the darkness of the hallway. The leading vampire appeared in my peripheral vision, fast, elegant, so familiar it made my head hurt.

"What do you want with me?" I gasped out.

"I hear you were responsible for jailing my children," said the Crow—it could only be him. "I wouldn't let an amateur spirit mage stand in my way, but since you insisted upon it, I feel no remorse for taking your life."

"I bet," I said. "I have to admit, I didn't guess a vampire might be behind all this. Using spells that kill the dead doesn't seem your sort of thing."

He took my arm and wrenched me through a doorway into a room panelled with the same dark wood as the corridor. Excruciating pain shot up to my elbow. I bit back a scream.

"What're you going to do?" I blinked hard, my eyes

watering. "Turn me into a lich and then a decaying corpse, like the others you experimented on?"

"You don't deserve that honour," he said.

"Honour?" I frowned, the pain making me lightheaded. "Did they volunteer for this shit?"

"Believe it or not, they did," he said. "They were willing to offer their lives for the purposes of furthering my research."

A vampire mad scientist. Who'd have thought it possible? "The liches who died didn't volunteer."

"Liches?" he echoed. "That's none of my business. I'm only concerned with my fellows."

Shit. It must have been the traitor lich who'd killed his own people, but the Crow's work was experimental, with an end goal. The spell wasn't just intended to kill, but to gain power.

"You," he said, "are going to stay here. I'll leave my children to stop you from getting yourself into trouble while I deal with your friends."

"Like hell." I reached for my pouch, but he wrenched on my arm with another dizzying current of pain. "What's the point of all this?"

"You will soon leave this world behind," said the vampire. "I will clean up this city and purge the undead scum so that the living can walk in the light again."

"Do you include yourself among the living or the dead?" Elements, my arm hurt. "Or does it depend on who you're talking to?"

The pain was making me loopy. I couldn't think clearly—which was no doubt the point. The three vampires closed in, their teeth bared in smiles. Ready to torture the spirit mage.

"Oh, come on, guys," I said. "Can't you at least give me a fighting chance?"

A foot slammed into my ribs, and pain engulfed my entire world.

21

"You should have got this by now," said a voice. "Try again."

I faced my mentor, my hands curling into fists as the energy of a node roared through my veins.

"Better," said Dirk Alban, stepping into view. "Show me again."

I did so, reciting the rules in my head as I did so.

Travelling through nodes is the first stage of spirit magic. The second stage is bringing the spirit across but not the body. The third stage is drawing on the node's strength to bolster your own.

The fourth? Moving the soul to another source.

In the real world, I lay on my back and stared up at the ceiling. The vampires had finally gone to hunt some poor humans down to sate the bloodlust brought on by the smell of my fresh blood, and they'd left me to nurse my injuries alone.

It seemed they enjoyed playing with their food. They'd thrown my pouch somewhere else in the room, but my cantrips might be in one piece—if I had the strength to reach them. Even moving my arm seemed an impossibly herculean act.

The world flickered out, revealing Dirk Alban's face against a backdrop of cool grey. And next to him…

"I want you to meet someone today," he said. "Someone you can learn from."

The Crow looked at me. His eyes weren't pale, but were ordinary brown, and he didn't have pointed fangs. He hadn't been turned yet…

The memory flickered out, and the world faded back into view. I might not have all the answers, but I'd seen enough to guess the truth.

"You were a spirit mage," I whispered to the darkness.

The Crow had once been a spirit mage alongside Dirk Alban. I'd thought mages couldn't turn into vampires, but it wasn't like I'd ever met a living spirit mage after losing my memory. Not until Mr Cobb, anyway, and he hadn't had any of his powers left.

"Liv," said a voice from among the hazy light above my head. "Shit. Don't be dead. Not now."

"Dex," I croaked out. "I'm not dead, but the three vampires haven't finished with me yet. How'd you find me?"

"I searched every house in the vampires' district until I found you." Dex's form appeared hovering above my face. "You have your cantrips, don't you?"

"Too far." Too bad he couldn't pick them up to toss to me, because my arms were lead weights. Pain continued to pulse through my body as I fought to keep my mind in the present. The Crow was a spirit mage. He must have kept his magic after being turned into a vampire, which meant *he* was the person who'd been creating the cantrips. Not the lich traitor, and not the people at the warehouses. No other explanation made sense.

"Look, I can't pick anything up." Dex's voice turned pleading. "Come on. You have to get up, Liv."

Oblivion beckoned behind my eyes. The Crow's human face swam to the forefront of my vision, alongside Dirk Alban's. The whole picture had a hazy dreamlike quality, but I could tell the difference between a dream and a memory. Dreams faded upon waking. Memories grew clearer each time they replayed. As though each recall brought me closer to the person I'd been before.

A sour taste filled my mouth. I'd worked with the Crow... trained with him. Like Dirk Alban. But he didn't want me to help him now, like Mr Cobb had. Why would he? He wasn't looking to take on the Death King's power via his amulet, but to destroy him using cantrips of his own creation. He didn't need another spirit mage standing in his way.

The question was, had he realised the Death King's soul amulet was a fake yet?

Dammit, Liv. Get up. Blood soaked into my jacket, into the carpet. Who was to say this poor human victim of theirs would be enough to sate the three vampires' bloodlust? I needed to get the hell out of here before they got bored of playing with me and decided to go in for the kill.

Pain screamed up my arm as I rolled onto my side, my fingers stretching out to grab the pouch containing my cantrips. Almost there...

With a burst of strength, my hand closed on the pouch, scrambling for a healing cantrip. A flash of light engulfed me, and at once, I began to feel sensation that wasn't pain creep back into my limbs. The agony dialled down, and twinges zipped through my muscles as they unknotted, freed of pain.

Except for the ache in my chest born from Brant's betrayal, and the gutting knowledge that I hadn't truly known him at all. Hell, I didn't know *myself*. Had I really been that person sitting eagerly in front of Dirk Alban and the Crow, waiting to learn from them? Maybe I hadn't known what they were capable of. The Crow had been human at the time, and for all I knew, he'd left that life behind after turning into a vampire. Unless the Order had hit him with a memory spell, too...

The door whispered inward. The three vampires were back, their mouths bloody from feeding on their prey. With the crimson stains on my clothes and hands, I still looked like I was bleeding, too... which worked in my favour.

Okay. I'm getting out of here in three, two...

Fire flashed before my vision as Dex descended on the vampires in a shower of sparks. As the vampires recoiled, I set off the cantrip hidden in my hand. The paralysing blast struck all three vampires at once, and I ducked between them. One tried to grab me and tripped, his usual coordination marred by his attempts to avoid getting too close to the fire sprite. Another cantrip sent smoke pouring through the room, and I sprinted out into the corridor and slammed the door behind me.

A heavy body struck the wood an instant later, shattering it to pieces. The vampire broke free with a furious lunge and a scream of rage. I flung myself flat and rolled over, past the splintered door. *What kind of vampire makes their doors out of wood?*

My hand closed around a sizeable shard of broken door, and I swung the improvised stake with everything I had.

The wooden stake speared the vampire's chest. He fell back, blood pulsing from the wound. From inside the room, the other vampires let out cries of fury mixed with despair.

Dex flew into the path of the door, but both vampires ran straight through him, propelled by their rage. I staked one of them in the throat, while the third sidestepped, his teeth sinking into my shoulder.

Pain shot through my arm once more, but it was a far cry from the agony they'd inflicted on me before. I used the stake to block a hammer-like strike that broke my weapon into two shards.

"Give it up, sweetheart," the vampire growled.

Dex flew down into my attacker's eyes, sparks flying from his hands. The vampire danced backwards, but not before I stabbed the improvised stake into his arm. Crimson soaked my fingertips, and the vampire's arm went limp.

With my free hand, I grabbed for another piece of shattered wood. My second strike caught him in the neck, and he fell to his knees, blood fountaining from the wound. His bloody teeth moved, forming words I couldn't read, before his head hit the carpet.

As his gasps petered out, I slumped against the wall, breathing heavily. My shoulder continued to burn, but I forced myself upright. "Dex... is the way out clear?"

"Yes..." He darted out into the corridor from behind a door leading into another room. "But there's something in here you'll want to see."

He lit the way into the adjoining room, halting above a dark-clad figure lying on the ground. His throat was a mangled mess, his pale skin streaked with bloody furrows.

My stomach lurched. Brant lay bleeding from multiple wounds, enough for me to confirm the vampires had used him as their snack rather than ambushing someone on the streets. A sob caught in my throat, anger and disbelief merging until I couldn't speak.

One thought won out: I wouldn't leave Brant in here to die, no matter what he'd done.

I hadn't a hope of carrying him single-handedly, but I reached into my pouch and grabbed my last healing cantrip.

Dex descended over my shoulder. "Liv, are you sure?"

"No." I turned on the cantrip before I changed my mind, then I gave Brant a shake. "Hey. Rise and shine."

His eyes flickered open. "Liv?"

"Can you walk?" I tried to keep my tone even, but relief seeped in all the same. "I think the three vampires are dead, but their sire might come back."

"You killed them? All three?"

"Of course I did." I grimaced when he leaned on me to push himself to his feet, not noticing my shoulder wound. "Their sire, though, he's a nasty piece of work. He left them to kill me. And you, apparently."

He mumbled something unintelligible under his breath.

"What was that?" I said. "Regretting working with him now?"

I might not want him to die, but I was a long way from

ever forgiving him. Unpacking that could wait until we were both back on safer ground, however.

Brant looked up at me, his face streaked with blood. "He owns my soul. If I tried to run, he'd find me."

"How long?" I asked. "How long has this been going on? He was the vampire at the fancy event you mentioned, right? The one who convinced you to bet your soul on a poker game?"

He flinched. "Yes, that was him. He has people everywhere. In the warehouses… even among the Death King's army."

"I gathered." My voice shook, my shoulder throbbing. "Is this guy the one who was supposed to be able to get my memories back, too?"

He was silent for a heartbeat too long. "I never lied when I said I didn't mean for this to happen to you."

"You of all people should know that when you play with fire, the consequences are on you." I backed down the hallway, heading for the door. "He's not in here, is he?"

"No…" He walked after me, his steps slow, uncertain. "No, he wanted me to stay out of his way. Because of you, he deemed me a flight risk."

"Oh, so it's my fault you turned traitor?" My hand gripped my sore arm. "I knew I shouldn't have wasted my last healing cantrip on you."

"You're injured." He reached for my arm and I slapped him away.

"Don't touch me."

His gaze dropped. "I'm—"

"Spare me the apologies and just tell me where your master went."

When he next spoke, his voice was thick with emotion.

"If he has the soul amulet, he'll have gone to... to his home."

"This isn't his home?"

"No, it's a safe house."

"Then you won't mind burning it to make sure those scumbags don't come back this time, right?"

He glanced behind him, a conflicted expression on his face. "I'm a dead man now, whether I leave or stay. If he finds out—"

"He already let his vampires feed on you. I reckon he's done with you, Brant." When he didn't move, I added, "He ripped your throat out. You'd be dead if not for me, and if you don't set this place ablaze, I will."

Flames sparked from his hands, spreading to the bodies of the dead vampires. The wooden furniture joined the blaze, and we ran out into the cold air, leaving the burning remains of the vampires behind.

22

Brant and I ran out onto the unfamiliar street outside the vampire's house. I let him overtake me, feeling another pang in my chest at the thought that he must know the area better than I did, and despite my shattered trust in him, I needed to rely on him to find the way to the Crow's house. To my friends.

As he took the lead, I gave him a warning look. "If you lead me the wrong way, I'll shove my D20s up your nostrils."

Dex snorted. "What're you looking for?"

"The Crow's place, and it's this way." Brant turned right. "I don't have any reason to lead you in the wrong direction, Liv. It's too late for your allies now, whether you go there or not."

No. It isn't. "Let's assume my allies are just fine, but they could use my help."

We found the first body a short distance down the road, ripped open as though by sharp claws. A phantom must be loose near here.

"How many of those spells does he have?" I remarked aloud. "If he hand-carves them all, he can't have a whole houseful."

Not enough for an army, surely. Then again, with the speed vampires were capable of moving at, carving several spells simultaneously wouldn't be a tall order. How had he escaped detection for so long? If the vampires stayed out of one another's business and none of them knew of his history as a spirit mage, though, I could see how he might have escaped their notice. And the Order might have marked him as dead for all I knew.

Dex flew in agitated circles above my head. "If one of those things is on the loose, I'm outta here."

"If you fly off alone, you're more vulnerable," I warned him. "If you ask me, the Crow won't have any phantoms inside his hideout. He wouldn't want them getting in his way when he gets his hands on the soul amulet. Right, Brant?"

From his pinched expression, I'd guessed right for once. Didn't mean I knew where my other allies had disappeared to. The last I'd seen, they were fighting the phantoms beside the node on the other side of the city, but the Crow thought he had the Death King's amulet. I needed to stop him before he realised it was fake.

Brant made a right turn down another dark street. "He won't be alone. If he's attempting a full spirit magic ritual, he'll need assistance."

"From other spirit mages?" I arched a brow.

"No," he said. "He wouldn't work with others. He doesn't like to share."

"That's why he wanted me out of the way." I shivered in the cold air, and my shoulder burned with pain, a reminder of the tooth-marks in my skin. I didn't have any more healing cantrips, and I could no longer trust Brant to watch my back.

But I wouldn't leave my friends to die.

"You're thick as pig shit," Dex informed Brant. "You knew the vampire was a spirit mage, but you still didn't even try to warn Liv?"

He glared up at the sprite. "I warned her not to get involved."

"No, you tried to encourage me to use spirit magic." I marched on down the darkened street. "I was your backup plan. You hoped I could save your soul. You still do."

"She's got you there," said Dex. "How about I burn off your hair, fire-boy?"

Brant hissed out a breath. "We're here."

I followed his gaze. A vast estate extended before us, so large that it made the other house I'd been trapped in look modest in comparison. Fences surrounded the pristine lawns, and its whitewashed walls gleamed in the light of lamps hanging from above each of its arched windows.

"How'd he afford *this* place?" I whispered.

"Vampires build connections fast," he said. "He buried his past when he turned."

"The Order should have found him first," I muttered. "They should have known he worked with Dirk Alban."

Brant shot me a worried look. "How'd you know?"

My hands fisted, sending another wave of pain through my shoulder. "You were counting on me never gaining my memories back, weren't you?"

Dex made a noise of alarm. "Incoming!"

Fire blasted from Brant's hands, and a curse exploded

from the bushes. Ryan walked out, their cloak smoking at the edges, and looked Brant up and down. "What's he doing here?"

"Making up for what he did." I shot Brant a glare. "I saved his arse from the vampires we left burning in the safe house. Where's the Crow?"

"My master insisted on going into his estate alone." They glanced over their shoulder at the estate. "He hasn't come out yet."

"And you didn't think to go after him?"

"He expressly forbade me too," said the Air Element. "Besides, that sprite of yours went looking for you, so I decided to wait and see if he found you."

"You did?" My voice rose in surprise. "Thanks."

"Anytime." As Brant shifted at my side, Ryan's eyes narrowed. "If you turn on us, prepare for a world of pain."

"Brant, you should go." To Ryan, I said, "The vampire owns his soul via some contract I'm not a hundred percent certain on. Even if Brant doesn't want to turn on us, he might end up forced to do so anyway."

From Ryan's expression, they wanted to leave Brant dead in a ditch somewhere. But all they said was, "I'm going to find my master."

"He can't have been hurt, can he?" Surely not. His soul was safely hidden wherever he'd put it when he'd switched it out for the fake. Then again, these people were messing with magic which could turn even a lich into a rotting corpse. Who knew what other tricks the vampire lord had up his sleeve?

Ryan stepped through the gates into the darkened garden. The windows were dark, too, their curtains closed despite the lights hanging above the arches.

"My master and I took care of the guards outside before he went in," Ryan explained.

"Including the phantom?"

They inclined their head. "As for Davies… I haven't seen him. I should have guessed he was working against us. He never liked the other Elemental Soldiers, but I never realised just how much."

"I know the feeling." I didn't look back to see if Brant was still waiting outside the gate. If he had any sense, he'd leave, before the person to whom he owed his soul stepped in to claim it.

I walked after Ryan, across the darkened grounds towards the vampire's estate. The Air Element's magic rustled the leaves of the bushes, and pushed the front door inward before we reached it.

I gagged on the smell of rotting flesh. A body lay sprawled across the doorway, a blank cantrip gleaming on its chest. A lich.

"The Death King didn't do that," I whispered to Ryan. "The Crow did. He's not very careful with his allies, is he?"

"He doesn't have to be." Trix popped up in the doorway, for all the world like he'd been there all along.

"When did you get in?" I said, bemused. "I thought you were at the comic con with Devon."

"Oh, I came back here after she went home," he said. "I intended to help out your friends, but the one who calls himself the Crow caught me. He had one of his vampires drain my blood until I passed out, and I only just woke up."

"You…" I trailed off, staring. Needle-sharp bite marks stood out on his neck. "How'd you survive that?"

"I used my elf healing powers, of course." He shuddered. "It was very unpleasant."

Beside me, Ryan's baffled expression mirrored my own. "Have you been hiding here the whole time?"

"I saw you coming, so I decided to wait for you to arrive." He shivered. "I heard voices downstairs… I think there's something trapped in here."

"Some*thing?*" I walked into the gloom, beckoning Dex to fly ahead of me to light the way. "Did you see the Death King?"

"No. I woke up in there…" He pointed through a narrow doorway into a sitting room where three bodies lay limp and unmoving on the ground. The vampires had come off worse in the end, it seemed.

"Why'd he bring you here?" I tensed at the sound of a sharp cry from below our feet. He was right, and the sound wasn't close to human. But whoever it was, their distress was unmistakeable.

Dropping to a crouch, I found the rusty handle of a cellar door. With a quick tug, I opened it, wincing when my arm burned with pain again. The piercing bite marks weren't deep, but it was a nuisance to do everything one-handed.

Dex flew under the trapdoor, lighting a set of stone steps leading into the gloom of a basement.

"He's not down there, I don't think." Ryan trod downstairs behind me, and my gaze alighted on a cage resting on top of a stack of boxes.

Dex exclaimed in alarm. "Storms and showers!"

"What's that?" I leaned forward to look into the cage—and recoiled. A transparent shape floated behind the cage bars. A sprite, like Dex, but paler. So pale I could hardly see it.

"That's an air sprite," Ryan said in a hushed voice.

"I'll get it out," said Trix.

"Are you sure?" I backed up from the cage, peering into the gloom. Nothing else of note filled the dark basement. The sprite must have been one of the vampire's experiments, too. I couldn't just leave it here, so I stepped back to let Trix reach the cage himself. His elf hands worked the lock with ease, and a moment later, the sprite zipped out, crashing straight into Dex. The ensuing shrieking echoed off the basement walls, loud enough to raise a slumbering vampire.

Oh, hell.

"C'mon." Beckoning, I climbed the stairs behind Ryan with Trix bringing up the rear, followed by the two sprites. We'd pretty much killed any chance we'd had of sneaking up on the Crow undetected, and when I tripped over a second trapdoor, the sound of voices below made me pause.

Ryan reached for the handle, only to recoil as though burned. "It's warded. They're downstairs."

Which meant the Death King must be down there, too. The unintelligible tangle of mutters didn't tell me who was on the winning side, though surely a fight would make more noise. If the vampire didn't have the Death King's soul amulet, he must have found another way to subdue him. *Crap.*

Dex disentangled himself from the air sprite and descended beside me. "If you're looking for a way into the murder dungeon, try the other one."

"What?" I twisted on the spot, seeing Ryan descending into the first basement. "What're you doing?"

"Stay back." Ryan disappeared from sight. A moment later, there came an almighty blast, like a torrent of air magic slamming into a solid wall. The whole house seemed to tremble with it.

"Dammit, Ryan." I halted at the top of the steps as another tremor shook the ground below my feet.

I dropped to a crouch and peered down, my eyes stinging from the explosion of dust. Below, Ryan had blasted straight through the brick wall of the basement into the neighbouring chamber. Brick dust clogged my throat as I climbed downstairs, coughing uncontrollably. Dex's bright form appeared to light the way to where Trix had joined Ryan at the foot of the staircase.

Piles of shattered brick lay around a sizeable hole in the wall adjoining a larger basement. Dex's light bloomed, alighting on the form of the Death King standing inside the chamber on the other side of the wall. He wore his human face, his brows raised in surprise at the sight of us. I climbed over the debris to his side. "What are you doing in here?"

He gave me an exasperated look. "Did you have to step over the line?"

I looked down at the lines of a circle below my feet, almost obscured by the brick dust. Shit. I'd stepped straight into a magical trap. "You might have told me it was there."

"*I* might have told you?" he said.

"I'm assuming the spell doesn't stop you from speaking." I coughed, the dust burning my eyes. "Where's the Crow?"

"Somewhere under that wall."

Oh. Ryan hadn't just interrupted the ritual; they'd knocked the wall onto the leading vampire's head. Awkward. Crumpled bricks and other debris covered the chamber. I squinted through the dust and saw a number of figures standing around the outskirts of the room, and they all held cantrips in their hands.

"Was this a ritual to turn you into a zombie, by any chance?" The circle was a complex one, even with half of it obscured by the collapsed wall. Trix and Ryan stepped through the doorway and stopped moving as a dark figure rose to block their path.

The Crow's face was flecked with brick dust, his mouth pulled taut with rage as he strode over to the edge of the circle. His pale eyes narrowed as he studied me. "You're a puzzle, Olivia. I have to admit, I thought you died along with Alban. I didn't know the Order took your memories. Then again, my own memories of that time are... fractured."

The breath caught in my throat. Had whatever fate had befallen Dirk Alban caused him to end up transforming into a vampire? I wished I'd been able to see more in my memories while I'd been the vampires' prisoner, but there'd been no time, and if I'd delayed, I wouldn't have got here in time. Even now, I had the sinking suspicion I might be too late to stop him.

Several bright gleams caught my eyes as the figures standing around the room closed in. Some were vampires, some mages, and I recognised the Fire Element among the latter. His expression was blank, but when his gaze connected with mine, he sneered at me.

Anger brewed inside my chest. He was no better than

any of the other scumbags who the Crow had lured into serving him.

I gave the Crow a defiant look. "I'm hard to kill."

"So I see." His gaze lingered on the blood on my shoulder. "You'd make a fine vampire… if there was room for another of my kind, that is."

"A vampire spirit mage." I forced myself to meet his hungry stare, the combination of the dust thick in the air and the blood loss making me lightheaded. "With the number of people you've killed, it's no wonder I didn't guess you were anything other than a particularly inventive murderer who likes to target the dead."

"It's harder than I anticipated to effectively use this spell on a vampire," he said. "I've lost many brave volunteers to the cause… the spell works better on liches and phantoms, as I've found, but I've kept refining the spell in the hope of finding a solution."

I cocked a brow. "Brave volunteers, huh. You really want to use the spell on yourself? You want power that badly?"

"No," he said. "I merely wish to return to life. I've been trying to find a way ever since the unfortunate accident which turned me, and I have no other options left."

My heart jolted. He was trying to find a way to turn himself into a flesh-and-blood human again? It seemed his claim to purge the undead from the city so the living could walk again was literal. He wanted to turn himself into a living, breathing human, no longer one of the immortal undead.

"Why don't you want to live forever?" I said. "I'd have thought becoming a vampire would be a sweet deal, considering the alternatives."

Considering Cobb lost his magic and I lost my memories.

"This curse has its downsides," he said. "Vampires' capabilities are limited, but spirit mages once ruled the world."

"The vampires rule over the city now, though," I pointed out. "What the hell did you do to the council? Do they know you're here playing with the forces of life and death?"

"They're investigating a disturbance at the warehouse, orchestrated by some of my allies," he said. "The vampire council will have to bow to me when they return to find that I have become myself again and am no longer subject to their rule."

"So you want to be the Death King, too," I said. "Like Cobb."

"Cobb hoped to take Alban's place," he said. "To become like him. But he wasn't strong enough. He lost his magic, and without it, he could never have been as great as I am. He had to resort to taking the power of the King of the Dead in order to gain a fraction of his former glory."

Keep talking, dickhead. Not that I could do much from in here. My allies, though, were outside the circle. I had to trust that they'd come up with a plan.

"What the hell do *you* want with the Death King's soul, if not to take his power?" The man himself hadn't moved or reacted to the Crow's speech. I could only assume he was contemplating his next move.

"To remove him, of course." He turned to address the mages and vampires around the outskirts of the room. "The power contained within this barrier should be enough. Go on. Speak the words of the ritual and free the

Death King's soul from its prison. I'm sure he will thank us for it, before he perishes."

The others inside the room spoke in unison, a chilling murmur that raised the hairs on my arms. Power surged through the circle's edges, and the cantrips in each speaker's hands all glowed at once. The Crow, meanwhile, held up a token of his own. The amulet containing Death King's soul. Or so he thought.

I backed up to the far edge of the circle. I had until he realised it was a fake to find us a way out, so I needed to act quickly. No normal cantrip would work as long as I remained in this trap, but perhaps I could use one of my other tools.

I tilted my head and caught Trix's eye from where he stood at the circle's edge. I looked down to where he pointed. A brick lay half in the circle. The barrier was designed to contain magic, but maybe I could work with this.

I dropped to my knees and scooped up the brick, readying myself to take aim. The vampire continued to chant, holding the Death King's soul amulet high so it could be seen by everyone in the room.

As the chanting continued, the Death King swayed on the spot, as though drained by an invisible force. *What's going on? I thought it was fake.*

The cantrips in the hands of the vampire's allies glowed brighter with every second that passed, so I couldn't delay any longer. I readied the brick, took aim—and lobbed it straight at the vampire's head.

He went down hard, cut off mid-chant. I grabbed another brick which Trix had thoughtfully shoved into the circle behind me and hurled it at one of the other vampires.

"Duck!" shouted Ryan.

A current of wind blasted over my head, straight through the circle and into the gathering vampires. They scattered, dropping cantrips everywhere, and chaos broke out.

23

The Air Element's attack blasted the vampires aside like skittles, and even the Crow staggered backwards, his forehead bleeding where I'd hit him with the brick. Trix jumped in a moment later, hurling a brick at the nearest vampire. The brick struck his forehead with a ringing thud, and he crumpled into a heap.

"Didn't we already drain you?" one of the vampires said. "How do you have any blood left in you?"

"I'm an elf," he said, which was enough of an explanation in itself.

Ryan blasted their way through the remains of the door, while Dex flew above the spell circle. "Damn, that's strong. Nasty piece of work, that. How's the deadly king holding up?"

The Death King remained stock-still next to me, his head bowed. He hadn't even noticed the vampires fall, nor that the soul amulet had been lost somewhere in the chaos. What in hell was he doing?

A bright flash caught my eyes. Davies stepped out of the ruins of the shattered wall, his hands alight with fire as he faced off against Ryan. Fire blasted from Davies's hands, but Ryan dispelled it with a wave of their hands. The flames hit the brick dust, extinguishing on the spot. If they started an elemental duel in here, we'd all be caught in the backlash if we weren't careful.

I turned to shout a warning, and the Crow's bloody face loomed above me, looking quite deranged. His hand shot out and closed around my throat. "You won't get in my way any longer, you foolish girl."

Panic sparked as his fingers tightened, still vampire-strong. I couldn't access my spirit magic from behind the circle's boundary. He could snap my neck in a heartbeat, and he knew it. I heard someone shouting my name, but the sound disappeared as a roaring noise filled my ears.

Images flickered behind my eyes. The Crow's face beside Dirk Alban's—Dirk shouting something—blood on my hands, dripping down the walls…

The vampire's grip broke and he twisted aside with a snarl, away from a torrent of flames. I dropped to the ground, gasping for breath, but it wasn't Davies's fire that'd caused him to let go. Brant, who'd crept up to the circle's edge, pressed something into my hand. My fingers closed on cold metal, too stunned to react.

"Too stupid to die, are you?" The Crow flew at Brant with vampire speed, and the two of them disappeared in a haze of brick dust. Alarm rose thick in my throat, mingling with the smell of burning.

I looked down at the item Brant had given me—a cantrip. The light was too dim for me to see the lines on the surface and figure out what it did, but I had nothing to lose at this point. The Crow's head rose from the dust, his mouth bloody—and I set the cantrip off in his face.

The vampire fell backwards, gasping, then recovered an instant later. Before my eyes, his fangs retracted, the inhuman glow of the living dead fading from his eyes until they were an ordinary blue colour once more. His whole countenance changed from otherworldly to human, his speed slowing, his features sliding from porcelain to imperfect. Human. Living, once more.

All the sound in the room seemed to fade into the background as the Crow regarded me, a slow smile creeping onto his mouth. "I've missed this more than you can possibly imagine."

A glow saturated his skin, and a torrent of light pulsed out from his palms, knocking back everyone who wasn't in the circle. My teeth chattered, my skin chilled with the backlash of spirit magic. He was a spirit mage entirely, a vampire no longer—and unlike me, he had full access to his knowledge.

I'll kill Brant. That is, if I didn't die myself first. Whatever power source the Crow was drawing from, I didn't have a clue—there were no nodes nearby—but he was more experienced than I was. And a stronger spirit mage than he'd been as a vampire. No wonder he'd wanted to return to life.

The duelling Elements had vanished somewhere in the gloom, leaving only the Death King and I to face off against the new threat. From the way the house trembled, the Crow would bring the whole place crashing down on our heads if he wasn't careful.

"Spirit magic and vampirism are not compatible," he said, cupping a swirling current of energy in his palms.

"Vampires require energy to function, so they simply absorb power rather than being able to use it in this manner."

His hands glowed, and he spun around, blasting another hole in the wall. The guy seemed to *want* to destroy the place. Yet the circle around my feet remained intact... and now I understood why the Death King had stayed put. Physical objects might be able to touch us behind the barrier, but not spirit magic.

"You can't stay in there forever." The Crow's eyes danced with madness, his mouth bloody from biting Brant, and it hit me that he was vulnerable to any damage as a regular human was now. He must have figured it'd be worth the trade-off. "Come out and face me."

"No, thanks," I said. "I think I'll let you wear yourself out first. Right, Death King?"

He *still* wasn't moving. What the hell was he doing?

The vampire—no, spirit mage—moved closer to the circle's edge. "Dead already, are you, Grey?"

The circle exploded. Light burst outward, knocking into everyone within reach. Even Dex flew through the ceiling and out of sight, while I toppled backwards right onto my bleeding shoulder. Pain screamed up my arm to my spine, and a fresh wave of plaster dust blurred my vision.

The Crow roared in fury. The blast had hit him in the face, and when he lifted his head, there was a hole where his nose should be, a dent in his face filled with crumpled bone and stringy muscle. Spirals of energy spun around his hands, and a rush of understanding seared my mind. He hadn't been channelling an independent source—he'd been using his own life force as energy to fuel his attack.

And the spell, like the others which had left a pile of dead liches and phantoms in their wake, gifted the user incredible strength fuelled by the user's own life force until it gave out entirely.

Brant wasn't betraying me after all.

The Crow snarled and grabbed for my ankle, but I kicked his hand away from me. His hands scrabbled, still leaking life energy, and the decay was already spreading from his face to his neck. His body was decomposing at rapid speed, his legs decaying beneath him, his face rotting away. I gave him another kick, and his body crumpled into a twitching heap. A scream rose up from his allies as they realised their master was dying, but most had already run. Brant lay unconscious on the floor, while in the cellar bordering this one, Trix stood surrounded by unconscious vampires.

"Dex," I called to the sprite, who hovered on the ceiling at a safe distance from the battle. "Where are the others?"

"The Elements ran. Well, one of them did."

Davies. I'd bet he'd run at the first chance of the tide turning on his master. And he'd called Brant a coward.

I stumbled out of the circle—or tried to. Instead, I walked into a solid barrier. *Ow.*

"Hey, Death King." I turned to his side and stifled a gasp. A thin line of bright energy pulsed from his hands into the circle itself. He must have been pouring his own life force into the spell all along, intending to protect us until he'd gained enough power to destroy the Crow and his people. Now he was *still* fuelling it with his own strength, and if he didn't stop, we'd both be stuck in here indefinitely.

He didn't look up, no matter how many times I called

his name. He was beyond reach, at least from here. But maybe… maybe I could reach him another way. It wasn't like I had any better ideas.

I slid out of my body and saw the transparent form of his spirit staring back—but not all of it. A familiar glow drew my attention to the soul amulet lying beside the rotting remains of the Crow.

"You brought your own soul?" I whispered. "What the hell were you thinking?"

"You're going to have to evacuate everyone before I can break the circle." His voice was quiet, but audible. "The whole house is going to be destroyed when I do so, and anyone inside might get caught in the backlash."

"Shit." I looked up for Dex. "Hey! Everyone, get out! This place is gonna fall down!"

The vampires were already fleeing—those of them who could still stand, that was. Brant still lay half-conscious and bleeding on the floor, and my heart dropped in my chest at the sight of him. I didn't want to watch him die.

Trix stepped in. Without needing to be asked, he grabbed Brant and threw him bodily over his own shoulder, jogging up the stone steps and out of sight.

I released a breath. "All right. How do I…?"

"Imagine you're drawing the power out of the circle and into yourself." The Death King placed a hand on my arm, which startled me as much as it had the first time he'd done it.

I reached for the energy current rippling from the circle's edge. I could feel the strands of power coming from the Death King and feeding into the barrier around us, and instinct took over. My hands closed around threads, pulling them away from the circle's edge. Shock jolted up my arms as the same power rippled into me, through my bones. I gasped aloud, the current threatening to carry me into its embrace.

It's like... a node...

The Death King looked me in the eyes. "Let go."

I released the threads, and the circle collapsed. Power burst from my hands, blasting through the ceiling and rippling through the house. The remainder of the stone walls fell down, the ceiling blew open, and the darkening sky of the world outside appeared above our heads.

In seconds, we stood in a halo of ruined walls, surrounded by the gutted remains of the house. I released a shuddering breath, and only looked up again when the Death King stepped out of the circle and retrieved his soul amulet.

I picked my way out of the ruins, too, my legs shaking. My gaze landed on the gates, the only part of the house which was still standing, and where the others stood at a safe distance—Trix, Ryan, and the two sprites floating above their heads.

"Did you get Davies?" I asked Ryan.

"He ran," they said. "Better than burning the place down while we were inside it."

Brant lay unconscious next to the others. He needed to be handed over to the authorities before he followed Davies and ran. If any vampires had survived, they were without a sire, and without a master. Most of them had either run or knelt down in surrender, prepared to hand themselves over.

I was more than happy to oblige.

24

I was in a shitload of trouble with the Order. Again.

As it turned out, blowing up a house in the middle of the vampires' district drew unwanted attention from all angles. The Order already had me on a watchlist after the incident at the airport, and since several of them also recalled seeing me enter the Order's HQ when it was on fire, they'd showed up at the shop in my absence. Since Devon refused to say a word against me, they put both of us under house arrest upon my return.

The vampire council had handed Brant straight over to the Order on the grounds that the Crow was an ex-employee and so was Cobb. According to Ryan, the Death King was pissed that he didn't get to handle the punishment himself, but I hadn't been back to see him since I'd been placed under house arrest. Even astral projecting was risky when Order members kept showing up on our doorstep as though hoping to catch me in the middle of an illicit action.

While I'd told everyone who would listen about how the cantrips from the warehouses were being misused, they'd remained in full operation in supplying the Order, which left it up to Devon and me to salvage a way to save our business. Fast.

On the Friday morning after the battle with the vampires, the two of us were arguing over the merits of admitting defeat and quitting the Order to sell Warhammer figurines when two Order employees, including Judith, sauntered into the shop. They halted in front of the desk, looking Devon and me up and down.

"Your friend's trial was this morning," said Judith smugly.

My throat constricted. "Your point?"

Since the Order had been occupied in fixing the damage caused to their offices by the fire, you'd think they'd have better things to do than to come here and bother Devon and me.

"Brant Edwards was convicted for illegal involvement in dark magic, but not for starting the fire in the Order's headquarters," said Judith's friend. "The perpetrator of that heinous act of arson has yet to be caught."

I folded my arms. "And your point is? Did you want Brant to be the one who set your headquarters on fire?"

"You were there." Judith looked me over. "Anything to say to that?"

Ah, hell. Of course she'd guessed I'd been into the building. "I know who started it because the Fire Element fled the Death King's territory and went rogue right before it caught on fire, while Brant was imprisoned in the Death Kingdom at the time."

"Convenient," she said. "And you happened to be

working for the Death King, too? Yet you still didn't see Brant Edwards as a threat?"

"If you're going to call me an idiot for trusting him, then get on with it." The Order couldn't punish me any more than I'd already punished myself. Despite everything Devon said to the contrary, I couldn't help wondering if I could ever have stopped him from turning onto the path he'd ended up on.

No sooner than I could have stopped the girl in my memories from trusting Dirk Alban, I'd guess.

"You were at the Death King's side when he destroyed the rogue vampire's house, according to all these reports," she said. "I find it interesting that you always end up at the centre of these incidents. Very interesting."

"At the centre of what?" I said. "The Crow had his pet vampires leave me for dead. It was the Death King he wanted. I was only involved because we—"

"You were working together," she said. "Despite our orders to the contrary."

"You try disobeying an order from the King of the Dead."

It was too late to dwell on what might have been. As my near-death experiences had shown me in a painfully clear light, life was too short for that. I'd made my choices, and unlike Brant, I had no regrets.

The door rattled inwards, and the two Order employees both startled as a shadowy figure passed into view. As though conjured by my words, the Death King strode between the two of them, wearing his human face and back at full power once again.

"Are you here to buy something?" he asked the two intruders.

"No." Judith and her companion exchanged alarmed looks. "We're going."

"Good." The Death King waited until the door closed behind them before approaching the desk. "You were somewhat difficult to track down."

I didn't move. "How'd you get my address?"

"Ryan," he said. "They looked it up."

"Great." Now I'd have no way of escaping the King of the Dead, in this realm or otherwise. At the very least, though, it meant his people would stop unexpectedly walking out of the node in the middle of the house. "What do you want?"

"I owe you a payment," he said. "It should be in your bank account within a week."

My mouth fell open. "What? But I didn't solve the murders."

Devon rammed an elbow into my ribs, and I bit my tongue. I got the message. *Don't turn down free cash, Liv.*

"You led me to the right solution," he said. "I apologise for the delay, but I was beginning the preparations of looking for a new Fire Element."

"Oh. That's... no problem." An apology? From the King of Death? Maybe I'd slipped into some bizarre alternative universe at some point in the last week. "By the way, the Order is angry with me for not taking their advice to stop working with you, and they're trying to find a way to pin the arson on me. If you hadn't already guessed."

"I expected they wouldn't let the issue drop," he said. "So I left them a message."

"Of what sort?"

The phone started ringing. Devon walked into the back to answer it, while I stared at the Death King. The guy had some nerve. But then again, given his position, there was little even the Order could do to challenge him.

"What did you do?" The words came out more accusing than I'd planned, but I couldn't suppress my irritation that I always had to fall back on the King of the Dead to get me out of trouble. For all the times he'd saved my neck of late, he had more secrets under wraps than the vampires did, and I could never be sure he wasn't pursuing some other agenda.

"I merely gave the Order a reminder of who is to blame for the current situation, and that they do themselves a disservice by ignoring what they have at their disposal."

That doesn't tell me anything. I heard Devon speaking on the phone and I wanted to listen in, but more questions that had sprung up since the battle sprang to mind. I'd had enough time to form a long list of queries concerning the stunt he'd pulled at the house, and why he'd seemed so certain the two of us could overcome the vampire. So many questions, I hadn't a clue where to start.

"You need to stop putting your soul amulet in peril like that," I finally said. "Why'd you do it?"

"I'm lucky to be more flexible with what I do with my soul than most," he said.

"And it almost killed you." I shook my head. "I'm beginning to think you became immortal because you'd have died otherwise."

"That's not far from the truth," he said.

Right… he'd already hinted that he'd had no choice in the matter. "Brant said… he said you turned the other liches so that they'd have to obey your every command."

He arched a brow. "And has anything in recent times compelled you to trust his word?"

Ouch. Guess I deserved that one. "I'm just saying, this spirit mage business has done a fine job of wrecking my life without turning me into the living dead on top of it. And you seem to have a short life expectancy, too."

Stop talking, Liv. I wasn't doing myself any favours by needling the Death King, yet he continued to watch me with nothing more than mild surprise in his expression. Or indifference. I really couldn't tell, even when he wasn't wearing his usual mask.

"I already told you I have no intention of turning you into a lich."

"The Crow ended up as a vampire, and Cobb ended up with no magic," I said. "Like I said… people who dedicate themselves to spirit magic seem to have a short lifespan whether they're dead or alive."

"What do you want me to tell you?" he asked. "You chose to continue practising spirit magic."

"I did." And despite the Order's attempt to put a new stranglehold on my life, the glimpses into my own history I'd seen refused to leave me be. "That doesn't change the fact that I don't know who you really are. Was that your name? Grey?"

"Does it matter?" His tone was non-confrontational, but it brought a chill to my skin all the same.

"You were a spirit mage," I said. "So how…?"

"A curse." He spoke in a low voice. "Not something that is likely to affect you."

A curse, which forced him to turn lich or die? "How? I mean—when?"

"It originated in the spirit war," he said. "I wasn't alive in those days, so I can only guess at how it started."

"You weren't?" I had it wrong. I'd assumed he was centuries old, but he wasn't, not at all. If he hadn't even been born before the war had started, that would make him close to my own age. He'd died young. Really young.

Sadness swept through me, inexplicably. The murmur of voices from the back room died down, and he shifted position, clearly ready to leave. "Your sprite is still at my castle. Does that bother you?"

"He is?" I frowned. "Why?"

"Ryan has taken a liking to him, along with the air sprite you rescued," he said.

"Oh." I didn't know what to say to that. "Good. Uh. I've been thinking about your offer…"

"And?" His tone was expectant, his stance still indicating he intended to leave.

"I… might need lessons in spirit magic," I admitted. "After the Order takes away the house arrest order on me, I mean."

"I wouldn't trouble yourself by worrying about the Order," he said. "But yes, my offer stands. If you are willing to risk that step."

"I think I'll have to." As recent events had proved, I wasn't alone as a spirit mage, and my lack of knowledge had cost me. If my history contained any more lessons which were essential to survival, I'd need to be ready.

Devon walked back into the room. "We got a mass order for cantrips from the Order. Apparently, the fire destroyed most of their stock."

"And you're ready to make more?"

"You bet."

I looked up at the Death King, only to find he'd vanished before I could ask if he was responsible for this new development.

Not that I needed to ask. *The Death King strikes again.*

I wouldn't grow complacent. He might be on my side for now, but when he'd stopped thinking he owed me a favour, things would go downhill fast. But I was content to enjoy the rewards of our near-death experience. Elements knew I needed them.

———

It was D&D night, and our team was assembled and ready for action. Devon sat in the prime position at the head of the table, and I found myself missing having Dex around to play NPCs. He'd been a real riot during our last game, and while I was glad that he'd made a home for himself in the Parallel, I missed his company all the same.

With luck, the Order would cave to the Death King and lift the house arrest directive by early next week, and then I could get back to work.

Trix was back in the game, while the others gathered around the table with cartons of takeout and stacks of character sheets. Just as Devon called the game to a start, the doorbell rang with a strident *incoming!*

"I'll get it," I said.

If the Order had come to crash our games night again, I'd be having words with them. Same with the Death King, for that matter. He might have pulled us out of dire financial straits—again—but D&D night was serious business.

I opened the door. It wasn't the Death King, or even

the Order. Instead, Ryan of all people stood on the doorstep.

"Oh, you do know how to ring the doorbell," I said. "Word of advice—knock in future. You might have guessed there's no volume control on that thing."

"Hey, Liv!" Dex flew in circles around Ryan's head, accompanied by the air sprite. The second sprite already looked much happier than it had when I'd found the cage in the vampire's basement, and now resembled a humanoid figure surrounded by a halo of greenish light.

"What the...?" I stared between the two sprites. "What are you two doing here?"

"I invited the air sprite to stay with me," Ryan explained. "She was terrified after being trapped in that cage. Dex helped her get settled in, and in the end, they both stayed. I didn't throw them out, so they took that as an invitation to make themselves at home."

"Your boss said they were both staying with you, but I didn't know." Despite my bad experiences at the hands of Elements lately, I didn't think of Ryan as a villain. Not like the Fire Element. On the other hand... I knew why they were here. This was the Death King's doing. He knew I wouldn't work for him, so he'd sent one of his people over to convince me instead. "Did the Death King send you? Because we have a new job from the Order which is going to take up all our time for the foreseeable future."

"I know." They peered over my shoulder, gaze snagging on Trix. "What're you doing in there?"

"Playing D&D," I said. "You know what it is, right?"

"Of course I do," they said. "I did grow up in this world, but I never had a regular gaming group I could meet up with. Since taking on the job as Air Element, I've had even less time."

I hesitated, feeling the others watching me. Even Dex. I'd never been a fan of mages, and after Brant's betrayal, I had even less reason to trust them. And yet. "You want to play D&D with us?"

A smile formed on their face. "If it's okay with your friend."

I went into the back room, where Devon gave me a questioning look. "Ryan's here to play, believe it or not. Do we have room?"

"The Air Element wants to join us?" she said. "Sure, we have room. But they'll have to come up with a character."

"Not a problem." I beckoned to the two sprites to follow the Air Element into our house. "You two can't hold dice, but Dex had a great time playing a fire demon last time. What do you think?"

"You bet," said Dex, and the air sprite nodded vigorously.

It looked like we had enough room at the table for a few more.

ABOUT THE AUTHOR

Emma is the New York Times and USA Today Bestselling author of the Changeling Chronicles urban fantasy series.

Emma spent her childhood creating imaginary worlds to compensate for a disappointingly average reality, so it was probably inevitable that she ended up writing fantasy novels. When she's not immersed in her own fictional universes, Emma can be found with her head in a book or wandering around the world in search of adventure.

Find out more about Emma's books at
www.emmaladams.com.